"*Daingerfield Island* is a splendid first novel, a legal-political thriller that grabs your attention on the first page and keeps it throughout. John Wasowicz gives this book an excellent sense of place, with details of Northern Virginia and D.C. that paint a picture but don't distract. Well done."

—Paul E. Fletcher
Editor-in-Chief, *Virginia Lawyers Weekly*

"*Daingerfield Island* is a top-notch political thriller that moves with breakneck speed!"

—Meaghan Beasley
Marketing Manager, Island Bookstore, Kitty Hawk, Duck & Corolla, NC

DAINGERFIELD ISLAND

John Adam Wasowicz

DANGERFIELD ISLAND

Editor: Clarinda Harriss
Graphic design: Ace Kieffer
Cover art: Alex Herron Wasowicz
Author photo: Aron Wasowicz

BrickHouse Books, Inc. 2016
306 Suffolk Road
Baltimore, MD 21218

Distributor: Itasca Books, Inc.

ISBN: 978-1-938144-55-4

Printed in the United States of America

In memory of

Paul M. Herron

Oh what a tangled web we weave
When first we practice to deceive.
But when you're practiced quite a bit
You really get quite good at it.
—Nicholas Elliott

Table of Contents

CHAPTER 1

Sunday, October 31

HER BODY floated face down off Daingerfield Island at dusk, her long dark hair spreading like an inkblot on the water.

A mile away, cars snaked across the 14th Street Bridge out of Washington. Traffic should have been light, it being Sunday. But the roads were clogged, filled with motorists, many in costumes, everyone in a rush to get somewhere. Throughout Washington, children began flooding neighborhood streets, parents lighting their paths with flashlights and jack-o'-lanterns. At door stoops, candy spilled out of bowls into the open bags of trick-or-treaters. In Dupont Circle, high heels were strapped on for the annual drag race. Halloween was on.

Overhead, airplanes roared their descent to Reagan National Airport, touching down at four-minute intervals after navigating their way up the Potomac River, flying fortresses gliding along a liquid highway.

A Metro train leaving L'Enfant Plaza burst out of the ground and zoomed along the overhead subway rails paralleling the bridge, the windows of each car, like tiny movie screens, displaying commuters in costumes.

Weathermen reported rain working its way across the Blue Ridge. Not to worry. Tonight's air would be dry and cool, the evening perfect for little ghosts and goblins trespassing across front lawns strewn with papier-mâché gravestones.

As his nonstop flight from Los Angeles approached the airport, Jack Smith turned his head and stared at the reflection in the plane's window: old, worn and gray, the face of a Washington warrior weathered by bureaucratic infighting. His jaw was square, his dark eyes as clear as ever. He nodded approvingly.

Smith's eyes shifted to the ground below. The traffic snaked along, a string of white and red lights. Daingerfield Island crouched off to one side, separated by a tiny inlet from the airport's landing field downstream of the bridge.

As the airplane came in low, Smith surveyed the restaurant on the island in the gathering dusk. There were two wooden decks, devoid of umbrellas and furniture as fall slipped toward winter; an almost vacant parking lot; and several rows of sailboats at anchor, and dozens more stacked and racked at the far end of a pier.

He could see the woman's body dancing in the water below, about twenty yards off the bulkhead.

Suddenly a bicyclist approached, heading south along the Mount Vernon Trail. Smith turned his head to follow the movement, but the airplane was banking. No luck. Everything was moving too fast. The wheels dropped from the belly of the big-bodied plane as it made its final descent.

Turning from the window, Smith closed his eyes. He fastened his seatbelt a little tighter, then pressed the button to put the seat upright. It needed no adjustment; it had been in the upright position the entire flight.

This day marked special significance for anyone in the intelligence business, the anniversary of the infamous Halloween Day Massacre of 1979. With his eyes now pressed shut, Smith recalled how Admiral Stansfield Turner eliminated eight hundred human intelligence-gathering positions, decimating the operations corps with the stroke of a pen.

Jack Smith had survived, but whatever youthful romanticism he had brought with him from college had died that day. He had grown jaded early, and never recovered. Over time, between black ops, drone strikes, enhanced interrogation techniques and renditions, all his enthusiasm had drained away, leaving only the cold heart of a cynic.

"Sir?"

Smith opened his eyes. He looked up at the flight attendant who was standing over him, a look of concern on her face. The plane was already on the ground and most of the passengers had disembarked. He closed his eyes again, briefly.

**

AS SMITH'S PLANE was landing, the bicyclist, David Reese, was cruising along the waterside path.

When he reached Daingerfield Island, Reese slowed his pace, hesitated, then stopped and dismounted. No way, he thought, squinting toward the water. He cocked his head, trying to see it from another angle, any angle that would allow him to ride away with a clear conscience.

A sound ricocheted across the inlet from the satellite parking lot directly to his north. Reese's gaze swept across the water, catching sight of a man slamming the back door of a white van and walking around to the driver's seat, a phone to his ear.

Reese looked back at the thing floating on the water. He engaged the kickstand on his bike, then removed his helmet, hanging it on the handlebars. Then he took off his glasses and drew out a soft piece of tissue from the pocket of his nylon racing pants and cleaned the lenses. As hard as he tried to make the image go away, there it remained. No mistaking it.

There was a body floating in the Potomac River.

Reese recalled reading about Lenny Skutnick, who jumped into the water a mile upstream to render assistance to passengers of Air Florida Flight 90 when the plane glided between two spans of the 14th Street Bridge and crashed into the icy water back in '82. Reese thought about plunging into the water, but he was not an experienced swimmer. He pulled out his cell phone and dialed 911.

"There's a body floating in the Potomac, just off Daingerfield Island." He took a deep breath. "I think she jumped in the water. She's not moving. You've got to get a rescue crew out here right away!"

"Stand by," instructed the operator, coolly and calmly. "Emergency vehicles have already been dispatched," she announced to his surprise. "Please await their arrival."

As she spoke, the shrill sound of sirens filled the air. Reese could follow the unseen emergency vehicles by the sound of the sirens, growing ever louder. First they reverberated along the parkway, then along the tree line. Reese calculated their arrival time.

Thirty seconds.

Ten seconds.

One second.

An ambulance and a fire engine braked in front of the restaurant, their sirens running down. Two EMTs jumped out of the ambulance. Reese directed them to the bulkhead that supported the slimy bank of the Potomac.

A firefighter raced ahead of the EMTs, stripping off his yellow coat as he ran. He pulled the black boots off as soon as he stopped, then plunged feet first into about five feet of water. He landed chest high and struggled out toward the listless body.

As the firefighter reached for the victim, Reese became aware of people suddenly filling the paved surface that ran along the bulkhead. Eight, maybe ten, emerged seemingly out of nowhere. They looked like carbon copies of the same person, muscular, with trimmed hair, and dressed in dark suits with plain ties.

"Are you the one who called in the drowning?"

Reese turned to find a badge in front of him. The man holding it was dressed in civilian clothes. He was tall, heavyset, a caterpillar mustache that matched his bristling eyebrows. His longish hair was streaked with gray. His eyes moved slowly, like lights in a watchtower, beacons seeking trouble.

"Yes," Reese replied warily. A breeze ruffled his mop of reddish hair and he reached up to smooth it down.

"What's your name?"

Before Reese could answer, a splashing sound on the water drew their attention. They turned to observe the rescue operation.

"Let's get a better look," said the cop.

Reese followed the detective through the growing throng of rescue workers and spectators to the edge of the bulkhead.

A fireman grabbed the woman's shoulders and turned her over. Quickly, he performed some perfunctory mouth-to-mouth resuscitation. Receiving no response, he cupped her chin in his hand and began a scissor kick, pulling her to shore.

An EMT plunged into the water. She and two firemen on shore stretched out their arms to receive the body.

"She's already cold as ice," the fireman told a rescuers, struggling to raise the victim into their hands.

Reese stood transfixed. At age 24, Reese had never seen a dead body before, nor been this close to what might be a crime scene. His mind was jumping ahead to what might happen. "This is unbelievable," he whispered to himself.

"I've been at this for twenty years, and after a while it gets tiring," said the policeman, who was now watching the crowd instead of the body. He introduced himself to Reese. "Detective Harry Bullock. Homicide."

The night sky pulsated with blue, red, and white lights from the emergency vehicles, painting Reese, Bullock and the others in colors, flashing hues on their faces and clothes, on the grass and trees, on the water, on a purse lying on the bulwark, on the entire rescue operation. The colors kept flashing at warp speed.

Blue. Red. White. Blue.

A rescue worker knelt beside the woman's sodden body. Mouth-to-mouth resuscitation was tried one more time, unsuccessfully.

Reese pulled out his phone and quickly snapped a photo. The entire scene was bathed in red. He clicked on the woman's face, shrouded in wet hair, like seaweed, a necklace hanging from her neck.

The body was being raised onto a stretcher. The EMTs were wheeling the gurney to the ambulance and the vehicle was driving away.

Reese spotted something glistening in the grass where the

EMTs had performed mouth-to-mouth. He stooped to pick it up, thinking it might be a coin.

Bullock, who had been watching the crowd, turned. "What's that?"

Reese jumped. "Nothing," he replied, holding the tissue he had used earlier to wipe his glasses. Without really knowing why, he was reluctant to share this tiny souvenir. He stuffed the tissue back into his pants pocket. "Just something I use to wipe my lenses."

"Okay." There was no reason for the detective to be suspicious. "I'm going to have to get some details from you," Bullock said.

"Do I need an attorney?" Reese asked tersely.

"I don't see any need for one," the detective responded. "You're not a suspect, just an eyewitness. I need a statement. Who, what, when, where, why. It shouldn't take more than a few minutes."

"Do you suspect foul play?" Reese asked.

Bullock sneered. "Yeah. Which doesn't mean there was any. But I always start out suspecting foul play."

Reese smiled uneasily.

More flashing lights as an Alexandria Police cruiser pulled up and two young cops emerged.

"Boys," Bullock called. They walked over, deferentially. "There's a purse over there," he said, pointing. Sure enough, there was a big black purse on the bulkhead, nearly invisible in the darkness against the black backdrop of the water. "Take it to the station without getting your prints all over it. If there's a wallet in there, check the ID. Have Sergeant Cook inventory the contents."

The rookies nodded.

"And try not to shake it like a tambourine. I don't want to disturb the order of things. Understand? I'd like to know what was on top, what was on the bottom."

Bullock suggested to Reese that they go over to the restaurant to talk. Reese got his bike and wheeled it over to a rack outside the restaurant, securing it with a bike chain. He grabbed his helmet, then followed Bullock into the restaurant and slid into a booth opposite him. Police and firemen milled about outside, moving at half speed and talking to one another. The light show continued.

Blue. Red. White. The colors had become synonymous with the night.

A waitress brought two cups of coffee. Reese dropped his helmet on the vinyl bench beside him and reached out to wrap his fingers around his cup. In his interest over the detective's work, he had stopped paying attention to the fact it was cold outside. Light nylon racing pants and a windbreaker were not enough protection for a late October evening.

"Why did you instruct them not to disturb the order of things in the purse?" Reese asked.

"Are you a lawyer?" Bullock pulled out a pad and paper.

"Not yet," Reese responded, surprised. "I work at the Library of Congress now. But I've been accepted at American University's law school. I'm putting it off for a year, so I can work and earn some money."

"Thought so," Bullock nodded. "The way you ask questions. I can always ID a lawyer. They're a type." He hesitated. "I don't like lawyers. They're arrogant. Think they're smarter than everyone else."

Then, after another moment's hesitation, he answered Reese's question.

"Sometimes the way stuff is layered is important. It's like an archeological dig. It tells you things."

Bullock eased his way into the interview. He got the correct spelling of Reese's name, David A. Reese, and his basic contact information, including where he lived, an apartment complex in Alexandria.

Then the cop got down to business. "So, tell me what happened. What'd you see? Every bit of it."

Reese had finished his coffee. His fingers were warm now. He tapped them on the wooden table as he talked.

"I was riding along the bike path to Alexandria. I'd come over the 14th Street Bridge. I saw this thing in the water. A body. So I pulled out my phone and called 911."

He stopped for an instant.

"Anyway, the emergency vehicles got here really fast. A fireman and an EMT jumped into the water and pulled out the body. You saw that yourself."

"That it? See anything else? Anything strange? Anything out of the ordinary?"

"No."

Reese dipped his hand into his pocket and wrapped his fingers around the tissue. "No, not really," he said. He wondered how quickly he could get home to Mai Lin.

CHAPTER 2

LOU MOULTRIE LOOKED DOWN at his shaking hands, resting on the keyboard. Then at the clock in the right-hand corner of the computer screen. 7:00 p.m. Once he hit *send*, there would be no turning back. He tried to contemplate the consequences, which was difficult, since he was not entirely sure what he had here.

The operation at Daingerfield Island had gone terribly wrong. Part of him now wanted to walk away from the computer and stop thinking about it. Instead, he had continued to sit there, scrolling through old emails in his government account, then his personal account. After cleaning out the emails in his inbox and sent folders, he opened spam. His first inclination was to delete all of the emails. They constituted nothing more than junk mail: dating services, financial gimmicks, and offers for services he would never use and had no interest in trying.

For some reason, in an abundance of caution, he skimmed the emails in the spam folder. That was when he found it: an email that had been sent to him a week before. How it ended up in the spam folder was anyone's guess.

The message, when he opened it, alarmed him. After long thought, he composed a note to the head of operations, Jack Smith, attaching the email to his note.

> Jack: I'm back at my house now. I happened to go through some old emails in my personal account and ran across one that is, well, somewhat disquieting. From Eve. We can discuss more fully tomorrow. Lou.

Smith would not appreciate this intrusion into his personal life, even if it were from an old friend who served as best man at his wedding.

On top of that, Smith and his deputy, June Webster, would be aggravated by the botched operation planned for Daingerfield Island, which had fallen apart as soon as that bicyclist arrived and called emergency services. Moultrie wondered if Smith or Webster would blame him.

Everything on Daingerfield Island had seemed fine at first. Then came the sound of the sirens and all those busy, helpful rescuers dragging the body out of the water.

As the situation devolved, Moultrie quickly departed. Plenty of other agents remained on the scene to deal with loose ends.

Moultrie looked at his trembling hands one final time. He hit *send*.

CHAPTER 3

"LADIES AND GENTLEMEN of the Jury, *Fatta la legge, trovato l'inganno.* Do any of you know what that means?"

The speaker paused, then continued: "You're thinking it's something from Cicero, or maybe Marcus Aurelius. If there's a playwright among you, you're wondering if it's from Shakespeare. After all, every really good quote is from Shakespeare, or the Bible. Right?"

His lips were red, and moved slowly and deliberately. The voice was gentle but commanding. The eyes were warm and dark, playful and steely, inscrutable. He knew the jurors would love that line. Laugh at it, in fact.

"Actually, I don't know where the expression originated," he went on, "but that's beside the point. I'm only concerned with its meaning. Loosely translated, it means 'Every law has its loophole' or 'Make a law and a way will be found around it.' Something like that. I don't speak Italian, so I'm not a hundred percent sure myself."

The speaker's eyes stared into the rear-view mirror, checking for signs of sincerity.

Elmo Katz, practicing his opening statement, was stuck in bumper-to-bumper traffic on the southbound George Washington Memorial Parkway. He was handsome by any standard, tall and thin, with a sardonic smile and wiry hair. But the twinkle in his eye and the way his mouth twisted into a sweet smile were what people remembered about him. That and the way he could make words sing.

Fatta la legge, trovato l'inganno. He could not speak Italian, but he had memorized that line about laws having loopholes to use in his opening statements. He did it to suggest to jurors that he was not one of *those* lawyers who succumb to a credo like that. The irony was that he actually used every conceivable loophole known to the legal profession to crack a case. He just professed to do otherwise because it was an effective tactic.

Practicing criminal defense law in Northern Virginia was hard-

11

ly what might have been expected of a precocious kid from Chicago who had graduated from Georgetown University near the top of his class and been offered positions paying three times as much at the most prestigious law firms in the District.

But Katz was never some ordinary kid.

His name – Elmo – was a gift from his parents. "El" was for the "L," the Chicago Transit Authority's train system. The Duke Ellington Orchestra might have memorialized taking the A Train from Harlem in Billy Strayhorn's famous tune, but it was the "L" where his parents had first met, and it was love at first sight for two young students attending the University of Chicago. "Mo" was for Motown Records, which his mother adored. A Detroit girl, she had spent her youth dancing to the latest tunes by Smokey Robinson, the Supremes, the Temptations and Martha Reeves and the Vandellas. Mix the DNA of a Jewish kid from Brooklyn with that of a girl anxious to escape the slums of the Motor City, and you had a first-class, street-smart lawyer.

Straight out of law school, he had taken the Virginia Bar and accepted a low-paying job as an Alexandria City prosecutor. Three years later, he had made the leap over to specialize in criminal defense – the dark side, some said – when he opened a solo practice in Alexandria. Since then, he had plowed the fields of the local courthouses and built a reputation as a successful attorney, winning acquittals for hundreds of petit misdemeanants. It never paid much money – Katz had to supplement it by doing just enough boring civil litigation and some silk-stocking family law to pay the bills – but he derived enormous satisfaction from it.

Most of his clients were straight up guilty. The truth would not set them free, and neither would the facts. But technicalities did the trick; things like jurisdiction, identification, and the circumstances surrounding the arrest, search or collection of evidence. Those things could set a guilty man free, and Katz had made himself an expert on such trivia.

Katz glanced at himself in the rear-view mirror again. Yes, he was vain, but vanity was part of his charm, or so he told himself. He resumed reciting his opening statement.

"I tell you that quotation because I think many people, perhaps even some of you, believe that's what criminal defense attorneys – and attorneys who file tort claims or medical malpractice claims – are all about. We're perceived as always trying to find a way around things, to find some loophole to get a client off.

"But that's not what you're going to see today, ladies and gentlemen. You're not going to see my client trying to jump through some loophole. You're actually going to see the opposite. You're going to see him face the charge head-on, element by element. And, by putting the facts up against the elements needed to convict, we will show that the evidence does not constitute guilt beyond a reasonable doubt."

Suddenly Katz felt uneasy. He glanced to his left. Emergency lights were flashing out on Daingerfield Island. Blue. Red. White.

His phone, resting in his crotch, vibrated. He grabbed it. Joey Cook was calling.

"Where are you?" Katz asked. "And what are you doing?"

"I'm just crawling out into the fresh air. You?"

"Preparing for my next trial," Katz confessed.

"Reciting your opening statement." Cook laughed. "You're always polishing that thing, aren't you? Hell, half the clerks in the courthouses can recite that thing verbatim."

Katz ignored the jibe. Like any good actor, constantly rehearsing made him appear spontaneous. "There's nothing wrong with practicing, Joey," Katz pointed out.

Cook, a police sergeant, was permanently assigned to the Property Room in the Alexandria Police Department, the result of disciplinary action for fixing traffic tickets. He spent his days in a purgatory of computers and a squawk box, delving into the goings-on of everything and everyone in the criminal justice world of Northern

Virginia. Every once in a while, he did what he was actually supposed to be doing: inventorying guns, drugs, pornography, stolen merchandise, and sundry other illicit and illegal wares.

By spending all his time watching and listening, Cook knew who had won or lost a case, what evidence had been excluded and why, whether there had been problems with a Breathalyzer machine, which cops were cheating on their spouses or subject to internal investigations, whether any local judges had complaints filed against them, which prosecutors were angling to sleep with the staff in the Circuit Court Clerk's Office, and who the cops were hunting down at any given moment. That made Cook an invaluable contact.

"I've got something for you," Cook said.

"Wait a minute," Katz said abruptly. He put down the phone and turned up the radio to listen to the half-hour news bulletin. Alexandria Police were identifying Libby Lewis as the victim of a drowning earlier that evening at the marina at Daingerfield Island.

'Lewis, forty-nine, worked as chief of staff for the Senate Intelligence Committee,' the newscaster said.

Katz turned down the volume and reclaimed his phone. "Did you hear that? I think I just drove by it. Libby Lewis, some Hill staffer."

"Of course I heard about it. What's not being reported is they suspect foul play. Our buddy Harry Bullock's investigating it. He'll figure it out."

Bullock. Katz's heady days as a prosecutor had included some wild cases with that crazy cop.

"So, I got a tip for you," Cook went on.

"Lay it on me, Joey."

"Fortune's case. There's a chain of custody problem."

Katz snapped off the radio. He tapped the brakes. "What sort of problem?" he asked.

"The sort that results in acquittals," Cook replied. "I checked the prosecution's witness list against my custody records. The drugs were submitted by an Officer Cecil Dixon, except there's no Officer Dixon on the witness list. The only police who've been subpoenaed are the officers who stopped Tony and slapped the cuffs on him."

Katz quickly ran though the facts in his head. "Yeah, but that shouldn't be a problem." Katz tried not to get excited. "He might just show up without a subpoena. Or, if he's not there, they'll figure it out soon enough and have someone call him to come in."

"No they won't." Cook repressed his laughter. "Dixon's on vacation for the rest of the week, visiting family in Oklahoma."

Katz quickly processed the information. Without Dixon, the prosecution would be unable to admit the drugs as evidence. The case was as good as over.

"Pretty sweet," Cook said. "But I guess Kathy White will see a train wreck before it hits her," Cook continued, alluding to the prosecutor. "She'll move for a continuance."

"She would if she could, Joey, except the case has already been up for trial twice already," Katz replied gleefully. "First, the drug results weren't back from the lab. Then the certificate of analysis wasn't filed on time."

"You didn't stipulate to its admissibility?" Cook asked. Almost every defense attorney did.

"Joey, you know better than to ask me that. I don't stipulate to anything. How do you think I win half my cases?"

Cook changed the subject. "What time we getting together?" he asked.

Katz had two tickets to a Halloween charity fundraiser staged by the law enforcement community to raise money for rehabilitating juvenile offenders. It was being held at a mansion along the Potomac. He had asked Cook to go with him, since Abby Snowe had turned him down.

"Meet me about eight-thirty," Katz answered. "We'll smoke some cigars, have a drink."

"Sounds good. Have costume, will party."

After he hung up, Katz called and left a message for Suzie Marston, his secretary, who doubled as a clinical psychologist for his clientele. "Snooze, about the Ashford settlement. I just remembered something. I need to pursue the Wolfeman's offer now that the depositions are over." Katz sensed it was his best opportunity to leverage a win. His trusty secretary would understand that instinctively. "I put a draft document on your desk before I left the office tonight. Increase the settlement by fifty grand, to three hundred thousand. I think it'll work. I'm feeling lucky. No huge rush on this, but I don't want it to languish."

As Katz ended the call, Detective Harry Bullock was departing Daingerfield Island, and Jack Smith was stalking impatiently toward the airport exit.

CHAPTER 4

THE WHITE VAN had pulled out of the satellite parking lot at Reagan National and circled the airport twice before stopping at the arrivals curb. The driver put the vehicle in park and waited.

Inside the terminal, Jack Smith fidgeted with his phone. Five minutes later, he emerged, walked straight to the van, opened the back door and threw his bag onto the seat. Then he pulled himself up into the front passenger seat.

"Sir." The word sounded like a salute.

"Let's make this a quick trip, Hughes," Smith instructed. Normally a driver from the motor pool was assigned to transport Smith. Tonight was different. Hughes, one of Smith's best operators, was positioned behind the wheel, a man sworn to the boss's darkest confidences.

The van maneuvered through a maze of arriving, departing, and parked cars and vans. Smith sat quietly as the van traveled north on the parkway toward Langley. He stared blankly over the gorge cut by the river at the spires of the Georgetown University chapel on the opposite side of the Potomac; then at yellow rectangles, the lit windows of houses along Canal Road in the far northwest corner of the District; and finally at the dark green and black woods as the van glided up the parkway.

The van stopped at the main gate that led to the George Bush Center for Intelligence. Two vested sentries with long guns greeted it. Taking one look at Smith, the sentries quickly ushered the van into the compound after verifying credentials.

Smith pulled his phone from his coat pocket and called Nate Harding, the best backup man in the business. Smith had brought Harding up slow, from the minor leagues to the majors.

Harding answered his phone promptly.

"Sorry to bother you," Smith said. "It's just that I may need to call upon you for some help."

Harding had already heard about the drowning on the news. "Daingerfield Island, you mean," he said.

"It's very dicey," Smith replied. "We had an operation this evening to apprehend a terrorist. It appears as though the plan may have gone awry."

There was a thoughtful pause. "Why was this your operation?" Harding asked.

Smith smiled to himself. The real question Harding was asking was whether it should have been an FBI operation. "They're mired in their own problems," Smith answered with a disdain that dated back to the rivalry between J. Edgar Hoover and 'Wild Bill' Donovan. "We got a special pass to play in our own backyard this time."

Harding stifled his doubts at such cavalier flouting of the agency's charter and, out of a sense of loyalty, asked how he could be of service.

"If the police conclude the Lewis woman's death isn't an accidental drowning, but possibly murder, they're going to launch an investigation," Smith said. "We can't have that, not now. We're very close to nabbing this terrorist. I have a series of options in mind. We'll have a new plan up and running within a day or two."

The driver was pulling up to the headquarters' front doors.

"We'll need a decoy," Smith went on, "a scapegoat. Someone who can be charged with a murder so as to stop the police from snooping around."

Harding's facial muscles tightened. "Wow," he said, although that was not what he was thinking, which was more along the lines of 'Are you fucking serious?' Yet he repeated himself. "Wow." Then he added, "So that's me?"

"I hope not, but, yes, maybe," Smith said. "It will only be temporary, just long enough to catch this bastard. I'll be back in touch, probably as early as tomorrow. As soon as I have a better idea how this is shaping up. Thank you, Nate."

Smith hung up and exhaled slowly. He still exercised dominion over Harding, as he did over Hughes. He turned to the operative and asked, "Everything go okay?"

"Yes, sir," the man replied. "No glitches on my end. Everyone is blaming that damned bicyclist for scaring away the terrorist before anyone had a chance to nab him. Sirens and everything, just like a carnival."

Smith's eyes narrowed. His lined face showed no hint of what he was actually thinking. It was important to maintain that all-seeing, all-knowing façade.

The van stopped. Smith looked out the window. He slowly filled his lungs with cold air, as though inhaling a drug.

My God, he loved this place. The buildings. The campus. Everything about it. Each time he entered, memories flooded his mind. Plots, confrontations, strategies, decisions on what to reveal and what to obfuscate, how to complete the mission. At all cost, complete the mission.

His mind wandered back to the days when legends roamed, men like 'Wild Bill,' Alan Dulles, Frank Wisner, and Jim Angleton. These were men who provided the DNA essential for the propagation of a special class of clandestine service member. Smith possessed that DNA, though of a slightly more perverted type.

In his early years with the CIA, he had believed forthrightness and fortitude would win the day. Slowly, reluctantly, when those virtues did not always work, he had adapted, doing whatever it took to survive, no matter how deceitful or duplicitous. And he developed a personal mantra: *Fight. Fight hard. Fight dirty. Prevail.*

"Shall I hang around?" asked Hughes.

Smith looked at him blankly, then nodded. "Yes. Stay on your phone, Hughes. I may have something you can do for me."

Smith grabbed his bag from the back seat and alighted from the van. He headed up the stairs and through the glass doors to the entrance of the main building. He swept his badge over the top of the turnstile and nodded to the two guards at a table located to the left.

His cell phone rang. That ring. The one he had programmed to provide advance warning of her calls.

He muttered to the guards. "What was that line from Faulkner?" They looked at him with blank stares, oblivious to what he was talking about. "'The past is never gone. In fact, it's never even past.' Something like that."

Everyone in the CIA knew that particular ring by now. They had heard rumors about the divorce, read about it online, or discussed it with somebody in the agency about how he had cleverly outmaneuvered his ex-wife. Always up to his tricks, Black Jack. Legendary shenanigans. This time he had used them to leave her high and dry, and vengeful.

The phone emitted that ring again. He stiffened, turned aside and answered it. Out of respect, the guards pretended not to listen.

"Hello, Eve," Smith said, keeping his voice low.

Yet another motion had been filed by his ex-wife to nullify a portion of their property settlement agreement. Everyone seemed to know about it. Someone even included it in a blog of the sordid doings of agency bigwigs. The audacity of having served it on him here, where he worked, had set the agency's rumormongers buzzing like an agitated beehive. But, in a funny way, he had asked for it, or so the blog said, by handling his post-divorce motions on a *pro se* basis, without counsel.

"I'm sorry, Eve," Smith rolled his eyes in disgust after pretending to listen to her rant a few moments. "I know. I know it doesn't seem fair." He listened again, feigning empathy. "I wish I could help you. I really do. I'd like to do more, but we have a final agreement. It's the law. The PSA is final."

More waiting. Then, "Hauling me back to court isn't going to gain you anything. It's a waste of our time. Maybe you don't have anything better to do, but I do."

More listening. Then, "I have to go."

Smith hung up. No one acknowledged hearing, though everyone passing through the lobby had heard it. These conversations were whispered about throughout the building. How he had screwed the ex-Mrs. Smith. How she would never give up. How she hounded him. All to no avail.

Smith walked down the hall to the elevator, his back rigid with indignity. The car's doors slid shut on his lone figure. He let his face relax into a grin as the elevator took him silently up to his office on the third floor.

Once ensconced in its seclusion, he opened his email account. The first thing his eyes fell upon was a report from June Webster giving the gory details of the foul-up at Daingerfield Island.

Below Webster's email report was a message from Lou Moultrie. Smith clicked it open and scanned the text. Immediately he understood the significance, as well as the peril. He steadied himself, considering options.

The phone rang. It was Detective Harry Bullock, another puppet on Smith's string. "Things fell apart really fast after that kid summoned the EMTs," Bullock said. "I was all set to nab our lone wolf, but he obviously panicked and fled."

"What happened to the bait?" Smith asked.

"I've got control of it," Bullock answered.

"Okay, good," Smith replied. "I'll give you further instructions later."

The call ended.

Next, Smith called Hughes.

"It's a good thing I asked you to hang around," he told the van driver. "Something's come up. Something big. Turns out we've been played, by one of our own. We're going to have to act fast. How quick can you get up to my office?"

Ten minutes, he was told. He cradled the phone. Hardly enough time to do what now had to be done. Smith reached out and called Will Painter in the IT section, another one of his lackeys.

"I need you to send a message," he instructed Painter, giving him June Webster's email. "Make the source look like Lou Moultrie. Say you took the flash drive from Libby Lewis's purse. Indicate it'll be returned in the morning. Add a line that you're afraid you might have been followed from Daingerfield Island."

Smith nodded as Painter repeated the message back to him. He checked the time. 8:15. Then he continued, "Send it in an hour, understand? Oh, and Painter, this is for your ears only. After the fiasco tonight, I don't want to hear so much as a whisper of this in the building."

A knock came at the door. Hughes was early. Smith hung up on Painter and opened his office door. He closed it after his guest entered.

**

SMITH STOPPED in the men's room on the way to the Operations Center. He was already late. The arrangements with Hughes had taken longer than expected, but that was no problem. It was fortunate that he had checked that email from Moultrie when he did. He tried to imagine the predicament he would be in otherwise.

He splashed cold water on his face and checked his appearance in the mirror. He made sure his gray hair was properly brushed, the cold expression in his eyes sufficiently foreboding. His complexion was slightly flushed, an adjunct of age. He grabbed a paper towel, ran cold water on it, and dabbed his cheeks.

Show time.

Inside the war room, blue lights from computer monitors ringed the perimeter like fluorescent pearls. The room had the cool elegance of a lounge, with lights on each table covered by cool lampshades. Maybe the Rat Pack would drop by later tonight.

As Smith stepped inside, analysts raised their faces from their computer screens. Their eyes and glasses reflected the light from the monitors. Their heads turned in unison as June Webster, head of the section, spoke.

"Welcome back," she said with a tight smile, staring at Smith with dark eyes.

"How did it go?" he asked, pretending not to know.

"Not well." Admitting failure was always difficult for Webster, as it was for all of them. Smith showed no emotion. His thoughts were elsewhere, plotting the night's activities, and beyond.

"Perhaps we need to reconnoiter," he said.

"Perhaps."

Two months earlier, an alarming terrorist-related blog had been posted, its point of origin the Washington metropolitan area. Intelligence experts had confirmed the existence of a lunatic who was threatening mayhem in the shadow of the nation's capital. Another lone wolf, a type whose actions had become a routine occurrence, too often leading to bloody violence. The Navy Yard. A movie theater. Too many schools.

Smith had argued passionately for the agency's involvement in apprehending the terrorist before he had a chance to carry out his threats. The FBI's lapses in performance had embarrassed the administration and enraged Congress, making the bureau unsuitable for this operation, he claimed. Finally getting a reluctant green light for the CIA to take the lead, Smith had developed a plan as bold and audacious as any he had launched in his notorious career.

He proposed luring the terrorist into the open with an enticing invitation to participate in a terrorist plot, one devised by Smith.

What could be more tantalizing than planning the assassination of Jumaa al-Issawi, the flamboyant Arabian sheik who was arriving by train from Richmond to Washington on Tuesday, the 9th of November? Praised by The Washington Post, Le Monde, Politico, Belgium's Le Soir, The New York Times, MSNBC and others, al-Issawi advocated dialogue between radical terrorist groups and the West. Extremists would welcome his elimination, Smith said.

Information offered on a thumb drive promised to include details about the time, the route, and the car in which al-Issawi would be traveling. With that knowledge, a successful attack could be launched, perhaps by laying an IED along the tracks, or hiding in the brush along the route with a sidewinder missile. The bait had even informed the terrorist of the most vulnerable location along the tracks, just to be helpful.

Libby Lewis, Chief of Staff to the Senate Intelligence Committee, had been enlisted to help carry out the plan. Through a series of carefully orchestrated emails, tweets, blogs and computer entries targeted to specific audiences, all conducted under Smith's watchful supervision, Lewis had adopted the persona of a Capitol Hill staffer hellbent upon al-Issawi's demise.

A rendezvous was scheduled between the lone wolf and Lewis. The thumb drive containing the encoded data was prepared. The deal was on, the trap set.

Arrangements had called for sharing the flash drive at Daingerfield Island on Halloween. A dozen agents were stationed onsite, all prepared to take down the terrorist and charge him with conspiring to commit terrorist acts.

For Smith, a hand-to-hand trade had major drawbacks. Lewis could get hurt, especially if the buyer was fool enough to let her see his face. If the apprehension of the terrorist did not go smoothly, if he escaped or struggled, and managed to fire off a clip, someone else could get injured, maybe even killed.

If that happened, what would the media report the next day? 'Terrorist Nabbed at D.C. Marina.' Highly unlikely. More like: 'Sting Operation Goes Haywire: Fed Agent Killed.'

So Smith had built in hints of suicidal tendencies in Lewis's emails and other communications, just enough clues to enable him to stage Lewis's suicide at the exchange place. That would leave the bait untended.

A cadaver would be placed in the Potomac River to make the terrorist believe the hysterical Lewis had despaired and done herself in. Seeing the body, and a woman's bag lying on the bulkhead, the terrorist would instinctively go for the purse, or so Smith theorized. As the terrorist reached for the purse, he would be apprehended. Terrorist plot squashed. Headline to read: 'Ingenious Plan Foils Terrorist Plot.'

June Webster had objected. "It's completely unnecessary," she said, a polite way of calling it idiotic. Others agreed with her, but only behind Smith's back. In his presence, no one questioned the strategy. In fact, they praised it as brilliant cloak-and-dagger stuff reminiscent of the good old days. Against that backdrop, Webster had no chance.

Only days before the exchange, Smith had abruptly announced that he was needed on an investigation in Los Angeles. Ignoring Webster's loud protests, he had flown off and left her holding the bag. Now she and her whole section were stuck with the fallout of failure.

"About fifteen minutes before the target was slated to arrive, a bicyclist discovered the body and called EMTs to the scene," she explained to the gathered experts. "The whole thing fell apart with a great big bang. The sound of sirens ended the operation before it started."

Smith showed his disgust. "And the flash drive? What became of the flash drive? Was it left in the purse?"

"We're trying to figure that out now," Webster answered. "It's hard to know what's what right now. Fog of war, you know. We should have that information soon enough." Secretly, she welcomed the failure of the operation. It had always felt a little too theatrical, too old school.

A young aide entered, holding Webster's ID badge in his hand. "Excuse me for a minute," she said. "I'm having my badge updated." She reached for her purse, removing her Virginia driver's license from her wallet. "Have this photo swapped for the one in my ID," she explained, handing the driver's license to the aide. She looked at Smith. "The photo taken by security is hideous," she explained.

Even in the middle of a crisis, vanity ruled, Smith thought.

"Bring the new ID and the license back here," Webster said. "If I'm not around, give them to Derek." She pointed to Derek Fine, who stood silently at her side, slender and obsequious. The blue monitors cast an ominous glow over his face. The aide departed, clutching his responsibility, and Webster turned back to Smith.

"So, where were we?"

"We were trying to determine the whereabouts of the flash drive, June." Smith shook his head. "I can't understand it. After all the advance planning, the choreographing, the dozens of agents stationed at Daingerfield Island, and the hundreds of hours spent planning the takedown. I can't understand how you allowed it all to collapse like this." He headed to the door. "Figure out how to salvage this project," he bellowed as he stormed out of the room.

Webster retreated to a corner and surveyed her crew. Young people filled the space, all of them dedicated to the mission. They were working on a Sunday night, and it was Halloween. Granted, it was not Thanksgiving or Christmas. But some of them might already have children of their own. Others surely had parties to attend. Now that she looked at them closely, she saw a few were in Halloween costumes.

"I appreciate everyone being here tonight," she said, raising her voice to be heard. "Let's see if we can wrap up this caper in a reasonable time and get out of here."

**

BACK IN HIS OFFICE, Smith remained calm as he considered his next action. He had to stay ahead of everyone by at least two moves. Tomorrow morning, he concluded, clues linking Harding with Libby Lewis's death would have to surface. The police would inevitably follow those leads, and Harding would become the temporary fall guy. Yet Harding, like Moultrie, might turn into a liability. So, like Moultrie, he would have to be neutralized as soon as his usefulness ceased.

Hughes should already be on his way to clean things up.

CHAPTER 5

THE UNMARKED white van traveled south through dark shadows of solemn trees cast by a full moon. At the seven mile marker of the parkway heading to Mount Vernon, it turned left, crossing the northbound lanes and stopping at a closed gate that led down to a parking lot along the river. A sign on the side of the drive read: "Park Closed at Dusk."

Hughes exited the van. He removed a key from his pocket and opened the lock that secured two links of the chain wrapped around the bar of the gate. He unwound the chain, pushed the gate open, returned to the van and drove through. Then, after placing the van in park, he returned to the entrance, closed the gate and wrapped the chain around the posts, leaving the opened lock dangling from one of the links. He returned to the van and drove down to the deserted parking area.

Stars sparkled in a black sky. The air was growing cold. A train's horn sounded somewhere out in the distance. Sound travels far on a clear night.

**

A MILE AWAY, behind a ranch house abutting a broad creek that flowed into the Potomac, Lou Moultrie stood on his dock, looking up. He raised the glass in his hand and placed it over the moon like a stamp, staring at the colors shining through the ice cubes, bourbon and crystal.

He took a big gulp of booze and headed back to the house.

It had been a mistake from the outset. The plan was flawed. He had said nothing, just like the others, standing mute before Smith's insistence that it would attract the terrorist like a moth to a flame. Now he understood the reason.

As Moultrie ruminated, Hughes was pulling a small rubber raft out of the back of the white van and carrying it down to the water's edge. Then he retrieved the remainder of his belongings, placed them in a plastic bag, and put the bag in the deep pocket of the dark vest he wore. He launched the raft silently.

Once on the water, Hughes turned his craft to the right, moving against the current under the stone bridge that fed into the same creek that flowed behind Moultrie's house.

Moultrie stepped off the dock and walked up the flagstone path to the back of his house. He pushed the screen door to the side before opening the glass patio door and slipping through it. The door behind him remained unlocked.

Suddenly he heard a commotion. Noises on the front walk. The sound of feet running up from the street. The front doorbell rang. Moultrie hurried to the foyer and opened the door.

"Trick or treat!"

A fairy princess and a big fat tomato stared up at him. He grabbed a ceramic bowl off a table beside the door and told the children to help themselves. They did, plunging their tiny hands into the bowl and pulling out as many miniature candy bars as their hands could hold.

No matter. It was unlikely that there would be many more goblins tonight.

The children turned and scurried back to their parents with their loot.

Moultrie smiled wanly. He had children, somewhere. A son and a daughter, both fully grown and long since moved away. He had no idea where either of them had settled. He had never met their spouses, assuming they were married, or seen their children, if any.

His family life had fallen apart long ago, a consequence of being wedded to the system. It demanded total allegiance, depriving him of a normal life. As the final irony, his abject loyalty had subjected him to a buffoon like Jack Smith, who ran around on cloak-and-dagger missions that bordered on the insane.

Moultrie closed the front door. He grabbed his drink and

stepped into the study to refresh it. After he took another gulp, he stepped over to the computer.

Why had Eve reached out to him? Did she really believe he had the balls to confront Smith? Well, he had surprised even himself by firing off that email. Maybe she had read him right, after all.

He heard more noises from outside and the sound of approaching footsteps. Another group of goblins had formed at his front step, giggling loudly. The doorbell rang.

"Trick or treat!"

As Moultrie returned to the front door, the raft was approaching the dock at the edge of his property. The man who navigated it grabbed hold of the planking, pulled the raft alongside, and secured it with a rope. He retrieved the plastic bag from his vest pocket, removing the handgun and silencer.

His rubber soles were silent as he walked along the dock to the house.

**

A U.S. PARK POLICEMAN was making his rounds along the parkway from the southern edge of Old Town Alexandria to the scenic majesty of Mount Vernon, eight of the most beautiful miles of urban highway in America.

The officer stopped at the entrance to the park overlooking the Potomac River about a mile north of the Mount Vernon mansion. He noticed the lock dangling from the chain wound around the gate. He got out of his cruiser and inspected the situation, spying the white van in the parking lot below, glistening by the light of the moon. He drove down to inspect the vehicle. He did not find anything out of the ordinary and assumed a fisherman was somewhere along the shore. He took the license number of the van, along with its make and model, and departed. The officer left the gate unlocked. The fisherman meant no harm and would be gone in an hour or so, he reasoned.

LOU MOULTRIE was putting the remaining candy away and turning off the front porch light. It was too late for any more trick-or-treaters. He poured himself another bourbon, then walked a wavering path into the family room and turned on the television.

His cell phone rang.

Moultrie went toward the hall table to answer it. He thought he saw something from the corner of his eye. The phone rang a second time. He turned his head and noticed the sliding door to the patio was partially open. He tried to remember. Had he closed it?

Before the thought could be processed, the first bullet struck his skull, jerking his head and torso backward. The glass flew out of his hand. The phone rang a third and final time. Two more bullets were fired from the muffled handgun in rapid succession.

The shooter moved into the room and pointed the gun down at Moultrie's chest. One more bullet was lodged in the heart for good measure. The shooter couldn't hit a target at thirty feet, but close range was not a problem.

CHAPTER 6

DEREK FINE stood in the hallway, furiously punching the password into his smartphone. He had mistyped it twice already. Then success. He texted:

She's headed back to her office.

As Fine sent the message, June Webster was racing down the hall. Jack Smith had been observed entering her office about ten minutes ago. Creating a debacle out of tonight's events was one thing, but invading her privacy was totally unacceptable.

She burst through the door. "What do you think you're doing?"

Smith stood in front of her desk. He had already slipped his phone into his inside breast pocket, right after reading Fine's warning. He dropped the papers on the desk.

"When did this happen?" he asked indignantly. "Why wasn't I notified immediately?"

Webster had entered full of her own indignation. Now she was forced to play defense.

"What are you talking about?" she bridled, pretending not to understand. But she knew very well what he meant. It was the recent report about Moultrie, questioning his loyalty.

"This taints the entire operation," Smith said, stabbing the dropped paper with a forefinger. "It was doomed before it ever got started. Moultrie might have sabotaged it."

"No, he didn't." Webster stalked around to stand by her desk chair. "Your plan never made sense anyway. And I don't even know where this report originated. It professes to come from the Inspector General. But I called over there, and they don't know anything about it."

"Quit defending Moultrie," Smith demanded.

"He's a good man, Jack," she said. "Once upon a time, the best man."

"Not any longer," Smith snapped. "He's a potential liability."

"You're the one who said we didn't need to worry about Moultrie," Webster reminded him. "You were defending his conduct just a week ago."

"I said no such thing," he replied with self-righteous indignation. "Those weren't my words. I said let's make sure we don't put him in a position where he can compromise the operation. That's exactly what I said."

Webster regretted her failure to keep a record of Smith's schemes. If this operation went south, as appeared to be the case, she knew he would shift the blame onto her. "I believe you're the one who entrusted Moultrie with a critical role in this operation," she said, her voice cold.

Smith smarted under the shaft of truth. "That's not entirely true either, and you know it, June. I never entrusted anything to him. It sounds to me like you're preparing your narrative. Maybe you can tell a congressional committee that story six months from now, but don't try to pull it off with me."

He stared at Webster. Stared through her.

With most people, Webster was assertive and intimidating. But one-on-one with Smith, she seemed to fall apart. Maybe because Smith possessed a character so duplicitous it distorted normal human interactions.

"Maybe you'll change your tune if I tell you he has the thumb drive," she said.

"He has the what?"

"The thumb drive," she assured him. "He emailed a few minutes ago. I tried to reach him, but no answer. As soon as things went south, he apparently slipped it out of the purse and took it home with him. He'll return it in the morning."

Smith's burning criticism did not subside. "Why did he grab the thumb drive? It should have been returned to this building, immediately. It contains important classified information."

Webster pursed her lips. "He says he might have been followed from Daingerfield Island. He might be in danger."

Suddenly Smith's complexion changed. "Then you'd better call again to check on him," he said. "Make sure he's okay. If there's no answer, send someone over. Do it right away. My God, we don't want anything else to go wrong tonight."

"A minute ago you loathed the man," she said.

"Not anymore," Smith replied. "Not if his life is imperiled. We have to do everything we can to safeguard our own. It's all we've got."

CHAPTER 7

THE POTOMAC RIVER glistened under the full Halloween moon. From the portico of the mansion, where eight large two-story-high beams supported the roof of a porch identical to George Washington's Mount Vernon, an expansive and manicured lawn rolled down to a tree line, which cascaded further down to the broad river. The moon's glow ran across the water, dancing and flickering over the wavelets.

"It's beautiful," Joey Cook observed.

"Aye, mate, that it is," replied Elmo Katz, wearing a billowing white shirt, black vest, swashbuckling red sash and black pantaloons. A bandana, eye patch, buckle shoes, and one loop earring completed the costume. "But with those on, how can you tell?" he asked, pointing to Cook's glasses.

Dressed like John Belushi's twin Blues Brother, Cook adjusted his sunglasses. "I can see just fine," he insisted.

"If you say so."

The Blues Brother and the pirate sat in rocking chairs on the porch under the moon's glow, sipping wine and smoking cigars. It was nearly 10 p.m. People promenaded out on the lawn and down the walk to the river.

Cook had already made an unsuccessful pass at a roller derby queen, who had swerved away and rolled over to a Groucho Marx clone.

"To quote Marx, 'A woman is an occasional pleasure, but a cigar is always a smoke,'" Cook said.

They smiled at one another. Cook was a prize, an aging cop with a dead-end career, facing the headwinds unflinchingly.

"I appreciated your call today," Katz said. The tantalizing tidbits of information Cook provided Katz were priceless, and Katz felt a need to constantly stroke Cook's ego to keep the pipeline of information flowing. "I don't want you jeopardizing your job for me. But

Fortune's a decent kid. With a little luck, Tony will settle down and straighten out."

"His girlfriend's expecting a baby any minute," Cook said, who knew Fortune in a previous life as a juvenile court probation officer. "I hope he grows up, for her sake. And I hope he quits taking risks. Always going to extremes. Usually to please or appease someone."

Katz stood up, placed his cigar under the rocker and crushed it. Fortune was his client, not his problem. "Let's go join the ball," he said.

As the two men moved toward the doorway, the roller derby queen suddenly bumped into them.

"Hey," she said to Cook, steadying herself against his broad shoulders. "I've been looking for you. Want to go for a whirl?"

"I thought you were with Groucho Marx," Cook replied.

"Don't be silly. Between a Blues Brother and a Marx Brother, I'm a sucker for that smooth Chicagoland sound."

Cook dipped his dark glasses and peered over them, making sure it was the same girl.

"Excuse me." Katz took his cue. Turning, he noticed Alexandria Sheriff Kevin Mulcahey, dressed impeccably in a three-piece pinstriped suit, and Jimmy Wolfe, dean of the defense bar, similarly clad in pinstripes, but thick vertical black and grey ones. "I'm going to check on the jailbird and his lawyer," he said. The duo had just finished speaking with the U.S. attorney, who was dressed as Liberty.

Phil Landry was rounding the corner, moving toward Katz. A second later, they found themselves abruptly face-to-face. "Excuse me," Landry said politely, and then, recognizing Katz, changed his tone, no longer sounding apologetic. "Mo," he said, "that outfit really suits you. A pirate, a buccaneer, a bandit."

"Where's your costume?" Katz asked, noting Landry's suit and tie. "Oh, I'm sorry, it looks like you're wearing one. You do a good job of impersonating a bureaucrat. You make a habit of that sort of thing?"

Landry, short and squat, a cop on detail to the Joint Terrorism Task Force, squared his shoulders. "Watch your step, Mo. One of these days I'm going to have you busted," he said loudly.

Katz smiled. Landry had had it in for Katz ever since he'd departed the commonwealth attorney's office, forever accusing Katz of bending the rules to get his client off for alleged criminal wrongdoing.

Mulcahey and Wolfe came up alongside. "Everything okay?" asked the sheriff. Both he and the denizen of the defense bar knew the score. No one wanted a scene at a social event. They got between Katz and Landry, separating the men from one another.

"You should be back at your law office, preparing for trial," Wolfe instructed Katz. "I understand you're going up against Kathy White in a drug case in the morning."

Landry scowled. "You'll use every trick in the book to help another crook get off, Katz. I don't know how you can live with yourself." Suddenly Landry's phone buzzed. As he read the message, an alarmed expression crossed his face. "I'd like to stay a little longer and bust your chops, Mo, but duty calls." Then he was gone.

CHAPTER 8

"OH, MY GOD," Mai Lin said repeatedly as David Reese told his story. It was after eleven, but neither of them could get to sleep.

Seeing a body in the water had been traumatic, of course. Still, there was something else, something bothering him as much as seeing a lifeless body in the Potomac, he told her.

"What is it?" she asked.

Reese removed a crumpled tissue from the pocket of his nylon racing pants. He unfolded the creased paper and showed her the tiny photo wrapped inside.

"Where'd you get that?"

It was a head shot of a nice enough looking woman.

"I found it in the grass where they tried to resuscitate that woman," Reese told her, holding the picture by its edges. "I think it fell out of a locket around the dead woman's neck."

Lin shook her head. "Why did you have to pick it up?"

"I didn't know what it was. I just slipped it in my pocket at the time."

"You have to turn it over to someone."

"Okay," Reese said. "I will."

**

Two hours later, Lin sat by the window, looking at the moon as her boyfriend slept. The story Reese had told her about finding that body was harrowing. If the woman had been murdered, perhaps Reese could have been in danger, too. She looked at the bureau. The tiny photo lay exposed on top of a tissue, touched by moonlight streaming through the window and across the room. Somehow Lin felt it was going to bring them trouble, maybe even ruin.

CHAPTER 9

Monday, November 1

ONLY THE LIPS were moving. Raspberry colored. Moving slowly and deliberatively.

"Ladies and Gentlemen of the Jury: *Fatta la legge, trovato l'inganno*." Pause. "Do you know what that means?" He gave the words a chance to dance in the jurors' minds. "I know what you're thinking. Cicero. Maybe Marcus Aurelius. If there's a playwright among you, you're wondering maybe Shakespeare. I mean, let's be honest, everything is from Shakespeare. Right? Or the Bible."

The jury laughed.

Now his eyes were moving. Eyes warm and playful, inscrutable. "Actually, I don't know where that expression originated, but loosely translated it means, 'Every law has its loophole.' Or 'Make a law and a way will be found around it.'" His eyes examined the twelve people in the jury box.

Katz moved about easily in familiar surroundings this morning, having tried dozens of cases in this courtroom. Like all the courtrooms in Alexandria Circuit Court, this one had high ceilings, with large windows that looked out over the roofs of urban brick townhouses like something painted by Edward Hopper. Behind Katz, rows of benches were set like church pews.

Anthony Fortune sat at the defense table, as mesmerized as the jurors were by his attorney's performance. He had slicked down his black hair, tied it back in a ponytail, and given his thin face a close shave. Respectable. That was what they were going for.

Fortune's pregnant girlfriend, Maggie Moriarty, about to deliver any day now, sat in the first row of spectators, per Katz's instructions. Her flaming red hair, curly as a sheep's fleece, floated on her shoulders. Moriarty had once told the lawyer that she suspected her boyfriend sometimes got himself into trouble just to watch Katz in action.

Katz stopped midway through his opening statement. On cue, Moriarty uttered a loud moan. She rubbed her swollen stomach.

Neither of them had shared this stunt with Fortune, who turned around with a spontaneous expression of concern that registered with most of the jurors.

Katz continued.

"No effort's going to be made in this case to go around the law. There's no reason to do so when the law is on your side. The pillars upon which our legal edifice is constructed are intended to punish the guilty. They are also intended to protect the innocent. So I don't believe in running away from things.

"I believe in meeting the allegations head on. And I do so because they'll guide the deliberations as to whether the defendant, Anthony Fortune, is guilty of any crime." Katz paused to run a friendly eye across the riveted jurors.

Walking around the podium, Katz stopped and rested his arm on it.

"You know, folks, truth is never as simple or as neat as a prosecutor makes it out to be. Truth is messy stuff. It's filled with strange twists and turns, most of which we're only half-conscious of in our daily lives because we're so busy with, well, living. With surviving.

"And, truth is, when you look at all the evidence here, there's not enough to convict this man of a crime. Oh, there's a scintilla, a little dab of what looks like guilt. But there is not enough evidence to show guilt beyond a reasonable doubt."

At the defense table, Fortune looked up admiringly out of the corners of his eyes. Katz was polished, persuasive, handsome, funny, and engaging. Yet, despite the outward appearances, Katz was feeding the jury a line, plotting to find a way to get an acquittal. The irony was not lost on Fortune.

"Thank you." Katz finished.

The judge turned to the prosecutor. "Call your first witness," she said briskly.

**

WITH MECHANICAL precision, prosecutor Kathleen White presented her case-in-chief. She began with the officer who had stopped Fortune.

A brake light had been out, the officer testified. The routine traffic stop had escalated when the officer smelled marijuana. Back-up was called. Fortune was asked to step out of his car. He stumbled. After backup had arrived, Fortune was put through a series of field sobriety tests. He passed, but refused to take a Breathalyzer test.

"What happened next, officer?" White asked.

"The defendant was placed under arrest."

"For what reason?"

"Refusing to take the Breathalyzer test, ma'am. It's a class one misdemeanor."

"And then what happened?"

"We conducted a search incident to a lawful arrest."

"And what, if anything, happened during the search?"

"Drugs were found in the glove compartment of the defendant's car, ma'am."

Katz rose. "Objection."

"State your grounds," the judge said.

"It has not been established that the car my client was driving belonged to him. He was certainly driving a car. But whether or not he was driving his own car, and whether or not he knew there were drugs in the glove compartment, and whether or not he possessed those drugs, are all questions that are in dispute, your honor."

White retorted, "I request that the Court instruct defense counsel not to testify, your honor. I still haven't heard the grounds for the objection."

The judge, a formidable black woman with twenty years on the bench, looked at Katz with a wry smile. The attorney knew how to put on a show. He reminded her a little of herself about thirty years ago.

"The last response will be stricken from the record, and the jury is asked to disregard any suggestion as to ownership of the vehicle at the time of arrest," the judge said. Then she looked at White and told her to proceed.

Turning back to the officer, White asked, "What did you find?"

"I found a small metal pipe and a glassine envelope containing what I believed to be marijuana."

"And what did you do?"

"I placed the envelope with the leafy matter I suspected as marijuana in a large plastic bag, sealed it, covered it with a piece of tape and signed my initials on the tape."

The prosecutor showed the officer a plastic bag and asked if he could identify it. He did, pointing to his initials on the tape.

"What did you do next?" she went on.

"I searched the trunk and found six more ounces of what appeared to be marijuana."

Next, White established through DMV records that Fortune was the owner of the car, removing any legal argument Katz might be planning of 'constructive possession.'

At eleven-thirty, the judge took a fifteen-minute recess, an indication she intended to hear testimony until one in the afternoon before breaking for lunch.

Katz and his client stood as the jury retired.

"That was a cheap trick," Kathy White said after the room cleared. Fortune and Moriarty had gone outside. "Having that pregnant girlfriend issue that mournful sigh. I thought you had more class than that."

Katz ignored the dig.

Fifteen minutes later, the judge resumed the bench. Fortune and his girlfriend were nowhere to be seen. Fortune was an old enough hand at this to know never to rile a judge. A judge was queen in her own courtroom, and this queen was getting angry, threatening to resume the case and issue a contempt of court citation. Just before she did so, Fortune sauntered back into the courtroom. Katz signaled that he should immediately take his seat.

"Where the hell have you been?" Katz whispered. "You know the rules." Luckily, the jury had not been summoned back into the room yet. "How many times have I told you that?"

"I had to call around for Mass times, Mr. Katz," his client replied. "It's a holy day and Maggie wants to go."

Katz shook his head. He wanted to be mad at Fortune, but, truth be told, he had great affection toward his client, often thinking of him as a younger brother. But for God's sake, Mass times!

No sooner had Katz finished admonishing his client than prosecutor White rose. "Your honor, before the jurors are summoned back into the courtroom, I'd like to take care of just a few *pro forma* matters. The first of which is to move the baggie identified by the officer in as evidence."

She nonchalantly walked over to the clerk's table and laid the baggie down.

Pro forma.

The judge asked, "Any objections, counsel?"

Katz eyed the court reporter and the bailiff. He stood up, stepped behind his chair and grabbed its back. "Yes, your honor."

"State your objection," said the judge.

"In presenting her case, the prosecutor makes it appear as though the arresting officer maintained custody over the drugs that were seized in the defendant's car. That's not exactly what happened. Officer Riley took possession of items in the vehicle that he believed to be narcotics, as he testified. And he placed those items in a box, sealed it, taped it, initialed it, and then gave it to another officer who arrived at the scene.

"That other officer – whose name is Dixon – placed the box in the evidence room. Officer Riley later took the box to the lab, and returned it, but the carrying of the evidence from the scene to the property room was done by Officer Dixon. The bag and the certificate can't come in as evidence because there's been a break in the chain of custody, your honor."

The judge, who hid her pro-prosecutorial bias well, appeared unfazed. This was, after all, easy enough to remedy. The prosecution could simply call Officer Dixon. Problem solved. She looked expectantly at White.

"Your honor," White said, "the prosecution requests a brief recess."

The judge knew this was never going to fly with Katz.

"The officer was not subpoenaed for trial, judge." Katz was ready, his lines all rehearsed. "He's not on the prosecution's witness list. I'm told he's actually out of town. Ms. White knew that he wasn't here when she moved the drugs into evidence.

"I object to any postponement in the proceedings, however brief," Katz went on. "This case has been continued twice already, both times on motion of the commonwealth. I move for a dismissal with prejudice."

White's silence admitted the truth. The judge looked disgusted but pounded her gavel.

"Case dismissed."

Katz started to agitate.

The judge added, "With prejudice."

Fatta la legge, trovato l'inganno.

Recalled and dismissed, a couple of jurors smiled, happy to see justice done.

White gathered her papers, shoveled them into a case and left. She was not really angry, just pretending to be. They both knew she had tried to sneak one by him.

Why be upset? It was only a matter of time before she got Fortune on something. Of course, if she was careless, Katz would try to do the same thing to her again.

Katz lingered after Moriarty and Fortune left, arm in arm and cooing like doves. Victory always tasted sweet. He spent a few minutes talking with the bailiffs and cops in the hall, then worked his way out of the court. He noticed Phil Landry's awkward figure, or thought he did, turning a corner far down a hallway.

**

BACK ON the street, Katz stopped on the front steps of the courthouse and checked his emails. One caught his eye. It read:

Need urgent help in criminal matter. N. Harding.

Katz propped his briefcase against the stairs, ran the cursor across the phone number at the bottom of the message, and hit the dial button.

"Harding," a voice answered on the first ring.

The voice did not betray it, but Nate Harding had done a lot of soul-searching over the past few hours. It began after he scanned the online news about Lou Moultrie's demise. Granted, it did not rate much of a headline. The drowning at Daingerfield Island had grabbed the main spotlight. Moultrie's death was being reported as the mere consequence of a residential B & E.

The previous evening Harding had spoken twice with Jack Smith. At first, Smith would only say that things were 'dicey.' It was all shaping up, he insisted. He had assured Harding that he would be in touch the next morning.

The time clock had been advanced to midnight, however, when the second call came. Harding's services were definitely needed. Libby Lewis's death was going to be declared a homicide. Someone had to step in as the would-be suspect. But only for a couple of days, Smith said. Only until the terrorist could be identified and captured. Then everything would be cleared up.

At Harding's insistence, Smith reluctantly shared the plan that had gone so terribly awry at Daingerfield Island. It all sounded crazy and confusing and twisted. That was how Smith operated. Every operation was a Rubik's cube.

Nate Harding sensed some sort of connection between Moultrie's death and events out at Daingerfield Island. He remembered Moultrie as one of Jack Smith's golden boys once upon a time, and as best man at Smith's wedding. Reminded of Smith's coldness, ruthlessness and cunning, and tendency to dump fellow agents into the cesspool, Harding decided he would need a hedge if he got involved in this latest caper.

"This is Elmo Katz," the lawyer was saying. "I received an email with this number on it."

"I appreciate your calling me back so quickly, Mr. Katz." Harding paused. "I'm not sure how to begin. My name is Nate Harding. I may be the subject of a police inquiry into a serious crime.

"It involves a woman, Libby Lewis. You may have heard about the drowning last night off Daingerfield Island. I have a bit of an emergency and need some quick legal representation."

Katz paced in front of the courthouse. "What sort of emergency?"

"My yacht, the *Won Way*, is being searched, right now, as we speak." Harding tried to keep his voice even and professional. "I found the police at the boat when I arrived a short time ago. I'm over at Dyke Marsh. It's located off the G. W. Parkway, just south of Alexandria, across from the Belle Haven Country Club."

"I know where it is. I'm standing outside the Alexandria Courthouse now."

"Can you come? Now?"

"I'll be there in fifteen minutes," Katz assured him.

CHAPTER 10

DYKE MARSH lay about a mile from the southern tip of Alexandria City, along the Potomac River. A narrow road led to a small, unimpressive marina housing a few dozen vessels. From the tip of the marina one was exposed to a view of the Woodrow Wilson Bridge to the left and, to the right, the widening river bound for the Chesapeake Bay.

As his car turned into the marina, Katz found Nate Harding standing in the middle of the road. He was in his fifties, tall and beautifully tailored from top to toe. Everything about him was angular: facial bones, figure, clothes, even movement.

"I realize these are highly unusual circumstances," Harding explained after their introductions. "I appreciate your coming on such short notice."

Harding pointed toward the water. "There's a police officer directing a forensic crew to swab the deck of my boat for evidence. My inclination is to let them proceed. I just need to think it through. Will you help?"

"I'll give it a shot," Katz promised.

They walked down to the boat while Harding explained that the police were convinced he was involved in the murder of Libby Lewis the previous day. Katz nodded. He had heard some of it on the radio news.

"Your Fourth Amendment rights prohibit the police from snooping around," Katz advised. "They need to secure a search warrant based on probable cause. In the absence of a warrant, we'll get them the hell off the boat."

Harding shook off the advice with a sideways nod. "They're not going to find anything. By permitting them to continue, I can demonstrate I have nothing to hide. I may be doing myself a big favor."

Yellow crime scene tape blocked access to the vessel and parking spaces at the edge of the pier. A four-member team wearing plastic gloves and plastic shoe coverings swarmed over the boat's deck. More were below. Cameras clicked as swabs, tweezers, fingerprint powder, and electronic devices were employed to gather hair, fluids, prints, and fibers for transport to the lab for further examination.

A silhouetted figure stood sentry, one leg perched over the starboard side and the other planted firmly on deck.

"Bullock," Katz shouted. "You'd better have a search warrant."

The silhouette turned its head and scowled.

"I'm serious," Katz continued. "If you don't, I'm calling the cops and alleging trespass."

"I am 'the cops,' Mo."

While Bullock was not taking Katz's threat seriously, the same could not be said for the forensic team, who had overheard him, as he intended. The team members had stopped working, with gloved hands holding tweezers and cameras in freeze frame. They had probably questioned the legality of the search from the moment they arrived. Bullock's reputation preceded him.

"Show me a warrant," Katz demanded. He and Bullock stood face to face now. "If you don't have one, stop the search and get the hell off of the boat."

Katz directed the next statement to the forensic crew at large. "If you are not operating under a warrant, everything you've obtained to this point is tainted and inadmissible in court. In addition to filing a motion to suppress the fruits of this illegal search, I will file suit against you, each one of you, individually and severally, for violating my client's right to privacy."

That always scared them.

Bullock raised his hand like a cop directing chaotic traffic at an intersection.

Katz smiled and lowered his voice. "I can't believe you're still pulling this shit, Harry. When are you going to learn?"

They had been partners once upon a time, a fly-by-the-seat-of-your-pants cop and a hotshot prosecutor.

Bullock, who was a sergeant in those days, had done the dirty work in the street, while Katz turned it into poetic justice. Making a deal with a snitch in a drug case or getting someone to turn state's evidence in a particularly gruesome homicide was Bullock's forte. It was less than dignified but, in front of a jury, Katz made it look that way.

Together they had racked up a string of convictions considered unwinnable by the police department, the majority of the prosecutors in the commonwealth attorney's office, and almost everyone in the defense bar.

Bullock was, at best, overzealous. He suffered from a disorder best described as law and order naiveté. Stop. Arrest. Convict.

At times, Katz considered Bullock a certifiable nut case. He was so fixated on stopping bad guys that he was hardly a force for good. Bullock was a menace to the force, actually.

"Mr. Katz your attorney?" Bullock asked Harding as he stepped off the boat.

"Mr. Katz is indeed my lawyer," Harding replied stiffly. "But he advises me, that's all. I make my own decisions. If the police want to search the boat, I don't necessarily have any objection."

Katz felt played. It was not simply because he thought Harding had made a miscalculation. It was something worse, more sinister. Katz's instincts were telling him that Harding had summoned him for the sole purpose of having counsel present before giving the police consent to search the *Won Way*. Katz was just window dressing.

Assuming a search proceeded without a warrant, and incriminating evidence was uncovered, a defense attorney could argue the evidence was inadmissible because of a lack of consent, i.e. a knowing and intelligible waiver of the Fourth Amendment. But, if defense counsel was present when the consent was given, that was another story.

"I don't have anything to hide," Harding continued, as though an explanation was needed. "If a search is going to clear my name and eliminate me from a list of suspects, then I very well might consent to the police doing all of the forensic testing they want."

The policeman turned to his crew. "Don't start packing up yet, folks. We might be going back to work in a minute or two."

Turning back to Harding, Bullock said, "Take all the time you need to consider your position, sir. We're not in any hurry."

Katz marched Harding away from the boat and, hopefully, away from the terrible decision he was making.

"This is no time for vindication," Katz whispered. "Right now, this is an open-ended investigation. There may or may not be sufficient evidence to bring an indictment. If there's an indictment, there may not be sufficient evidence to convict you. What in the hell are you trying to accomplish?" Katz wondered if Harding was even listening.

Across the way, the detective was keeping his eyes trained on the two men, hoping Harding would disregard his attorney's advice and give in.

"This is the moment they decide whether to label me a suspect or leave me alone," Harding said, his jaw taut.

Suddenly Harding's phone buzzed. He yanked it out of his pocket, glanced at a message, and tucked it away. Thirty seconds later, another phone rang. Katz glanced over as Bullock took a call.

"Here's my analysis," Harding continued. "This forensic team isn't here by coincidence. Someone saw me and Libby on the water or at the marina. That's probably enough for probable cause. So even if your policeman friend doesn't have a warrant, I'm pretty sure he could get one."

Clients seldom had that kind of objectivity when it came to evaluating their own cases because it was their life, reputation, or freedom that was on the line. They rarely thought rationally in moments like this, and relied on counsel. That was not happening here.

Harding, whoever he was, acted cold and calculating.

"I give you my permission to search the *Won Way*," he yelled to Bullock. "Please proceed. You aren't going to find anything."

Katz's instincts were screaming that this was a horrible mistake, but he tried to remain stoic. After all, Harding was hardly the first person who had consented to a police search in the mistaken belief that cooperation provided the key to vindication. Except, of course, most of those people made split-second decisions without any opportunity to consult an attorney, and they were either drunk or high at the time.

"I think you just made a colossal error." Katz had to say it.

"I disagree," Harding shrugged. "Anyway, I know a restaurant about a mile away. Unless you've already written me off, let's meet there and work out the details of your legal representation."

"I haven't written you off." Not by a long shot, Katz thought to himself.

**

SMITH SLAMMED DOWN his phone as fleeting satisfaction turned to seething anger. It was not every day he pulled strings from both sides of the stage, as he was doing now. First with Harding, telling him to consent to the search, and then with Bullock, the local cop he had positioned at the center of the effort to run down the lone wolf, reminding him how to conduct the search. Yet the pleasure he derived from directing the show was dashed by Bullock's news that Harding had retained Elmo Katz, the same attorney Smith had used in his divorce case.

Smith turned to the laptop that Hughes had obediently dropped off earlier, the one that had been seized from Moultrie's residence. A careful scan of Moultrie's email folder confirmed the communication from Eve. Smith methodically deleted her incoming messages and Moultrie's to him. Next he would instruct Hughes to ditch the computer. Nobody would ever know those emails existed.

CHAPTER 11

IT TOOK KATZ ten minutes to find a parking space. When he got to the entrance of the restaurant Harding had indicated, he saw a bright red Audi parked right in front. The license plate read 'Won Way'.

Nate Harding was seated at the lunch counter. He rose, and they found a table at the far end of the restaurant, a long narrow shop shaped like a shoebox with booths along one wall and the counter on the other.

After they were seated, Katz lowered his voice and asked for particulars on his client's involvement in the Libby Lewis case.

Harding acknowledged having Lewis on board his boat a few days earlier. "It was innocent. We went out for an afternoon on the water. Now the police think I killed her."

"Did you?" Katz asked bluntly.

Katz was always direct with his clients. There was no room for niceties when it came to criminal misconduct. The only thing that would save a client was if the attorney knew exactly what had happened. If Katz knew the truth, he could maneuver, sometimes around the truth, sometimes through it. But he needed to know it.

Katz curled his hand into a fist and placed it under his chin, a knuckle touching his lower lip.

"On my way over from Dyke Marsh, I listened to the news." Katz spoke slowly. Trying to navigate. "They were calling it a suicide last night. Now there's speculation it was murder. I wonder what's changing everyone's thinking so fast."

Nate Harding immediately went for a conspiracy. "I have a lot of enemies, Mr. Katz. They would love to have something pinned on me."

They sat in silence about two minutes, eyeing each other curiously. Then Katz said, "Tell me what happened."

Harding sighed. "Where do I start?"

"At the beginning."

"Alright. I've known Libby for years. She's a bit younger than me, under forty. We were attracted to each other the moment we met, but we didn't start a full-fledged relationship until the last few months.

"She's single and I'm divorced. Neither of us was looking for permanence. The relationship was all about sex. Always about sex."

"What kind of sex?"

"Nothing kinky, if that's what you mean."

"Go on," Katz urged.

"Recently the relationship hadn't been going well," Harding continued. "She'd been seeing someone else. I broached the subject once, but she didn't want to talk about it. I was grateful that we avoided it, to be honest. We both knew things would get heated if she leveled with me. So we talked around it." Harding looked off to the side. "Until we went out on the boat, that is."

"So you went out on the water with her yesterday?"

"That's right. It was perfect conditions, sweater weather but with the sun shining. She lives – lived – in Arlington. I live in the District. We agreed to meet at the marina in the mid-afternoon. She brought a bottle of wine along, which we drank at the pier. Then we went to the boat. Everything was going well, really well."

A waitress brought two glasses of water and placed straws on the table. Katz and Harding both ordered coffee.

Harding continued after the waitress left. "I made the mistake of asking if she was seeing someone. It was the first time I'd asked straight out. She responded by saying I didn't have the right to interfere with her life. I told her I had every right if we were going to continue a steady relationship. She got angry. It escalated from there."

"Escalated how?"

Harding took a straw and struck it on the table like a dagger, removing the wrapper with his fingers. Then he plunged it into the glass and drew water greedily into his mouth.

"I lost my temper and struck her," he said. "She fell and hit her head on the deck. At first, I thought, 'no big deal.' I was terrified, of course, but it wasn't a serious blow. I never intended to injure her. I expected her to get up."

"She didn't."

"That's right."

"What happened next?"

"I knelt beside her. I cried out her name. She didn't respond. I felt her pulse and couldn't find one. I realized something terrible had happened."

Tears appeared in Harding's eyes. "I never intended to harm her, Mr. Katz. I certainly didn't mean to kill her. I never even meant to strike her. It just happened. Heat of passion, you know."

Every client acted as if they were an attorney and everyone had a defense. They were all instant experts at self-preservation.

"What did you do next?" Katz moved him on.

"I dropped her body over the side, near Daingerfield Island."

Harding pressed his lips together. "I'm in trouble, Mr. Katz. I know it. That's why I sought you out. I know all about your reputation. I'm counting on you to get me out of this."

Katz lowered his voice. "You could have helped yourself at the time."

"How?"

"By doing just about anything other than dumping the body in the water. All you did was strike her. If you had stopped there, you'd be in trouble, but nothing like this."

Harding stammered, "I panicked. I just wanted it to be over. I thought it was plausible that, when her body was found in the water, it would be ruled a suicide."

"Really? You thought that was a smart way to have it be over? So you dumped the body over the side of the boat like a bag of trash."

Harding said nothing. The waitress returned with the coffees, placed them on the table and withdrew hurriedly, sensing the tension.

"This isn't something you can pretend away, Mr. Harding. Frankly, your action was one of the dumbest things I've ever heard from a client."

"I don't need to be lectured, you know. I can do that on my own."

Katz changed tack. "Did anyone see you during all this drama?"

"No. I'm sure no one did."

"What did you do next?"

"I returned to the marina. Then I drove her car up to Daingerfield Island. Her purse was in the car. I wiped it off with a handkerchief and placed it on the bulkhead, to make it look as though she'd jumped into the water.

"I called a taxi and returned to the marina. I wiped down the deck with bleach. Then I went home. About an hour later, I heard about the drowning on the news."

Katz summarized. "You managed to take an involuntary manslaughter charge, at worst, and transform it into first degree murder."

"Maybe, maybe not," Harding retorted. "No one saw me. Daingerfield Island was deserted when I got there. So was the marina. When I got back, there was nobody around. It was Halloween. Everyone was going someplace else to party."

"Except your taxi driver," Katz played along.

"They won't find him."

"They'll check every manifest of every taxi driver in Northern Virginia," the lawyer said. "They'll find him and then they'll squeeze him, because he's probably illegal or carrying enough baggage to be easy prey for the police."

"Then you'll be able to destroy the driver's credibility. Right?"

"An ID from the taxi driver will only be one data point." Katz let his exasperation show. "There's also the forensics. They are going to find stuff on the boat, no matter how well you cleaned up. That dumb move, letting Bullock search it, might blow up in your face. And the handbag. What about that? Were you wearing gloves?"

"No," Harding admitted, "but I wiped the surface of the purse clean."

"I'm sure you did."

Their conversation lapsed. They drank their coffees. Katz retrieved the smartphone from his pocket and texted Curtis Santana, his private investigator.

> With client at restaurant on S Washington St, down from the Bankruptcy Court. He's driving a red Audi. Parked in front. Need you to shadow him.

He hit *send*, then put away the phone and looked up at Harding. "Okay," he said, "given what you just told me, why let Detective Bullock search your boat? There have to be forensics on board linking you to the crime: hair, prints, fiber. Those experts are going to have a field day. What got into you?"

"I don't know. For a minute I was feeling invincible. It seems ridiculous now. I should have listened to you." Harding hesitated. "What are my chances?"

"Not good."

"You mean they're likely to arrest me?"

Katz laughed grimly. "I'm not talking about being arrested. I'm talking about your chances of spending the rest of your life behind bars."

"My decision to allow the police to search the yacht shouldn't be interpreted as a desire to admit guilt." Harding sounded downright pompous. "I intend to fight. You understand that, right? You'll defend me?"

"Of course I'll defend you. My leveling with you doesn't mean we don't put up a fight. A lot of strange things happen when you take a case to trial. You enter the theater of the unknown. If you get indicted, we'll plead not guilty at the arraignment. They'll set bail and we'll try to get you out pending trial.

"Whatever happens after that will be determined by the evidence. If it's a strong case, you may change your mind and instruct me to plea bargain. If there are problems with the prosecution, which is normally the case, the prospects grow for an acquittal or a hung jury.

"We're a long way from anywhere now. We'll strategize along the way, depending on how things shape up."

"I like you, Mr. Katz." Harding smiled. "I'm going to holler from the highest steeple I'm an innocent man. I'll do all I have to do to get myself off."

They shook hands. The conversation ended, Katz paid the bill and they walked out of the restaurant together. Harding got into the Audi and drove off.

As soon as Harding left, Katz phoned Santana. "Where are you?"

"I'm on Washington about two blocks north of the intersection with King Street."

"Well, slow down. Our client just left. If he's going back into D.C., like I suspect, he's going to drive right by you in a matter of minutes. You need to follow him."

"What's going on?"

"I just met with a guy named Nate Harding," Katz explained. "He called as I was finishing up with Tony's trial. Claims to have killed that woman at the marina last night. Except his story's been rehearsed."

Katz paused, then added: "I'm not sure what we're dealing with. It's all a ruse of some sort. Whatever it is, it's not a murder."

"He retained you?"

"Us."

Before they ended their call, Santana told Katz the news about Lou Moultrie's death.

"I didn't hear about it in the courthouse this morning," Katz said, surprised. He knew of Moultrie as the best man at Jack Smith's wedding.

"Moultrie was shot multiple times, from what I heard. There was an intruder, but the authorities are pretty sparse on the details."

"Does it strike you as odd?" Katz asked. "There's a drowning out at Daingerfield Island at dusk, and later in the night a CIA veteran is shot dead in his home."

"Yeah," Santana said excitedly. "And a red Audi just flew by me. I got to go." Santana ended the call and swung his car around in the opposite direction.

CHAPTER 12

WASHINGTON STREET had a traffic light at every inter-section, from one end of town to the other, a stretch of about two miles. To keep pace with the Audi, Santana did not have to stay right behind it, or even in the same block. He just had to stay synchronized to the lights. There was no problem if one light turned red; the next one was timed to follow suit in ten seconds or less. As a result, the private investigator fell a block and a half behind the red Audi.

The light ahead turned green. Santana stepped on the gas and shortened the space between the vehicles by half, and then by a single car length between them. Both vehicles exited Old Town and headed north toward Daingerfield Island and Reagan National Airport.

After Harding passed the airport, the lanes expanded from two to three. His Audi moved into the right lane. Without signaling, the Audi swerved suddenly into the turnoff lane to Gravelly Point, a park directly north of the airport that was a favorite place for people to watch the underbellies of airplanes as they came in for a landing on the tarmac.

Since he was directly behind the Audi, executing the same maneuver would have raised a suspicion. Santana was forced to remain in the right lane, heading toward the turnoff for the 14th Street Bridge.

A half mile down the road, Santana signaled, slowed, and jumped the curb, pulling off onto the grass a short distance before the bridge. Turning on his emergency blinkers, he put his Fiat 500 in park, then jumped out and ran back toward Gravelly Point.

Curtis Santana was a bundle of taut muscles developed in karate studios and boxing rings. Today, he wore khakis and an aged leather bomber jacket, with running shoes for mobility. Like any good investigator, nothing about him was memorable.

The parking lot was half filled. He spotted the Audi as he walked across the unoccupied soccer field. Harding was sitting alone in his car. Slowing, the investigator veered toward the riverbank. A casual glance around showed nothing unusual, just a guy sitting in his car, maybe working things out in his mind. Santana turned as though admiring the river view, but kept the Audi within sight.

About a minute later, a car pulled up. The driver got out and Harding did the same. Together they walked toward the river, directly toward Santana. They had their heads down, looking at their shoes instead of at one another. Santana took the opportunity to begin walking diagonally toward the parking lot.

Santana had no trouble recognizing Jack Smith as the man meeting with Nate Harding. For a time, he was even close enough to overhear their conversation.

"Why in the world did you do that?" Smith was saying to Harding. "Don't you trust me?"

"Listen, I honestly didn't know about the relationship. It's purely coincidental. I just thought I had to be represented, that's all. If only for the look of the thing."

"Do you expect me to believe that? Really? It was all over the media. In the *Post* and all the Washington blogs."

The roar of a jetliner approaching drowned out all other sound. Then the jet appeared, passing directly over them before gliding in for a landing on the tarmac at the north edge of the airport.

". . . did not do any research, if that's what you're alleging." Harding said, sounding defensive. Jack Smith was clearly agitated, and Harding seemed anxious to defuse the situation. Santana could tell Katz's client was jittery, as though the last thing he wanted to do was suggest to Smith that he doubted him in any way.

"It doesn't require any research, Nate," Smith said. "You know that. You just run a quick search on any website and the stories pop up." Smith folded his arms. "All I asked you to do was be available in case we needed you to play a role in this case for a couple of days. Nothing so dramatic that you should run out and retain counsel."

"That's what I'm saying," Harding protested. "It would look odd if I weren't represented by somebody."

Smith grimaced. "I don't know if I can trust you, Nate," he said. "I need someone I can count on. Someone who's a team player."

As the two men continued to walk toward the water, their voices fading, Santana strolled through the parking lot. Once at the end, he receded into the landscape and returned to his stranded car. Fortunately, no police officer had come upon the scene to investigate why an automobile had been pulled off to the side of the parkway with its lights blinking.

**

AS HE PULLED away, Santana rang up Katz. "Your suspicion was dead on."

"What happened?"

"Harding pulled off at Gravelly Point," said Santana. "He was joined by none other than Jack Smith, your erstwhile client."

Katz reacted with a look of surprise.

"They took a little stroll down by the river," Santana continued. "Smith is furious, accusing Harding of betraying his trust."

Katz reflected on his role as Smith's divorce attorney. "Smith knows it's no coincidence Harding retained me. It's a way for Harding to assert a modicum of control in their relationship. After all, I know some of Smith's secrets."

"What's going on, Mo?" asked the private investigator.

"I'm not sure, exactly," Katz confided. "Harding has confessed to a crime he didn't commit. I don't know why, but it obviously has something to do with Smith. Probably some sort of spy shit." Katz didn't know any better way to describe it. No matter. Santana understood what he was trying to say.

"It's confounding as hell," Santana said.

'We should have a better idea in a couple of hours about the Lewis case," Katz said. "I heard Jordin Deale is going to hold a press conference this evening."

"What for?"

"She's going to announce it's either a suicide, an accident or a homicide. My guess is a homicide, and our client Nate Harding's going to be indicted."

Santana grunted. "Later," he said.

As Katz ended the call, he wondered what they had gotten themselves into this time.

CHAPTER 13

ALEXANDRIA COMMONWEALTH ATTORNEY Jordin Deale anxiously awaited Detective Harry Bullock's arrival in her office. "What have you got?" she demanded when he finally arrived.

"Several things," Bullock replied in a voice that satisfied Deale's ire. He propped an evidence bag on the chair in front of her desk.

"We recovered a purse belonging to Miss Lewis. Her phone was inside it. The last number she dialed, at right around 3 p.m. yesterday, was Nate Harding's."

"Is the phone in there?" asked Deale.

"It's at the lab," Bullock answered. "They're running forensics and pulling text messages, emails, phone numbers, contacts and addresses. There's a treasure trove of communications between the two of them. They had a thing going on."

Deale cocked an eyebrow.

"Maybe it was getting messy," Bullock teased, suppressing a grin.

"What else?" Deale asked.

"Harding's fingerprints are on the purse. He'd wiped most of it, but missed a couple on the clasp. Her own have been wiped or are just smudges. Clear sign somebody rubbed it down after she handled it. So far as I can tell, Harding killed her on the boat and dumped the body overboard. He returned the boat to Dyke Marsh, where she'd parked her car, and drove it up to Daingerfield Island. There he planted the purse on the bulkhead to make it look like an accidental drowning."

"What about her car?"

"It's impounded. They're running forensics on it. The steering wheel's been wiped, but Harding's prints are on the dashboard."

"How did he leave Daingerfield Island?" Deale asked.

"We're looking into that now. Perhaps he had an accomplice, or maybe he used a cab. Either way, he goes back to Dyke Marsh to get his own car and then drives home, cool as a cucumber."

Deale ran her manicured hands down her pearl necklace as though she was stroking worry beads. Forensics were still being prepared. They'd found their likely suspect, but the evidence was still being gathered.

Deale looked at Bullock. She was trying to avoid making a decision.

"It's enough, Jordin," Bullock assured him. "The guy did it."

Deale was less than sure. She was looking for just a little more. "Wasn't there any blood found on the boat?"

"Nothing we can confirm," Bullock admitted.

"Why not?"

"Well," Bullock stammered. He scratched his cheek where a half day's growth of dark beard showed. "There were some flecks of blood on board the boat, all right." He looked at Deale. "But we've got nothing to compare it to right now. We're getting a search warrant for the Lewis woman's place, since her body was cremated early this morning."

Deale jumped out of her chair. "Cremated! What the hell is that about?"

"I know," Bullock said in a voice as dumbfounded as hers. "I don't have any details. All I know is that's what happened." He fell silent. Then he shrugged. "Listen, I went ballistic when I heard about it, too. There's no good explanation. It defies logic. All I can say is we're looking into it."

"Did the coroner get a chance to finish the autopsy at least?" demanded Deale.

"He's sure her death was caused by blunt force trauma," Bullock said cautiously. "I'll have to check with him about any other test."

"We're all going to look like idiots if this case goes south," Deale muttered.

Bullock tried his best to put the prosecutor at ease. "Look. Don't worry. It won't. Go south, I mean. In the end, you'll be a hero. I have a good feeling about this one."

Deale still hesitated. "Listen," she said, "it turns out Daingerfield Island was crawling with LEOs that night. There was either a convention for local cops, to which I was not invited, or some kind of operation was in progress, about which I was not informed. On my turf!"

Bullock shook his head. "I know. I saw them."

"What have you uncovered about it?"

"Turns out it was some exercise being run out of Langley. I'm having a difficult time prying information out of folks. Most likely nothing to do with the woman found in the water. I'm not sure. Give me a few days."

"Well, find out," she instructed. "U.S. Attorney Douglas was also kept in the dark."

Bullock nodded.

"Okay," Deale said, throwing her hands up. "Let's go ahead and do this thing."

Show time would be at seven – an evening news extra.

**

BULLOCK PLACED THE EVIDENCE BAG on the counter at the entrance to the property room. Joey Cook was in the back, playing on his computer. "Hey, Sergeant Cook," Bullock hollered, striking the counter like a drunk in a bar. "Can you get over here? I need you to check in these items from the Lewis case. I don't have a lot of time."

Cook hurried up front. "What's the good word, detective?" he asked. "I hear Ms. Deale is going to announce an arrest warrant tonight." He noticed Bullock was dressed in a suit and tie. "Are you going to be standing beside her in front of the cameras?"

"Just do me a favor and put all this back on a shelf," said Bullock, pushing the evidence bag toward Cook. Bullock was holding a thumb drive in his hand. "Everything except this. I'll maintain possession of it."

"What for?" inquired Cook.

"I'm going to have forensics see what's in it, if that's alright with you," Bullock replied sarcastically.

"I can do that for you, detective," Cook said. "Save you a trip. Standard operating procedure." Cook punched some letters on the keyboard at the end of the counter. A list of items appeared on the computer screen, the same ones Cook had inventoried Sunday night. Bullock was shaking his head, rejecting the sergeant's offer. "Then you'll have to sign out for it," Cook said.

"No need to," replied Bullock.

Cook noticed the thumb drive had been deleted from the inventory.

"Something wrong?" asked Bullock.

"Not a thing." Then, taking the thumb drive from Bullock's hand, he said, "I'll just put it in an envelope for you."

Cook disappeared into the shadows of the property room. Before Bullock could protest, his phone rang. Gus Wadley from the motor pool was updating Bullock's profile and needed the detective's customer identifier on his Virginia driver's license. "For Christ's sake," Bullock muttered as he pulled out his wallet and removed the license, squinting to read the tiny identifier number to Wadley.

An instant later, Cook reappeared with the thumb drive encased in a plastic bag. "Here you are," he said.

Bullock stuffed the baggie in his coat pocket and departed without saying a word.

CHAPTER 14

KATZ WAS in his office, finishing some fast food a little after seven and staring at his laptop screen, which was streaming the commonwealth attorney's press conference.

Katz's office at 771A Duchess Street was a tiny townhouse. The building was situated equidistant between the Alexandria City courthouse on King Street and the federal courthouse in the Eisenhower Valley. This provided a kind of symmetry, since half of Katz's clientele was tried in federal court, the other half in state court.

The building's front door opened directly into a spacious reception area, where during office hours Suzie Marston acted as greeter or wrangler, as needed. Her constant companion was Thunderbolt, a stray wire haired terrier who had adopted Katz's firm as his permanent abode.

Behind the reception area, a library and a small office were tucked in the far corner of the building. The furnishings throughout were spartan. Katz's office desk, inherited from his father, was an old teak Scandinavian style. The finish had rubbed off along the edge from two generations of use and was now grey rather than brown.

Dozens of manila folders lay in neat stacks on top of the desk. Most consisted of only a few pieces of paper: a uniform summons, handwritten notes on yellow legal paper from the initial interview, and a copy of the relevant state or federal criminal code.

Three larger files, off to the side of the desk, contained divorce papers, and the two bulky files next to them were filled with civil litigation filings. This was the desk's high rent district. These files paid the bills and let Katz dabble in the stuff he preferred, criminal law. Scattered among the files were a yellow legal notepad, a coffee cup filled with pens, pencils and markers, and another cup with dregs of yesterday's coffee.

Two broken-in leather chairs faced the desk. Beyond them, a bookcase was filled with files, folders and law books, all untouched and resting under a thin layer of permanent dust.

Katz, seated in one of the leather chairs, leaned in closer to his laptop as Jordin Deale began speaking.

"I'm here to announce a charging document against Nathaniel Harding in connection with the death of Libby Anne Lewis," she said.

"On the night of October thirty-first, Nathaniel Harding struck and killed Libby Lewis while the two argued on board his yacht, the *Won Way*, on the Potomac River. Mr. Harding proceeded to dump her in the river, where her body was eventually found just off Daingerfield Island.

"Initial signs pointed to suicide. Then law enforcement received a phone call from an unidentified eyewitness who claimed to have seen Mr. Harding and Miss Lewis sailing together that afternoon. Forensic examinations followed: of the boat; Miss Lewis' purse, recovered at the scene; and her motor vehicle, also located on Daingerfield Island."

Katz typed and sent a text message:

Jordin, I represent Nate Harding.

Next, he pressed the speaker button on his office phone and called Harding. "Are you watching?"

Harding answered immediately. "Yes. I just arrived home. I'm prepared to turn myself in."

"Good," Katz said. "I've reached out to the commonwealth attorney."

"The media and some friends are already deluging me with emails. What should I say?" Harding asked.

"Nothing," Katz warned him. "Anything you say can be used against you."

Harding inhaled deeply, then said, "Then maybe I should say that I'm innocent. What about that?"

Katz shot back, "What about listening to me for once?"

Harding was being stubborn again. "I should turn myself in. Then I can get released on bond and we can set about preparing our defense."

That was a stretch, namely believing, even for a minute, that Harding was going to be released on bond. Katz could not think of a sitting judge in the state court who would allow Harding to go free pending trial.

"Highly unlikely you'll be released on bond," he said. "Don't forget, this is a murder charge."

"You're not making me feel good," Harding replied.

"I think my job is to be honest with you. Truth is you're unlikely to be released on bond immediately."

"I want a bond, Mr. Katz," Harding insisted. "I don't care how high it is. I just don't want to be confined to a cell. I'm counting on you."

Katz kept his eyes on the computer screen. Deale was off camera now. Hopefully, she was reading his text message. Detective Harry Bullock had taken the podium.

An incoming call lit-up another button on the office phone. The screen showed it was from Joey Cook. Before Katz could get to the call, he received a text from Deale that read:

Glad he's well represented. Will he turn himself in?

Katz replied:

Yes. No need to send U.S. marshals out. I'd like to make arrangements for an agreed upon bond. Half a million?

The delayed response showed that Deale was trying to think two steps ahead. When it arrived, it read:

Will call off the dogs if you turn your client in at 10 tomorrow. Not opposed to bond, but will have

to be high. Can't commit now. Confirm he'll show
and we'll figure out the rest later.

The noncommittal nature of Deale's text was disconcerting. What was she planning?

Another incoming call from Cook appeared on the phone. Still no time to answer it.

"The commonwealth attorney's calling off the marshals provided you turn yourself in tomorrow morning at 10 a.m.," Katz said to his client. "There's no promise about bond. Deale is amicable, but noncommittal. Basically all she wants to do is to get you in custody. No guarantees to anything."

"Will you at least ask for a bond?" Harding asked.

"I already have."

Harding was prepared to move, and he wasted no time. "I'm at my home in Friendship Heights. I can't stay here tonight. I'm vacating. I need to avoid the cameras and this circus atmosphere. I'll find a hotel and see you in the morning. We can proceed to court together."

They ended the call. Then Katz replied to Deale:

We're on. See you in the morning.

A moment later the commonwealth attorney returned to the podium, smiling for the cameras.

"Nathaniel Harding's lawyer, Alexandria attorney Elmo Katz, has contacted me. Mr. Harding will turn himself in tomorrow morning at 10 a.m."

After the press conference ended, Katz finished his Chinese food. A third call came in from Joey Cook. "I see you landed yourself a big one this time," Cook began.

"It's going to be an interesting case," Katz said without elaborating.

"Bullock came over before the press conference," Cook said.

"He dropped off an evidence bag. Funny thing, though. He kept one of the items collected from the purse, a thumb drive. He said he was taking it to forensics. I almost laughed. The man's so lazy he probably doesn't even know where the lab is located."

"I don't see anything sinister in what you're describing," Katz said.

"There's something else. The thumb drive was missing from the inventory. If Bullock doesn't return it, no one will know it ever existed. Fortunately, I downloaded a copy of its contents onto my computer before letting him take it out of the building," Cook said.

"How were you able to pull that off?"

"I had a little help from the motor pool," Cook replied, without elaborating.

"I love you, Joey." Katz laughed.

"I didn't do it just for you," Cook said. "I did it to preserve the evidence."

We'll see, Katz thought to himself. We'll see.

**

NATE HARDING got in his car to drive to the Key Bridge Marriott in Rosslyn, where he would spend the night.

He trusted Jack Smith, but only so far. He had shown that by retaining Katz – despite Smith's fury. He was also skeptical about what Smith planned next. He knew Smith well enough to know every move was triangulated, with multiple parties working at cross purposes and without anyone knowing the whole plan. It was never a question of outfoxing Jack Smith. That could not be done. It was simply an issue of doing enough to guarantee one's own survival.

CHAPTER 15

Tuesday, November 2

AS THE MORNING RUSH HOUR COMMENCED, cars approached the District from all directions. They came down Connecticut Avenue from Chevy Chase and greater Montgomery County; east across the Anacostia River from Prince George's; and across the 14th Street and Memorial Bridges from the City of Alexandria and Fairfax, Prince William and Loudoun Counties.

With this as a backdrop, a demonstration unfolded to protest Jumma al-Issawi's scheduled visit to D.C. the following week. The Memorial Bridge was the pressure point.

An organizer blew his whistle. The throng quickly made its way across Constitution Avenue and up Henry Bacon Drive, adjacent to the Vietnam War Memorial. Within minutes, they had arrived at the Lincoln Memorial.

Traffic snarled as Phil Landry drove his car across the bridge. Faint drumbeats could be heard, then the clanging of cymbals and the intermittent sound of the organizer's whistle. The drumbeats and cymbals grew louder. The sound of protestors followed, first distant and then loud and threatening.

The throng erupted from the Lincoln Memorial and onto the bridge, filling the spaces between cars. Protestors surrounded the cars, barking slogans, beating drums, blowing whistles, and crashing cymbals.

The chanting resonated across the bridge and the Potomac River, over the Lincoln Memorial and down to the Reflecting Pool, and onto the Mall. Suddenly the throng enveloped Landry's car. The crowd was screaming. He could not make out what they were saying.

A protester approached Landry's car and slapped a flyer under the windshield wiper. Landry braced himself for contact: windows could be smashed, metal dented, lights broken. He reached across his ribcage exposing the holster strapped across his chest.

But none of the pieces of that particular nightmare scenario materialized. The crowd swept by his car like a storm, more threatening than damaging.

Landry whistled a sigh of relief. He surveyed the crowd as it moved on. Posters disparaging al-Issawi disappeared over the horizon. The protestors had retreated and were moving across Independence Avenue and into West Potomac Park.

Grabbing his phone, Landry texted Senator Abe Lowenstein. Their meeting would have to be postponed.

**

AN HOUR LATER, he was in Lowenstein's office.

"I came as quickly as I could," he said to the chairman of the Senate Intelligence Committee. "That demonstration over Jumma al-Issawi created havoc."

"For or against?"

"Against, although these days it's hard to know which side anyone stands on anymore. They just want something to yell about."

"Why are they opposed to a man who encourages dialogue?"

"No one wants dialogue," Landry replied. "They all prefer warring factions."

The senator nodded. "So about Halloween night," he began.

"I got a call late in the evening," Landry said. "Agents had been dispatched to Moultrie's home, apparently after receiving a distressing email from him. I got out there as quickly as I could, but it was already too late."

"What's your suspicion?"

"Impossible to say for sure. It could have been a residential burglary with a tragic ending, but the probability is that the lone wolf followed him home from Daingerfield Island."

Lowenstein shook his head. "Honest to God, what a screw up."

"Yeah," was all Landry could muster. "I've seen some crazy shit in my day, but never anything like this, not even for a Jack Smith operation."

Lowenstein nodded. "When I was briefed about it, it seemed convoluted." The briefing had been conducted under the guise of providing the senator with privileged information about a clandestine operation. Not that the old man had been fooled by such an overture. He knew they conducted the briefing only to cover their collective asses. After all, it was beyond the agency's jurisdiction. And now it was haywire. "I should have raised an objection."

"Why didn't you?" asked Landry curiously.

"I didn't want to stand in Smith's way if it was going to expose a lone wolf who's threatening the nation's capital. He's a very persuasive man. Hell, he still might pull it off."

Fair enough, Landry reasoned. Still. "I suppose hindsight is twenty-twenty," Landry said. "But look where we are now. The terrorist didn't take the bait. Moultrie's dead. And the thumb drive with all that real information is missing."

Lowenstein reflected on the bizarre sequence of events. "There's a lot of room for mischief in the spaces between those actions," he finally said. "Between idea and reality, between motion and act."

Landry recalled that line from a college English course. T.S. Eliot's 'The Hollow Men.'

"Where do things stand now?" Lowenstein asked.

"There's already been a press conference about an arrest."

"I caught it on the news last night," the senator said. "It was the top story."

"It's just a ploy to buy time," Landry explained. "Probably to try and lure the terrorist back. Smith used a cadaver as a prop for their little drama at Daingerfield Island. Then he had the body cremated."

Lowenstein laughed. "Jack Smith does have a flair for the dramatic. And, I have to say, getting Nate Harding involved was perfect."

"Oh, lots of people can't stand Harding," Landry said. "The

74

man's despised in this town. He's far too altruistic. They'll be disappointed when they learn it was a fabrication. Some would probably be happy if they could turn this fiction into reality."

"You should keep an eye on how the trial is proceeding," the senator instructed him.

"I've got it covered from a couple of angles," Landry replied, without elaborating.

"With Smith in charge, who knows what the hell will happen."

"That's true enough," Landry said. "Maybe Smith is setting up Harding for a real fall. Have him convicted of a crime that never happened."

The senator had watched Jack Smith a long time, always from a distance, and a considerable distance at that. After all, everyone watched everyone else in Washington. Watched how they handled adversity, which was sure to strike, sooner or later. Watched who survived, who fell, and who advanced.

"I can't believe Jordin Deale would have approved something like this," Lowenstein said soberly.

"I don't think either she or the U.S. attorney know most of it," Landry said. "They're probably being fed a fair amount of disinformation. A lot of things aren't being shared. The endgame is capturing a terrorist. If it succeeds, everyone will come out heroes. Until then, I think they're tightlipped and manipulating everyone in the system."

"The end may justify the means, but they're running a terrible risk if things go wrong," the senator said. "Then there won't be any way to sweep all of this under a rug."

"Not that Jack Smith cares," Landry said. "He doesn't give a damn about the criminal justice system. Just look at the way he handled his divorce. He bought an attorney who was as unscrupulous as he was, and, together, they destroyed his wife, psychologically and financially."

"Is that a fact?" asked Lowenstein. "I never paid much attention to it."

"And Harding just retained the same attorney to defend him against these criminal charges."

Lowenstein rubbed his chin. "As insurance against Smith?"

"No doubt. Odd thing, I had a premonition about Katz when I was at Moultrie's place Sunday night. Not sure why. I immediately enlisted a guy to monitor some of the attorney's activities."

"Good," said Lowenstein. "We'll have to see how the court proceedings go. The arraignment is at 10 this morning." He looked squarely at Landry. "After all this *sturm und drang*, what's the status on finding the terrorist? You know, the one they were supposed to be trapping?"

"There's a trap being laid for next Tuesday," Landry said. "They'll catch him then."

CHAPTER 16

NATE HARDING arrived at Katz's office around 9. A small group of reporters was already waiting on the doorstep. Harding fought his way through the crowd and into the building. Katz stepped out into the reception area to greet him, then led Harding to the inner sanctum of his office.

"They're already gathering for the lynching," Harding grumbled.

"This is nothing." Katz recalled the few cases of any real notoriety he had handled. All circuses. "Just wait until we get to the courthouse. They'll be swarming all around you."

"Am I going to have to say anything?" Harding asked, suddenly looking anxious.

"Not a word," Katz calmed him. They both sat down, Katz behind the desk and Harding in front of it. "When we arrive at the courthouse, you'll be taken into custody. The deputies will fingerprint you and take a photo. Then you'll be brought up the back side of the courthouse and placed in a holding tank."

"Sounds delightful." Harding sounded disgusted.

"When the case is called," Katz continued, "you'll be brought into the courtroom. I'll be waiting for you there. We'll proceed to the arraignment."

Harding bent his head.

"It could be worse," Katz said. "Oftentimes, you sit in jail a few days on a charge like this before going in front of a judge for arraignment. They're circumvented standard operating procedure for you."

"I should be grateful?"

"Yes, if it enables me to convince the judge to set bond at the arraignment."

"And what exactly will happen at the arraignment, and afterwards?" Harding asked, hesitantly.

"The judge will read the charges and I will enter a plea of Not

Guilty on your behalf. It's a pro forma proceeding, the first step in the process.

"Hopefully, a bond will be set. Later, we'll arrange for a preliminary hearing. If probable cause is established at that hearing, the case goes to a grand jury. If the grand jury returns an indictment, you'll stand trial, where the evidence will have to prove guilt beyond a reasonable doubt."

Harding filled his lungs with air, then exhaled. "Jesus," he exclaimed.

"We're a long way from there," Katz said in a calming voice. "A lot can happen. Let's just take this whole thing a step at a time."

Harding grimaced. "I'm not crazy about spending the night in jail waiting for a formal bond hearing."

"I understand," Katz replied. "But my concern goes a lot deeper than whether you spend a couple of nights in jail."

They slipped out the back of the townhouse and up the alley to avoid the media, not that it mattered. When they arrived at the courthouse, they were inundated by more reporters, thrusting cameras and microphones in their faces.

Vans were parked along the curb from one end of the block to the other. Telescopic antennas reached up to the sky. Reporters sat in directors' chairs, film crews huddled on street corners, and so many wires were strewn across the brick sidewalk that it looked like a multicolored snake pit, with the snakes anchored by duct tape. Katz and Harding stepped over the wires as they walked under the entranceway and into the courthouse.

A security detail of deputies from the sheriff's office awaited their arrival. Katz and Harding were whisked through the metal detectors. Harry Bullock was standing by the elevators, waiting for them.

Things went as Katz had explained. Bullock took Harding into custody to be fingerprinted and photographed.

In the meantime, Katz ascended the spiral staircase from the lobby to the second floor. The long hallway was packed with reporters, bystanders, courthouse regulars, and attorneys who had stuck around to watch the action.

Deale was waiting for him inside courtroom 1. "Quite a scene, Mo," she said. "Not the reception you're accustomed to with a typical client."

It was true enough, but Katz didn't appreciate the suggestion that he might be out of his league.

"By the way," she added, "a couple of folks from the Joint Terrorism Task Force are going to come down to observe the proceeding. They're going to sit at counsel table with us. Do you have a problem with that?"

"Nope," Katz replied nonchalantly as they separated, although Deale sounded as though she was annoyed that the JTTF would be present.

There was a 2001 memorandum of understanding between the City of Alexandria and the federal government for concurrent jurisdiction of Daingerfield Island and the adjacent marina. Serious criminal charges like murder and rape cases were usually handled by the locals. Members of the JTTF rarely sat in and watched those proceedings.

Twenty minutes passed, without much happening other than the courtroom filling to capacity. Katz found time to wander back toward Deale. "As long as we're waiting," he said, "I wonder if we can agree in advance on a bond."

"I'm not in a position to reach any agreement, Mo," Deale told him, cold and distant. "I'd like to work out something with you, but I can't. So much of this is a perception thing. You're going to have to take it up with the judge. You understand."

A total brushoff. Katz was not entirely surprised. After all, he was being presumptuous, and they both knew it.

As Katz returned to his chair, the door along the far wall opened. Two deputies led Harding into the courtroom. Katz was pleased to see Harding still wearing a suit and tie, instead of being dressed in an orange jumpsuit with Alexandria City Jail stenciled on the back.

Katz and Harding shook hands. The client looked completely frazzled. They sat down side-by-side.

A clerk had prepared the warrants. She walked over and handed them to Katz, who inspected the paperwork carefully.

"What?" Harding asked, watching Katz's intense examination of the papers.

"Just thinking," Katz replied quietly. He handed the papers back to the clerk. *Fatta la legge, trovato l'inganno.*

Kathy White arrived. She was accompanied by two other people whom Katz did not recognize. The guys from the JTTF, he assumed. They sat in chairs inside the railing behind the prosecutor's table.

White felt Katz looking at her. She turned and winked.

"You know one another?" Harding inquired.

"Only on a professional basis," Katz replied.

Harding did not appreciate Katz's attempt at humor. "Who are those other people?" he asked, rolling his eyes toward the railing.

"Feds."

"Why are they here?"

"Maybe to study the proceedings to file federal charges against you if this state case goes south."

Harding appeared as though the blood had been drained from his body. "You're joking, right?" he asked.

Katz studied his client's face carefully. Harding suddenly had the look of a man who felt set up and betrayed. Katz decided he should take advantage of this momentary vulnerability, particularly if he was going to make sense out of what was really going on with the case.

"No," Katz said. "I'm serious."

An instant later, the Honorable Dan Osborne appeared.

"All rise," bellowed the bailiff as the judge took the bench. Beneath his black robe, the judge's Armani suit and handmade shoes peeked out with each stride. He wasn't called "Dapper Dan" for nothing.

The judge wasted no time. This was an arraignment, pure and simple. The circus atmosphere did not change that one iota.

Katz and Harding stood.

"The defendant has been charged with abduction and first degree murder. How does your client plead, Mr. Katz?"

"Not guilty to both counts, Judge Osborne."

The judge made a notation in the file and looked at his calendar, searching for a date for the preliminary hearing.

"I would like to be heard at this time on bond," Katz said. "I don't have an agreement with the commonwealth, but I don't think there is any objection to the court setting an appropriate bond at this time."

White made a 'think again' face as she stood and addressed the judge.

"The defendant has just been taken into custody, your honor," she said. "Given the gravity of the offenses, the prosecution will be requesting a very high bond. A risk of flight exists in any case where the accused faces a lengthy prison term and the nature of the murder suggests a danger to the community. We request a postponement until our office can assemble sufficient information about the defendant to enable us to seek an appropriate bond."

"Judge," Katz began.

The judge cut him off.

"This court will not under any circumstances entertain bond at this time," Osborne stated flatly.

"Any such motion is deferred until next week. Until then, the defendant is remanded to the custody of the sheriff's department." He looked at White. "This is not a blanket postponement for the prosecution. I expect you to move expeditiously. Otherwise, I will accede to defense counsel's request and set a bond based upon whatever facts are presented to me."

Katz tried to speak, but the judge pounded his gavel and rose to leave.

Four deputy sheriffs now surrounded Harding. As soon as the judge disappeared, Deale was on her feet and out of the courtroom, along with the two representatives from the JTTF.

White tapped her papers on the adjoining table with a cool air of satisfaction, stood, adjusted her suit, and, swinging the railing gate that separated the bench, jury box and counsel tables from the rest of the courtroom, walked out with a side glance at Katz.

Katz thought he saw her smile.

Harding's arms were handcuffed behind his back. He was escorted through a door to the side of the jury box. He tried to turn back to Katz, but the deputies prevented it.

Katz was not surprised by the outcome, although he still felt terrible. So he waited a few minutes and then got the deputies to take him to the holding cell.

"What happened?" demanded Harding. "You promised you'd be able to get me out of this place."

"I don't think I ever made any such promise," Katz replied.

"I am not prepared to spend time in jail, Mr. Katz. You have got to get me out of here. I am insistent. I will not be treated like some kind of caged animal."

"You heard what the judge said," Katz said, keeping his voice flat. This was no time to get emotional and no place to discuss any other delicate questions with his client.

Sensing Katz's finality, Harding calmed down. "So what do we do now?" he asked.

"We prepare for the bond hearing," Katz replied, frustrated. "The court's going to want to know two things, risk of flight and danger to the community. We'll offer to surrender your passport, agree to home detention, argue that the evidence is tenuous, highlight your ties to the community and show that you have no prior criminal record."

Katz assumed all of that was attainable and true, and Harding nodded his head in confirmation.

"We'll ask the judge to set a high bond, maybe a million bucks or more. You'll have to put up ten percent and post collateral for the remainder."

Harding did a quick calculation, his eyes blinking. If his bond were set at $1 million, he could post $100,000.00 no sweat, and he had collateral.

"That isn't a problem. I can handle the financial part of it," he said confidently. "It's the imprisonment that's a problem. I have claustrophobia. You understand?"

Katz nodded in feigned sympathy.

Harding shook his head. "I hope the old man isn't up to something."

Which old man? Katz asked himself. *Dapper Dan Osborne or Jack Smith?*

"This town is full of old men, all with their little agendas," Katz commented. "Personally, I have no idea. We're just going to have to wait and see."

**

KATZ DEPARTED, moving slowly through the courthouse and toward the throng that awaited him outside.

A bank of microphones had been set up at a podium at the main entrance. More than a dozen television cameras were pointed at Katz. He saw this as an opportunity, not for publicity, but as a way to entreat any eyewitnesses to come forward. Katz knew something was badly wrong with this case. Maybe someone out there could help him, someone with vital information.

Katz walked up to the podium and spoke into the microphones. "Nathaniel Harding is innocent of these charges. I'm not sure why he became the subject of an investigation surrounding the death of Libby Lewis. If anyone out there was on Daingerfield Island the night the murder occurred, they should come forward and report what they saw.

"We need to methodically piece together what actually happened out there. Once all the facts are assembled, I'm confident Mr. Harding will be acquitted of all charges. He didn't commit any crime that night."

Katz stepped back from the microphones. He made no response to the reporters' questions. Instead, he hurried back to his office.

CHAPTER 17

THE OFFICE PHONE was ringing as Katz walked in the door to his office around noon. Suzie Marston was away from her desk. Thunderbolt ran toward him with an excited greeting. Katz picked up the line on the reception desk.

"Hello," he said.

"I'd like to speak with Elmo Katz," said the man on the other end.

"Speaking," Katz replied.

"My name is David Reese. I listened to your press conference a little while ago. I have some information you might want." The voice on the phone sounded young, and a bit nervous.

"What sort of information?" Katz asked.

"I'm the one who reported that woman's drowning. I was biking back from the District that night. After I saw the body, I called 911."

"You discovered the body." Not a question. A statement. A hopeful one.

"Yes," Reese replied. "But ever since I learned about the murder, I've been worried. I took something from the scene that I found in the grass, a tiny photograph of a woman."

**

AT LANGLEY, the analyst monitoring Reese's phone sat up, suddenly wide awake. She could hear herself breathing.

She had been instructed to flag anything to do with Daingerfield Island. She quickly sent an urgent text to Derek Fine, with a copy to Jack Smith.

**

"YOU found *what*?"

"After the EMTs arrived," Reese explained, "I was talking with a policeman. At some point, I saw something in the grass. It was lying where the EMTs had performed mouth-to-mouth on the woman. I picked it up, wrapped it in a piece of tissue, and stuffed it in my pocket. Later, when I looked at it, I realized it was a photo."

Reese held the tissue in his hand, in the middle of which lay the photo, like a stamen in a flower. "It's a photograph of a woman with dark eyes and a thin, stern smile. It's about the size of my thumbnail. I think it fell out of a locket that she was wearing around her neck."

"Why do you say that?"

"The locket was hanging open," Reese answered. "I remember that. I even took a photo when the body was moved to a stretcher."

"Why didn't you share this with the police?" One possibility immediately leaped into Katz's mind. So before Reese could respond, he added, "Who was the policeman?"

"His name was Bullock," said Reese.

Outside Reese's apartment, Mai Lin was fumbling with a noisy ring of keys. Reese turned his head. As Lin opened the door, the keychain dropped to the ground. The crash of the keys and other assorted junk was joyous.

"Mr. Reese, are you there?" Katz asked.

Silence. Then, "Yes. Sorry. I'm still here."

Mai Lin was planting a kiss on Reese's neck.

"Listen, can I call you back in a few?" Reese asked. "Something's come up." And, with that, the phone went dead.

**

DEREK FINE slipped into the war room and joined the analyst gazing at her computer screen.

"Any more info?" he asked.

"The guy hung up. Said he'd call back soon."

"What precisely did he say he had?" asked Fine.

"Some photograph he picked up at Daingerfield Island," said the analyst. "A picture of a woman. It had fallen out of a locket."

"Does Smith know about this?" Fine asked.

86

"Copied him on the message to you." The analyst sounded defensive.

Although Fine had no idea whose picture had been in the dead woman's locket, his instincts told him the attorney would ask for it and he foresaw danger in giving the attorney a photo of an unknown person.

"Get some head shots of women who work here," Fine ordered the people seated at other terminals. "We may have to move fast on this."

**

KATZ SAT in silence. *What exactly had just happened? Was that guy for real? Would he call back?*

Time passed and still no response from Mr. Reese. Katz finished reviewing all of his messages, both phone and text. Impatience began to set in. Why didn't Reese call back? Where was he?

When the phone rang, Katz sprang to answer it. "Hey," he said.

"Hey," Reese replied, like an old friend.

"So," asked Katz, "what was the problem?"

"No problem," Reese answered, snuggling on the sofa with Lin. "My girlfriend just came home. We needed a few minutes to be alone, that's all."

Katz smiled. That settled it. The kid was authentic.

"Instead of picking up where you left off," Katz said, "let me ask you a few questions. It's David, right? Beginning with, who exactly are you?" He fumbled for a pen and paper.

"Yes, my name's David, and I was riding my bike on Halloween night," Reese explained. "I went into the District and made a big circle up the Mall, around the Capitol, and back across the 14th Street Bridge. Then I went south along the G. W. Parkway toward Old Town. It was the same route I travel every weekend. Except something different happened that night. I saw a woman floating in the water."

"Okay. Stop there, David," Katz interrupted. "Think back to the instant you first observed the body in the water. What did you see at that precise moment? Were there any boats nearby?"

"No."

"Did you see any people standing around? Did you see anyone at all, maybe someone in the distance, walking to or from a car, that sort of thing?"

"No, I didn't see anything."

"Sure? Smell anything funny? Hear anything suspicious? Sense anything threatening near you?"

Reese closed his eyes. "I heard the sound of doors slamming," he recalled. "It was an echo, across the water. I remember looking across that inlet there. You know, there's like that little lagoon there, at the base of Reagan National."

Katz could picture it. "I watch sailboats there when I'm driving on the parkway," he responded. "Go on. What did you see?"

Suddenly, Reese remembered the sound that ricocheted from the satellite parking lot. "A man was walking around from the back of a van to the driver's door. It was a large white van. It was a guy. I think a white guy. I don't remember anything else about him. It was a good eighty to a hundred yards from where I was standing. And it was dusk. I didn't see anything clearly. Oh, one more thing. He was on the phone."

"That's very helpful. What did you do next?"

"I dialed 911 and told the operator a woman had jumped into the water off Daingerfield Island."

"Is that what you said? That a woman had jumped into the water?"

"I think so." Reese hesitated. "I realize now it was wrong. I mean, I have no idea what happened."

"Then why did you say that?"

"It's just that the area was so still," Reese admitted. "Deserted. It was just her there, alone, floating in the water on her stomach, her hands out on either side of her."

"What did you do after you made the call?" Katz asked.

"I waited for the EMTs. Then I hung around, watching."

"And Detective Bullock showed up?"

"Yup," Reese answered.

"And did he interview you?"

"He did. He gave me a strange vibe," Reese said. "It was as though he was suspicious of me for some reason."

"That's not strange, David. That's what cops do. They're a little like doctors. They probe."

"I understand, but it was like he knew what had happened and was trying to find how much I knew. Does that make any sense?"

"Bullock's a good cop," Katz assured him. "I've worked with him. I know his level of professionalism." But a seed of doubt had been planted in Katz's mind. *What was Harry Bullock doing out on Daingerfield Island in the first place? He didn't patrol it. And was it coincidental that it should be Bullock at Dyke Marsh the next afternoon?* "Listen, could you send that photo to me?" Katz asked.

"If you give me your email address, I'll send it over now," Reese replied. "I already scanned it into the computer and enlarged it."

"That's fine, David," Katz said, reciting his email address.

**

THE STAFF SPRANG INTO ACTION. The email was intercepted and the attachment opened.

There was no time to look for another substitute. Derek Fine worked with what he had, a copy of June Webster's photo from her agency ID cropped into a neat oval. He substituted it for the picture emailed by Reese and sent the diverted email to its intended destination.

**

"OKAY, I've got it," Katz said.

Lin snuggled closer to Reese, relieved that the photo was no longer her boyfriend's problem alone.

"So are you going to share it with the authorities?" Reese asked. He sounded uneasy.

Katz thought about it for a minute. "Not yet."

"Can I destroy the original?"

"No, hold onto it for now. If a prosecutor or a cop asks you about the photo, turn it over and say you provided me a copy."

"Okay, I will," Reese said, and hung up. He turned to Lin. "Where should we put this for safekeeping?"

She opened her purse and tossed it inside. "Here," she said.

**

FROM HIS computer monitor at Langley, Fine watched Katz's computer screen.

The attachment was opened. A picture of Webster filled the screen. Mission accomplished. The lawyer had hardly noticed the brief delay. Fine keyed in a message to Jack Smith confirming what they had done. Then he maintained surveillance of Katz's computer, in the event that something else turned up.

CHAPTER 18

IN THE MIDDLE of the afternoon, Joey Cook stopped by Katz's office.

"What brings you here?" Katz asked, looking up from the piles of paper strewn over his desk. Cook tossed a small metal object at him. "Watch it!" Katz exclaimed as he caught it. "What is this?"

"Consider it a present," Cook said.

"No, seriously, what is this?" As Katz asked a second time, he realized he was holding a thumb drive with the information Cook had downloaded onto his personal computer. His expression grew serious. "Joey," he said. "Are you sure about this?"

Cook was a source of information, innuendo and rumor, all of which translated into a competitive advantage for Katz in the courtroom, as most recently exemplified by the outcome in Tony Fortune's drug case. This was significantly more than that.

"I'm not giving you anything you couldn't get through normal discovery, assuming the thumb drive is returned to the property room," Cook said, dropping into the chair opposite Katz's. "The thing is, I don't think Bullock has any intention of returning it. He never checked it out before taking possession, and he's probably the one who deleted the drive from the inventory of items found in Libby Lewis's purse." Cook looked despondent. "I've got a bad feeling, Mo."

Under normal circumstances, Katz might have refused to accept the evidence. Instead, he plugged the thumb drive into his computer. A folder appeared on the screen, labeled 'Lewis Drive.'

"Don't bother trying to open it up," Cook said. "I tried already, and failed. It's encrypted. You're going to need a pro to get inside. Maybe Curtis knows someone who can help you."

Katz yanked out the thumb drive. "Okay, I'll ask him," he said.

**

DEREK FINE was sitting in June Webster's office, a square box in the corner of a rectangular steel and glass building. Windows with southern and western exposures served as walls. They were black now, offering only the darkness of the early November night.

Webster was seated at her desk, her back toward Fine, punching at her keyboard and squinting at the computer screen. Fine sat at the opposite end of the office working his phone, his fingers sliding across its face. Their reflections and her desk light shone on the windows.

Neither spoke, each consumed in their own thoughts.

As he played with his phone, Fine reflected on the day's activities. He knew the importance of preserving the fiction that the corpse in the water was Libby Lewis until the terrorist was neutralized. Putting jewelry on the cadaver created an air of authenticity, and it probably belonged to Lewis. But if it did not, and the tiny photo was traced to someone unrelated to Lewis, it could raise questions and risk the operation's success.

A few minutes earlier, Fine had shared the news with Webster, deliberately leaving out the fact he had substituted her photo for the one transmitted to Katz. He did not tell her because he was afraid she would be upset with his decision. Better to bask in the glory of a half-truth than to risk the ignominy of the whole one.

Webster was paying no attention to Fine. It was a relief to take a break from the search for the terrorist, with everyone whirling about like dervishes. She was studying information harvested from her own private research. Her eyes raced across the headlines scrolling across her computer screen.

She scanned the items listed on the screen:

Wash Style & Social News Daily
Under fierce cross-examination, Eve Smith denied doctoring financial documents provided in Discovery. The allegation nonetheless tainted her credibility for the rest the hearing. It probably influ-

enced the court's decision to give spymaster Jack Smith the major share of the couple's assets. Jack F.X. Smith...

CNNT Press Release 091777

Today's announcement of Jack F.X. Smith's promotion was greeted with public praise and whispered criticism, coming less than a month after a highly contentious divorce...

"Have you ever looked at stories about Smith's divorce?" she asked without turning in Fine's direction.

Fine looked up from his phone's screen. "Sure," he said, surprised. "Everyone has. It makes for some pretty salacious reading." He paused before asking, "Why do you ask?"

She said nothing for several minutes, reading. Then she said, "The stories are very telling."

"How so?"

"Take the story about alleged doctored documents," she said. "Smith claimed his wife had tampered with some of the materials provided to him in discovery. That damaged her credibility and worked to his advantage in the distribution of their marital estate. Reading between the lines, though, you might conclude Smith doctored those documents himself and then blamed her to gain an advantage with the court."

Fine cocked his head. "It worked, if that's what he did," he said, recalling the story. "The press doesn't like him much, so the articles make him out to be somewhat deceitful. But all's fair in love and war, you know."

"That's what they say," Webster said, without signifying agreement. She swiveled around in her chair. Time to talk shop. "What are people saying about how the operation is being conducted?" she asked.

"Honest answer?"

She nodded. Truth to power.

"They think it's a disaster, the staging of a drowning and all," he said. "They're also worried about the monkeying with the criminal justice system. They think it's wrong, that he's subverting the system."

"And what do you think?"

"I think it's permissible if we get our terrorist to come out in the open."

His response did not seem to surprise her. "Well, we lost our quarry Halloween night," she said. "It looked amateurish. Our suspect freaking over the sirens and lights and taking off like a hunted gazelle. And poor Lou Moultrie scattering in the opposite direction with the thumb drive in his possession, allowing the lone wolf to follow him home."

She had a point, Fine admitted to himself.

"This entire drama has been totally unnecessary," she added, disgusted. "We could have caught our terrorist without any of these shenanigans. All he's really done is complicate things. That's his MO. It's absurd."

She should have stopped there. It was not appropriate to share her views about Smith with a subordinate. But she went on, "One of these days, people are going to quit interpreting Smith's actions as genius and see them for what they are."

"We're facing a little turbulence," Fine said. "There's no reason to panic. We just have to accept that it's an unorthodox plan."

She laughed. "No one is in a panic. But the plan is more than a little unorthodox. It's borderline criminal. Smith finds the edge of the map and races to it, all the time. You might be comfortable there, but no one else is, as you just confided in me."

She stood up and walked across the room. "Even if this had succeeded in the first instance, someone is going to inquire about the details. Someone is going to demand accountability." She already had someone in mind, namely Senator Abe Lowenstein. "No one can do this sort of thing and expect to get away with it. Not in this day and age."

Fine muttered, "*Fatta la legge, trovato l'inganno.*"

"I'm sorry?"

"There's a way out of everything. Haven't you heard Mr. Smith use that expression?"

"Yes, but I'm surprised to hear you repeating it."

Fine shrugged. "It's something his divorce attorney used to say, I'm told."

Back to the divorce. "Do people really gossip that much?" Webster asked.

"All the time," Fine laughed. "Right now, the hot topic is his ex-wife's incessant phone calls."

Webster smiled wryly. "Really?"

"Come on, boss," Fine said. "You haven't heard? She's calling him at all hours of the day and night, in and out of meetings, around the clock. She's taking him back to court."

Fine was unsure whether Webster was really that ignorant, hiding her head in the sand to avoid hearing the gossip, or if she was playing dumb to figure out how much he knew about the post-divorce proceeding.

"Why?"

"He outfoxed her. It's in those media stories." Fine pointed to the computer screen. "You can read about it yourself." He was uncomfortable talking about things that tarnished Mr. Smith's image. He rose from the chair and put his phone in his pocket. "If we're finished, I'd like to get back down on the floor."

Webster excused Fine and resumed her research.

An enormous amount of information about *Smith v. Smith* existed online. Smith was responsible for much of it, apparently having gone to extraordinary lengths to discuss his divorce in public forums to portray himself as a sympathetic figure. For example, the *Washington Style & Social News Daily* article included the following post-divorce quotes by Smith:

"I considered myself a goner when my ex-wife hit me with divorce papers. You know what working in the clandestine services can do to you. My only refuge was home. When she walked out on me, I felt adrift in the world.

"We had no children, so the fight was over money. She wanted everything. Pension, house, furnishings, cash, you name it. Virginia's an equitable distribution state, so she was automatically entitled to half of the marital estate, which was acceptable to me. But it wasn't enough. She wanted all of it."

In the weeks leading up to their hearing, Smith's attorney had encouraged settlement. Yet when the parties appeared in court, Jack Smith insisted on a trial, catching the other side unawares and forcing a settlement along terms dictated by his side. Those terms amounted to sixty percent of the marital residence to Mrs. Smith in exchange for a waiver of any interest in Mr. Smith's retirement accounts. Jack Smith walked away with a grossly uneven outcome that was 70-30 percent in his favor.

One of the articles questioned whether he felt she had forgiven him for his trickery.

"No," he had replied. "She hunts me every day. Hunts me and haunts me."

**

The door opened and Jack Smith entered. Webster started, quickly turning from her computer, sensing, as she did so, that he knew what she was doing.

"I've reestablished communication with the lone wolf," he said, excitedly. "He admits shooting Moultrie and stealing the flash drive. I provided him with the necessary information to access its contents. He now knows where and when to attack the train carrying al-Issawi to Union Station. He'll show up and we'll be waiting for him."

A lot had happened in a short time. Webster expressed surprise.

"Fortunately, it's fallen back into place," Smith said. "A week from today, we will avenge Lou Moultrie's murder and capture a terrorist. It's something to look forward to, don't you think?"

She rose from the chair. "Yes. Thanks for the update. Let me know if there's anything I can do."

"I'll let you know if I need you," Smith replied, dismissively. He walked to the door and closed it behind him as Webster stared at her reflection in the darkened window.

CHAPTER 19

"WHERE ARE YOU and what are you doing?"

Katz had been worried about Curtis Santana off and on all day. The investigator had been coy about his activities, providing little in the way of details. Like where his latest so-called surveillance was being conducted.

"I'm sitting on my bench," Santana replied innocently, reaching for a cup of coffee. He was seated on a bench at Haines Point facing the river, almost directly beneath the 14th Street Bridge. Katz called it the Santana Baruch Bench, a takeoff on Bernard Baruch, the diplomat known for conducting affairs of state on a bench in Lafayette Park across from the White House.

"Do you know what time it is?" asked Katz, trying not to sound worried.

"Nine. The sky is overcast. The forecast calls for rain," Santana joked. "I'm conducting surveillance."

"Where?"

"Your place. And someone just left by your back door."

"What the hell are you talking about?"

Santana looked intently at the small computer screen in his lap. He adjusted the phone mechanism wrapped around his ear. "I had a premonition your place was going to be hit. So I went there yesterday, after I tailed Harding, and set up some cameras around the place."

Katz anticipated the worst. "Is my place torn up, too?"

"Hardly scratched," Santana replied. Katz was relieved. "Very, very clandestine. They don't want you spooked."

"Who showed up?" asked Katz.

"A guy in a white van. He walked up to the front door and knocked, bold as brass. Very smooth operator. It looked like a house call by a remodeling contractor."

"Well, I do need some work done in the bathrooms and kitchen."

"Don't be too cavalier about this, boss," Santana admonished. "It's no joke, two bodies turning up on Halloween night. There's some connection between them. I'll lay odds Jack Smith has something to do with both those cases."

"Maybe," Katz replied.

"No maybe about it."

"What did the guy in the van want?"

"He searched through your house, quick but thorough. Whatever he was looking for, he didn't find. He left empty-handed."

Santana gave Katz a moment to ponder the situation and then continued. "I did a little digging into Moultrie's death. The killer apparently paddled up Little Hunting Creek on a raft. I figured the point of origin was the park where the creek flows into the Potomac River."

"So you checked the police logs for any activity in that area?"

"That's right," Santana said. "It turns out a U.S. park police officer ticketed a vehicle parked down there Sunday night. It was a white van."

"Good work," Katz said. "Why don't you drop by the office when you're done with your surveillance? I've got a few things to share with you as well."

Off the phone, Katz picked up a file. It was the Ashford personal injury case. Jimmy Wolfe represented the other side. He studied the file and then made another call. "Wolfeman," he began, once cued to leave a message. "I'll tell you straight up, it's going to take three hundred thousand to settle the Ashford case. The poor woman had burns on twenty percent of her body."

His client had suffered serious burns when citronella fuel poured onto a ceramic fire-pot exploded over her body like napalm. The medical bills were already more than sixty grand. Her lost wages were approximately half that.

"My girl's maimed for life. Your client's got deep pockets. I've prepared a settlement proposal. Suzie will send it over your way. Then let's talk."

**

SANTANA ARRIVED around ten. Katz locked the front door to the office and turned off the lights in the reception area. The two retreated to Katz's office, where Katz found a bottle of Green Hat gin and poured two glasses. "I got a call from a guy named David Reese who discovered Lewis's body in the Potomac," Katz said. "He watched my press statement. He saw a white van across the inlet at Daingerfield Island on Sunday night, with a guy standing beside it on the phone."

"White vans are like grains of sand on a beach, but maybe it's no coincidence," Santana said.

"I'm thinking it's the same van," Katz said.

"There are CCTVs all over Reagan National," Santana continued, referencing the closed circuit television cameras that had become a favorite of law enforcement. "I know the folks who operate the stuff at the airport. I can talk to them."

"I could get them with a subpoena," Katz said, "but the preferred way is to stay out of court."

"Plus, I've got the license plate of the van that was parked in your driveway, and a good photo of the man inside your place."

Good," Katz said. "Reese also found a photo that had fallen out of a locket Libby Lewis wore around her neck. He picked it up. He sent me a PDF." Katz walked over to the computer. "I'm emailing you a copy now. Try to figure out who this woman is as well."

"Will do, but how does that help you?"

"It's like anything. You grasp at every straw. Sooner or later you grab hold of something that matters. You know how it works."

"Have you told Kathy White?"

"No. I just got it."

Suddenly Thunderbolt appeared out of nowhere. The dog buried his muzzle into Santana's outstretched hand, his bobbed tail wagging furiously. "No treats today," the private investigator said, patting Thunderbolt on the head.

Next Katz explained the thumb drive. "I need someone who can crack open this thing and figure out what's inside of it," he said to Santana. "Cook made it sound as though it's impenetrable."

"I'll get started on it right away," Santana replied.

They had finished their drinks. Katz removed the cork from the bottle of Green Hat and refilled both glasses.

"By the way," Santana said, "apropos of nothing, I heard Smith is back in court next Friday on another post-divorce motion. He's pro se."

**

AS THEY TALKED, a figure crept into the shadows of the outer office.

"Hello?" Tony Fortune whispered softly. He stepped into the waiting area. "Hello?" he called again, a little more loudly. Still no one answered.

Katz and Santana were ensconced in the back of the suite, intent on their conversation.

Fortune stopped at Marston's desk. He flipped open a few files, running a pencil flashlight over them. Then he moved quietly toward Katz's office at the far end of the suite. He heard the two men's voices and froze.

Thunderbolt strutted out of the open office door, his tail wagging. The light from the office glinted on the dog's rhinestone collar. As a longtime client, Fortune was prepared. He pulled some shreds of beef jerky out of his jacket pocket. The terrier flopped down on the rug to devour the treats.

In the office, Katz and Santana finished their discussion with more questions left unanswered than when they started. The investigator departed by the back door.

After he left, Katz wrote a note to Marston:

When you get in, email Ashford settlement to Wolfeman. Also check with the clerk's office to see if Jack Smith's divorce case is on the docket 11-12. If it is, get copies of any filings. Thanks.

Katz walked out into the dark reception room and placed the note on Marston's desk. He paused. The room was eerily silent. Thunderbolt trotted over to Katz. The lawyer leaned over to rub the dog's head, looked around and then returned to his office.

Katz picked up the phone and called Harry Bullock's cell number.

"What do you want?" the detective groaned when Katz announced himself. "It's late and I'm off the clock. Been putting in too many hours on the damned Lewis homicide."

"My client wants some of his personal possessions that he left on board his boat," Katz explained. "I'd like to get over there in the morning to recover them."

"The boat's not at Dyke Marsh anymore. It's been moved up to the Columbia Island Marina."

"That's fine. I'll meet you there at ten in the morning."

As Katz hung up, he thought he heard a click at the front door. He listened intently for a moment, but hearing nothing further, he shoved the flash drive into his pants pocket and retreated to the sofa, where he would spend the night. Knowing his house had been entered made Katz uneasy about sleeping in his own bed. Thunderbolt jumped onto the leather sofa and curled up beside his feet.

CHAPTER 20

Wednesday, November 3

THE COLUMBIA Island Marina was off the G. W. Parkway north of the 14th Street Bridge. Each day, tens of thousands of commuters traveling on Interstate 395, combined with the traffic from the parkway, swirled around it like locusts, a year-round infestation, particularly acute in autumn and winter, when the loss of leaves on the trees eliminated nature's sound buffer.

Contributing to the clamor were airplanes taking off from the airport less than a mile away, trains delivering coal across a trestle to the power plant near the Capitol, and Amtrak trains and Metro cars rushing along their own sets of tracks across the Potomac – a veritable Times Square of mechanized motion.

The marina itself, on the other hand, was quietly nestled in a thicket of trees near the LBJ Memorial Grove. Day and night, the area was rich with the unnoticed comings and goings of hustlers and politicians.

As he pulled into the marina, Katz received a text message: 'Where r u?' Katz glanced around. He spotted Harry Bullock waiting in his unmarked cruiser, the driver's window rolled down, with smoke from his cigarette billowing out from it. His head was bent over his phone.

Katz pulled in beside the policeman's car. He wrote back: 'Look to your right, a-hole.'

Bullock took a long drag on his cigarette and blew out smoke, chuckling, as he read the response. He exited his vehicle without looking over.

Katz spoke first. "Did you plan to get a search warrant for the *Won Way* the other day?"

Bullock gave him an empty stare. "You know me better than to ask a question like that," he replied. "I'm too damned lazy." Then he got serious. "Your client's in a shitload of trouble, Mo. Lewis's car was seen at Dyke Marsh. It's a fair surmise that Harding killed her on the boat, put-putted upriver and dumped the body in the water. Then he doubled back, got into her car and drove to Daingerfield Island, and left her car and purse there. He tried to give it the feel of a suicide. But there are too many holes in his fairy tale. I'm not telling you anything you don't already know. Fingerprints. Taxi. Normal type of stuff we see all the time at a botched crime scene."

Katz shrugged. "You're dealing with a lot of speculation."

"Not so much."

"We'll see what you're left with after I file suppression motions."

Bullock stiffened. "Look, counselor. I'm not worried about what happened over at Dyke Marsh. Your client gave us consent. You were there, whispering in his ear. That makes you an accomplice, of sorts. You're the reason we'll win if you contest the matter."

Bullock took another deep drag of his cigarette and then flicked it in front of them, stepping on it eight steps later as they approached the boats docked at the pier.

"I thought you were quitting those," Katz said.

"Quitting is a process," replied Bullock.

Katz could see the *Won Way* ahead. A pair of uniformed policemen stood on the boat's deck. Strolling the shore of the marina were a couple of Coast Guard ensigns.

"You taught me pretty well," Bullock said while they walked. "*Schneckloth versus Bustamonte.* That's the case, isn't it? When a subject is not in custody and the prosecution argues consent, the court is going to require evidence that the consent was voluntary and not the result of coercion or duress, either express or implied."

"I'm not sure," Katz lied.

"Textbook shit," Bullock laughed. "I committed it to memory before I threw away those pages. Voluntariness is shown by the totality of the circumstances. Right? In this case, Mr. Harding had his counsel with him, and his decision was only made following prolonged and careful consultation with said attorney. I've got you, Mo."

Katz shook his head, smiling.

"You taught me good, counselor." Bullock slapped Katz on the back.

They had reached the side of the yacht. "Of course, not that any of it matters," Bullock said. "We went ahead and got a warrant. Just before we towed it up here. Deale advised it was the smart way to go. I checked with the prosecutor on the case. You know her. Kathy White."

"She was in court yesterday with Judge Osborne," Katz said.

"I heard," replied Bullock.

They climbed aboard the boat.

"Mr. Katz is the defendant's attorney," Bullock told one of the policemen aboard the boat. He ignored the Coast Guard, so Katz did too. "He's here to look around. I'll stay with him."

As they walked across the deck, Bullock confided, "I know you're not here to retrieve any items for your client. You want to survey the crime scene."

Katz tried to look surprised.

Bullock guffawed. "That's the first thing you did in all our cases," he said. "Get to the scene and look around. I've been expecting your call."

"I guess I did teach you right," Katz said.

"Yeah, so look around all you like," replied the detective. "Maybe you can get some nice images of the boat that you can present to a jury six months from now, when your client stands trial for murder."

Katz spent ten minutes looking around. Then he asked where the john was located.

**

ONCE IN THE bathroom, Katz removed the flash drive from his pocket. He searched for a hiding place. The hollowed-out inside of a small wall clock proved the perfect repository. Katz secured the gadget behind the face so it would not be knocked free. Then he flushed the toilet and washed his hands, wiping them on the sides of his pants.

Emerging into the corridor, Katz opened a door to the sleeping quarters. This would have fit in at any three star hotel, with a queen sized bed draped in blue chenille. He opened the sliding door of the closet, reached in at random and pulled a couple of shirts off their hangers. With a last glance around, he headed back up to the deck.

"Need more time?" Bullock asked, showing signs of boredom. "Maybe you should go back down and sit on the crapper to think about how to get your client out of this one."

"No," replied Katz. "I'm ready to go. Do you need to frisk me?" He held out the arm holding the shirts.

"Nah. I trust you, Mo. And just leave the shirts here. Like I said on the phone, no need for pretense."

Katz put down the shirts. He and Bullock stepped off the gently rocking deck and walked back across the parking lot.

"Find anything?" Bullock asked casually.

"Not really," Katz answered. "It was like you said. I just wanted to familiarize myself with the boat. It gives me perspective. That's all."

"I get you," Bullock said.

"One thing, though." Katz stopped. "Why was the yacht transferred over here? And who's maintaining custody over it now?" He pointed at the ensigns, who still loitered in the vicinity of the yacht. "The Coast Guard is part of Homeland Security. You know that, don't you?"

Bullock looked upset. "Yeah. I know. That's Phil Landry sticking his nose in where it doesn't belong. I wasn't consulted about moving the tub."

"So who has that kind of clout in a criminal investigation?" Katz asked, his head cocked. "Moving a major piece of evidence?"

"I don't see how it matters, really. Dyke Marsh isn't the crime scene, when you think about it."

Still.

As they approached their cars, Bullock suddenly froze in his tracks.

"Well, I'll be damned," he said.

Katz tried to figure out what was going on.

"There," Bullock pointed, eyes narrowed against the sun.

In the corner of the parking lot, hidden under some overhanging trees, two men were seated in a car. Katz stared at the unoffending vehicle, wondering what had attracted Bullock's attention.

Suddenly Bullock's heavyset shoulders blocked his view. The burly cop rushed toward the vehicle, his service weapon drawn and pointed in the air.

What the hell is he doing now? Katz wondered.

"Police," Bullock hollered. He flashed his badge, his gun still pointed to the sky. "Put your hands on the dashboard where I can see them. Now!"

The vehicle, already running, quickly shifted to drive. The accelerator pedal was pressed to the floor. Shooting out of its space like a rocket, the car swerved toward the policeman.

Bullock dove to one side.

As the car raced across the parking lot toward the exit, Bullock rushed back to his own car. Katz jumped in the passenger side, slamming the door as Bullock roared out of the lot in hot pursuit.

Both cars turned right onto the G. W. Parkway. The escaping vehicle sped away, careening on two wheels as the driver made another sharp right turn onto the southbound lanes of I-395. It was one of the few times of day when traffic was light on the southbound lanes.

"Couple of punks," Bullock muttered. "I can't wait to knock their heads together."

Katz had been privy to a lot of cases with Bullock: as a prosecutor, saving Bullock's hide for practicing vigilante justice was his almost daily chore; as a defense attorney, extracting a penalty for that vigilantism sometimes let the guilty walk. This was up there with the worst of them. Here they were, barreling down a major interstate at breakneck speed in pursuit of two men who committed an unspecified crime, if any crime at all.

Bullock rounded the corner and gunned the car up the access ramp. He turned on the car's flashers and siren, to no avail. Katz braced one arm against the dashboard and struggled to secure his seatbelt.

Bullock's cruiser narrowed the distance between the two cars.

"What did you see?"

"A drug buy," Bullock stated. "One of those guys was waiting when I first pulled up, before you arrived."

Both cars were traveling at breakneck speed along southbound I-395 in the direction of the mixing bowl in Springfield. If the cars got to that maze of thruways, Katz thought, shuddering, there was going to be a whole lot of twisted metal.

Bullock's speedometer topped eighty.

"I don't think it's such a good idea to pursue a couple of guys for some nickel and dime drug deal at this speed, Harry," Katz cautioned, his voice strained. "You cause an accident and the department is going to be liable. They'll have your shield and your earlobes."

They were now cruising at ninety.

"Call it off."

The good advice fell on deaf ears.

Katz persisted. "Look, you've got the make and model of the car. What you're doing constitutes reckless endangerment. If someone gets injured, you're going to be sued. It's not worth it."

"That so?" Bullock demanded. Basic police procedure was out the window. "Maybe you think I should slow down and let those dirtballs go." Bullock accelerated. The distance between the two vehicles continued to collapse.

"Couple of punks," Bullock repeated to himself.

The two cars raced by the soaring prongs of the Air Force Memorial. The escaping vehicle swerved into the fast lane, passing cars and vans and pickup trucks as though they were parked. Bullock maneuvered into the middle lane, behind an eighteen wheeler as they passed the Ridge Road exit ramp. Bullock yanked his car into the righthand lane and hit the brakes. The bulk of the truck's massive wheels blocked Katz's view of the getaway car.

Using the truck's mass as a screen, Bullock pulled back into the center lane. He hugged the back wheels of the eighteen wheeler, close enough to make his passenger flinch. Bullock veered slightly left for a peek at his quarry, then tucked in on the truck's rear like a chunk of mud.

Suddenly, there was a stretch of clear lane to their right. Bullock yanked his wheel and stood on the accelerator. Katz could feel a shudder run through the car's metal frame as it sat down and surged forward at a frightening speed.

The driver of the getaway car must have lost track of his pursuers because he had taken his lead foot off the gas pedal. The misjudgment had enabled Bullock to shorten the distance between the cars as he prepared to execute his next move.

Suddenly Bullock's car shot out in front of the eighteen wheeler.

"Brace yourself!" he yelled.

Bullock's car slid across two lanes of traffic and slammed into the other vehicle like a battering ram, pushing it violently to the left. Both cars' airbags deployed. Locked like battling sharks, the cars skidded up the highway in a screaming embrace. The truck driver swerved to the right to avoid a catastrophe.

Rubber burned, glass and plastic shattered, and oil and antifreeze spilled over the roadway. Finally, the two vehicles skidded to a halt, a mass of mangled metal.

Bullock punched his way past the air bag, cursing, and jumped out first, unscathed, his gun and badge in hand.

"What did I say?" he hollered, directing his ire at the two

semi-lifeless forms in the wreckage of the other vehicle. "Police! Put your hands on the dashboard where I can see them. Now!" He didn't seem to notice there was no longer a dashboard upon which to place anyone's hands.

"Punks," he added. "All you had to do was what I told you." Then he commanded them to get out of what was left of the vehicle.

The two men staggered out of the rubble of the getaway car, crawling on the road, coughing, their arms and faces dirty and bloody. Bullock shoved them closer together, yanked out a pair of cuffs and clicked the two together where they knelt.

Then the rain – promised since Halloween – began. It fell in torrents. Traffic came to a virtual stop as people hung out their windows to stare through the downpour. The entire interstate was soon transformed into a parking lot.

The sound of emergency equipment filled the air. Cruisers, fire engines and ambulances were fighting their way through traffic to the crash scene.

Bullock wiped his face. Water and blood dripped from his forehead. He put away his gun and badge and returned to his vehicle – or what was left of it – and opened the passenger door.

Katz fell out, dazed, half unconscious. Bullock dropped to his knees. "Hey, Mo," Bullock said, sounding worried for the first time. "You okay?"

Katz got his legs back. A little disoriented, but walking. He stretched his limbs and curled his fingers and toes to make sure everything was there and in working order.

A medic appeared at his side and cradled his arm. He tried to steady himself. Another uniform embraced him from the opposite side.

Katz could hear Bullock's voice, hollow and distant. "You okay, man?"

"Yeah, I'm going to be fine," Katz answered with little air behind the words. "But next time, call for backup."

110

A flotilla of cruisers encircled the cars. Police officers had sprung into action: placing pylons on the roadway, diverting four lanes of traffic into two, prodding the cars to move along. The occupants of the battered escape car were cuffed and taken from the scene in ambulances.

Someone pulled Katz's jacket off to check him over, then wrapped a blanket around him. Its wool quickly became saturated with rain and felt as though it weighed a hundred pounds. A hot cup of coffee found its way into his hand. Raindrops the size of quarters were falling into the cup, diluting it.

Katz kept checking whether his extremities functioned, curling his fingers and toes. One hand felt numb, but when he looked down it still seemed to be there. Finally, someone led him to a van of some sort and wrapped a neck brace beneath his chin.

He tried to object. A hand reached in with his forgotten jacket and an EMT accepted it. More fresh dry blankets were heaped on him. Their warmth was soothing. He closed his eyes and drifted away.

CHAPTER 21

THE FRONT DOOR to Katz's law office flew open.

Suzie Marston, tapping out a brief, looked up from her computer. "Oh, my God!" she exclaimed. Jumping up from her desk, she ran over to Abby Snowe, who stood in the doorway.

Rain swept in with cold air. A strong wind prevented the door from closing.

Marston wrapped one arm around Snowe and slammed the door shut with the other. "What were you doing out there? You're drenched!"

"Where's Mo?" asked Snowe, looking around. Slim, blonde and golden brown in sunlight, the downpour had transformed her into a wet knot of clothes and straggly hair.

"He's probably out with his new client, Nate Hardy, the guy accused in the Lewis murder case."

"Harding."

"I know, I know. Harding." Marston frowned, confused. Snowe and Katz had been on, then off, then back on, for as long as she could remember. "Are you assigned as the probation officer on the case?"

"Suzie, please stop talking about that case for one minute, will you?" Snowe implored. "Have you heard from Mo or not?"

"Why?" she asked, realizing something was wrong. "What's the matter, Abby? What happened?"

The telephone on Marston's desk rang.

"Hopefully, that's Joey Cook," Snowe said. "He called about ten minutes ago. There's been an accident. I told him I was heading over here. He should have an update."

As Snowe hit the conference button on the phone, the door opened again, bringing in another gust of wind along with two young people in yellow parkas.

Marston turned to the couple. "Who are you?"

"David Reese and Mai Lin," said Reese.

Snowe was on the speaker phone. "Joey? What's happened?"

"Bullock totaled a cruiser in a high-speed chase on I-395," Cook reported, his voice squawking from the tinny speaker. "He and Mo were out on Columbia Island. For some reason, Mo was in the car with him. Word is Mo's injured."

Snowe bowed her head. "Where did they take him?"

"NOVACARE," Cook said.

Marston stared at Reese and Lin. "Who are you again?" She noticed Lin holding a manila envelope.

**

Marston pulled her car up to the NOVACARE emergency room entrance and Snowe climbed out. An awning shielded her from the continuing rain as she sprinted into the hospital.

Upstairs, Katz was resting comfortably in a hospital room. He had been scrubbed and bandaged. His lower left arm was swathed in a soft cast. He had suffered only minor lacerations, a badly sprained wrist and some bruising where the seatbelt tried to bite him in half. Amazingly, they found he did not have a concussion.

"Well, at least you're dry," Snowe said, relieved after bursting into his room expecting the worst. She removed her soaking coat and disappeared into the bathroom with it. Returning, she gave him a kiss and took his good hand in hers.

Katz gave her the broad outlines of the drug deal Bullock had interrupted at the marina, the ensuing chase and the near-fatal crash.

"The man's an idiot," she said. "A complete moron! He really doesn't have an ounce of sense in that pea-brain of his." She could see Katz still had fond feelings toward his former police liaison. "Don't look at me that way, Mo. You know what I'm saying is true."

"Well," Katz interjected, "he did bust a couple of bad guys."

"And for this he risked lives, including yours, roaring down a highway in the middle of the day?"

"Everyone survived," Katz said, "and a couple of druggies were busted."

"Come on, Mo. Quit defending him." She flopped down into the visitor's chair.

He decided to change the subject. "You're assigned to my client, Nate Harding, aren't you? Judge Osborne wants a report before deciding on bond. Any conflict of interest problems?"

She pursed her lips. "Not that I know of at the moment."

"So we're straight?" he asked.

"We're straight."

This was no time for regret. Katz launched into his role as advocate for the accused. "You're going to find that Nate Harding is a pillar of virtue. No criminal record to speak of, great credentials, bedrock in the legal community."

Snowe greeted his words with skepticism. "It's a horrible crime," she said.

"Assuming he did it, and I don't think he did, it was probably in the heat of passion or some sort of accident gone terribly awry," Katz replied. "The point is, I don't see him as a present threat to the community. I think we can set a reasonable bond with stipulations, such as his surrendering his passport, even submitting to electronic monitoring."

She was noncommittal. "As soon as you're ready, we'll set a date and time to get this in front of the judge."

"Maybe you can talk to Kathy early on," Katz suggested, "and reach some preliminary agreement. Harding suffers from claustrophobia in those jail cells."

Curtis Santana rushed in. "Joey got the word out on the street," he said. "I drove here as fast as I could. A lot of people are worried. You okay, Mo?"

Katz smiled. "If I'd been killed on a wild goose chase with the likes of Bullock, I'd never forgive myself."

"The defense bar would never stop laughing about it," Santana admitted. "What the hell happened, exactly?"

Katz recounted the story. The drug deal had by now become a little more sinister, the chase a bit more harrowing. Taking that as a sure sign he was feeling better, Snowe leaned over and gently kissed his forehead.

"Time for me to go, sport," she told him. "Appointments to keep." She disappeared into the bathroom for a second to fetch her coat.

Marston, after having had trouble finding a parking space, finally arrived. The four spent a few more minutes talking, bringing Marston up to date and reassuring her that her boss might live. Snowe eventually repeated her farewell. Marston took the cue and headed for the door as well. She knew it was better to leave Mo alone with his private investigator.

Santana took the chair Snowe had occupied and pulled it closer to the bed.

"I thought maybe you'd left the flash drive in your car," Santana said. "You didn't, did you?"

"No," Katz assured him. "I'd already found a place for safekeeping. It's under the watchful eye of the long arm of the law, if that makes any sense."

"Well, that's good," Santana sat back and sighed. "I dropped over to Columbia Island to check on your car. Joey said you'd been there with Bullock to look around Harding's boat. The passenger's side window was smashed out. Someone had gone through the whole interior." He looked at Katz. "First your house and now this. We have ourselves a problem."

"At least I do," Katz agreed.

Santana pulled at his sparse beard, a sure sign of nervousness.

Suddenly the door swung open. David Reese and Mai Lin walked into the room. "I hope we're not intruding."

"That depends," Katz replied, surprised. "Mind telling me who you are?"

Reese and Lin introduced themselves. Reese shook hands with

Santana and Lin reached over the hospital bed and hugged Katz. Within minutes, they were engrossed in conversation like old friends.

"What happened?" asked Lin.

Once more Katz recounted his story, with even more details and flourishes.

Reese shook his head, seeing no humor in the situation. "I can't believe Detective Bullock did that. He should have called a dispatcher. Police Departments have protocols. He knows that. Pursuit under circumstances like that is extremely dangerous. Someone could get killed."

Katz gave him a halfhearted nod.

"I'm serious," Reese insisted.

"I don't disagree," Katz said. "Who's paying the price?" He raised his padded wrist.

"I agree with David," said Lin. "A couple of guys making a drug buy. That's no reason to rocket down the interstate and pull a life-endangering stunt. What was he trying to do? Get you killed?"

Katz felt Santana staring at him. They exchanged looks.

"What?" Lin asked, watching the two men. She looked at Reese.

"You guys really think Bullock might have done it on purpose?" Reese asked.

"It hadn't entered my head until just now," Katz said.

"Well," Reese continued, "The Department's Internal Affairs Division should make a case study out of this one. If Bullock's showing a pattern of this kind of recklessness, then hopefully someone will recommend taking him off the street."

Katz smiled. "Are you in law school?"

"I got accepted at AU and start next fall," Reese replied proudly. "Hey," he added, "maybe I can intern for you while I'm in school?"

"I'll consider it," Katz said. Then he asked, "How did you kids know to come here?"

"We went to your office just when Miss Snowe was calling the police department," said Lin. "She is very beautiful," she added.

"Why did you go to my office?"

"I brought a copy of the photo," answered Reese. "The one of Libby Lewis being pulled from the water that I took that night."

"We dropped off one copy with the prosecutor and left a second one with your assistant," said Lin.

Katz did not ask whether the couple had given Kathy White a copy of the tiny photo as well. He assumed they had not done so. No sense complicating matters now, he reasoned.

"We listened very carefully to your statement on the television yesterday," continued Lin. "We felt as though you were speaking directly to us. You said the pieces of this case have to be put together methodically and, once that happens, your client will be acquitted."

"We believe you, Mr. Katz," Reese added. "We want to help you put together the pieces."

Katz studied the young couple. They appeared so innocent and naïve. "Okay," he said. "We'll see."

CHAPTER 22

KATZ WAS discharged three hours later. A nurse had gently arranged his injured wrist inside a black cotton sling and given him a little something to ease the pain for the next few days. He threw the pills into a nearby receptacle.

As he waited for the paperwork to be completed, Katz watched an interview on the cable television in the reception area. The reporter, identified as Nick Mann, was interviewing Senator Abraham Lowenstein. Looking like any good actor, the politician's mane of white hair was sculpted, his jaw raised to hide any sag. He oozed sincerity.

"Senator," the reporter asked, "sources reported this morning an alleged plot in Washington to injure, kidnap or assassinate a foreign dignitary. As chairman of the Senate Intelligence Committee, what can you tell us?"

"Nick, there's enough chatter being picked up by our national security agencies to warrant a close look into the matter. The chatter before 9/11 was deafening, and yet we chose to ignore it. As a result, a bunch of thugs hijacked our airplanes loaded with our fuel off of our runways and flew them as missiles into our buildings, causing incalculable havoc on our way of life. That's not going to happen again."

"How do you intend to make sure it doesn't?"

"I'm holding a hearing next Tuesday, Nick, to discuss our preparedness in the wake of these rumors. If there's any legitimacy to them, I want the American people to be fully informed about any threat we're facing and the steps being taken to prevent it."

"Are hearings sufficient?" asked the reporter.

"If I thought for one moment that we faced an imminent threat," Lowenstein replied, "I would be calling upon our intelligence agencies to assume their battle stations rather than hauling them up to the Hill to discuss contingencies. I see nothing, however, that suggests a terrorist attack is imminent. I think we have time for a thoughtful, methodical and transparent discussion about what steps are being taken to abate any potential threat."

"Is that the sort of debate you want to conduct out in the open?"

"Of course," the senator answered unequivocally. "To the extent we conduct our business behind closed doors, the American people are deprived of an open discussion. In a representative democracy, that means the terrorists win, without even hurling a single explosive device. What are we shielding the American people from? The terrorists already know we've detected their scent, and they know we're all about the business of tracking them down and killing them."

"The recent death of Libby Lewis, a former staff member of your committee, created quite a sensation," Mann said. "There's been an arrest in that case, and the defendant is awaiting a bond hearing. Is there any connection between the murder and the rumors circulating in Washington about threats to members of the diplomatic corps?"

"Nothing's outside of the realm of possibility. We're going to do a deep dive into whether there's a security risk. Everything's going to be fair game."

"Who will be testifying before the committee?" asked Mann.

"Jack Smith, to begin with."

A nurse interrupted Katz's concentration.

"You're ready to go, Mr. Katz," she said. "Just be careful with that arm."

When he turned back to the screen, the interview had ended.

Katz went outside to where Santana was waiting for him. He was careful getting into Santana's car. "Can you drop me off at the Alexandria jail?" he asked.

"You're sure you don't want to go back to your office? Or home?" Santana turned on the windshield wipers. It was still raining heavily.

"No, I'm good," Katz assured him. "Things are happening. I've a feeling there isn't a lot of time."

**

TONY FORTUNE, christened Antonio Jose Fortunato, struggled to open the large heavy doors to the church, which were never locked. The latch clicked. The wind helped him out, swinging open the door with a wild rush as the rain swirled around him.

He had walked across the Key Bridge from Rosslyn to Georgetown. The church was about fifteen minutes from the foot of the bridge, down toward the waterfront. An old, nondescript building, it was built on a postage-stamp-sized lot bordered by an iron fence that touched the edge of Wisconsin Avenue as the street dipped below M Street toward the water.

The door slammed shut as he stepped inside. The church was a quiet refuge from the storm that raged outside. Parishioners sat motionless in pews, like patrons at a movie theater waiting for the matinee.

Tony moved down the side aisle. He felt unworthy to use the main aisle. He stopped and knelt at a marble step at the base of the altar.

In the shadows of the vestry, a priest watched, stroking a beard peppered with grey and black hairs. He had not seen Fortune in months. Perhaps he had come seeking God's grace in advance of his girlfriend Maggie's delivery.

Tony's body was heaving with emotion as he bent his face in prayer before the altar.

As the priest watched, his face began to show creases of worry. Had Maggie given birth to their child, or was it something other than that? The priest had no time to pursue these thoughts, as it was time to vest for six o'clock Mass.

120

CHAPTER 23

THE RAIN, which had been falling in torrents for hours, was now reduced to a sprinkle. Santana pulled his car to the curb in front of the Alexandria detention center. Katz slid out and headed toward the building. The glass doors opened and he turned to the right, heading toward the jail.

"Mr. Katz," a sheriff's deputy hollered from the information desk. Katz stopped and turned. "Sheriff Mulcahey asked that we flag you down," said the deputy. "He wants to speak with you if you've got a minute."

Katz reversed direction and walked a bit stiffly toward the elevator bank leading to the administrative offices. Five minutes later, he was sitting in the sheriff's office.

"We had ourselves a little bit of a situation earlier today," Mulcahey explained. "Your client received a visit from someone pretending to be a probation officer."

"What happened?"

"This guy came in with credentials from the Alexandria City Office of Probation and Parole. He asked to meet with Harding. Everybody knows your client is awaiting a bond hearing, so it didn't seem like any big deal."

"It sounds like it did to somebody," Katz retorted.

"One of the deputies on duty said the PO didn't look familiar," Mulcahey continued. "Plus, the word is out that Abby Snowe's got the case, and Kathy White's prosecuting. So my deputy takes it upon herself to look up the guy's name on the Probation and Parole website. She can't find his name, so she calls the PO's office. They confirm there's no probation officer with that name working in their office."

"Were you able to nab him?" Katz asked.

"By the time she came to me, and I contacted the front desk, the visitor had left," Mulcahey answered.

"Does Harding know what you know?"

"No. I wanted to share it with you first."

Katz thought for a minute. "I appreciate that, Kevin. Either Harding knows this person who visited him, or he was duped like everybody else. There's a CCTV in the room where they met, right?"

"Of course."

"What about audio?"

"I don't permit that in this facility, Mo," Mulcahey said. The sheriff respected privileged conversations, whether between inmates and POs, or inmate and their attorneys. He just housed the clientele.

"What about the identity of this guy?" Katz asked. "Shouldn't you have a copy of the credential he handed over to get into the jail?"

"We have his picture," Mulcahey said, "but there's not a matching image of him in any of the state or federal databases we've checked. The ID check has also come up negative."

No traces, which did not particularly surprise Katz.

"How are you going to handle it with your client?" asked the sheriff.

Under normal circumstances, Katz would not discuss his intentions with law enforcement, but he decided to make this an exception to the rule.

"I'm not sure. I think I'll scope it out first. See whether he says anything to me."

Sheriff Mulcahey shared his own observations. "This guy is strange, Mo. Everyone's noticed it. He acts like an untouchable. Doesn't seem to have any of the anxiety of someone facing serious jail time, particularly on a murder charge. What's up?"

"I haven't exactly figured that out yet, Kevin," Katz admitted. "All I know is this has all the trappings of some kind of staged murder. I'll leave it at that. Do me a favor. Watch Harding for me. Restrict visits as much as you can. Or at least monitor the visitors carefully."

"Will do."

KATZ HEADED over to the lockup. He took the elevator to the third floor, where a large metal door opened electronically, allowing him entry into an attorney-client meeting room. Once the door closed, Harding entered from the inmate side, wearing a green jumpsuit.

The place smelled flat and musty. That was something Katz noticed every time he visited a client in jail. No fresh air, only recirculated air; and no direct sunlight, only fluorescent bulbs.

"I'm in trouble, Mr. Katz," Harding said without preamble.

Katz played his cards carefully. "It's a serious charge, Nate," he said. "It's natural to be worried. If the story you told me yesterday wasn't true, that's no big deal. It happens in this line of business all the time."

There were two plastic chairs in the room, one blue and the other yellow. Harding sat in the blue chair while Katz remained standing. "It's a lot more than that," he said. "People might claim I was involved in a murder. I wasn't. In fact, there is no murder."

Katz tried to evaluate what had changed so quickly.

"What are you talking about, Nate?" he asked, temporizing.

"The other day, when we first met, you asked me to start at the beginning," Harding replied. "That's what I want to do now."

Katz sat down in the yellow chair.

"What happened to you?" Harding asked, indicating the sling on Katz's arm.

Katz replied, "Minor accident. That's all."

Harding lowered his voice. "There's a terrorist on the loose," he began. "I know this sounds outlandish. But it's true. And our counterterrorism folks are luring him into a trap before he can do any serious damage.

"There was a planned takedown at Daingerfield Island on Halloween," he continued. "The place was teeming with cops. The plan called for Libby Lewis to provide a computer flash drive to the terrorist. The flash drive laid out the travel route for a targeted assassination. The plan was to nab the terrorist, catch him in a conspiratorial act.

"A cadaver was placed in the water to look as though Libby Lewis had committed suicide. The thumb drive was in her purse on the bulkhead for the terrorist to pluck. The whole thing was staged."

"So what happened?" Katz asked.

"Things got totally messed up." Harding said, relieved to break his pact with Smith and to speak the truth. "Some civilian spotted the corpse and called the police. As soon as the sirens started approaching, everything went to shit. The trap snapped shut, but it was empty."

"Are you being honest with me this time around?"

"Everything I'm telling you is on the level," Harding insisted. "Maybe you have to suspend belief. I don't know. But you have to listen. My life may be at risk."

"Start all the way back at the beginning, Nate, like I said to you the other day," Katz instructed his client. "Walk me through it."

"Okay." Harding took a deep breath. "Years ago, when I was young and idealistic, straight out of law school, I was recruited to work for the CIA. But I crashed and burned. It wasn't because of anything that I did. It just happened. The director suddenly eliminated eight hundred operational positions. Mine was one of them."

"The Halloween Massacre," Katz said. "I've heard all about it."

Harding nodded. "Anyway," he continued, "I thought I was out permanently. But that's not what happened. Two years after I'd been let go, I got a call. I was asked to come back."

"Jack Smith called you."

"That's right."

"He was setting you up," Katz said.

"That's true, but, at the time, it was such an ego boost, hearing from him," Harding explained. "Being let go was devastating. Now I had purpose and belonged."

"And you felt like you owed it all to him," Katz added.

"That's what I didn't understand, Mr. Katz. Not at the time. But it's exactly right. I owed it all to him. The loyalty had to be unshakeable, and personal."

"Did you return as a regular employee?" Katz asked.

"No," Harding said. "He didn't want me to have a desk job. He said he wanted me to remain undercover. Be one of his ghost agents."

"And you went along?"

"Of course. It was my chance to get back in the game. Smith set me up in the private sector at first. Then he asked me to handle a clandestine operation. A small one. They were all small ones at first. But, as time went on, the operations got bigger and bigger."

"And he helped you grow financially," Katz suggested. It could have been asked as a question, but was not. They both knew the answer.

"Every which way," Harding said. "Financially, I was provided with a steady stream of checks. And he set me up in the job market, first on a few crucial boards and then in the public sector. I'm now in the Senior Executive Service at the Office of Special Counsellor."

This was vintage Smith. Finding out a man's weakness, and capitalizing on it. Harding was a romantic about the intelligence business, so he had been offered the ultimate cloak and dagger.

"When you get involved in something like this, they're supposed to take care of you, aren't they?" Katz said. "They're supposed to swoop in and rescue you if things get too crazy, like the marines do. Never leave a man behind."

"Except they don't always do that," Harding replied. "Sometimes they let you twist in the wind. It's like a Kafkaesque nightmare. They leave you dangling. I'd been promised they would pull the plug on this farce of a criminal case in a day's time. But look where I am."

Katz understood the pressure Harding was feeling. He decided to take advantage of it. "Smith might have killed Lou Moultrie," he stated flatly. "Or at least had it done. You've got to be worried he'll do the same to you."

Harding recoiled. "That had to be the terrorist."

"I doubt it." Katz poured it on. "Maybe Smith won't take care of you with a bullet, like Moultrie. Maybe he'll just leave you to rot here in jail to take the rap for a fictitious crime. How can you prove you're innocent if they manipulate the evidence and stack the deck against you?"

Katz could feel Harding's paranoia the way a doctor can smell a disease. "You are in over your head, my friend," Katz told his client. "Jack Smith is nobody's fool. I know. I learned all about his methods by representing him in his divorce case. He's relentless, Nate."

"That's what I'm afraid of, Mr. Katz," Harding admitted. "It's why I hired you."

"For insurance?"

"You could say that." Harding said. "I looked up his divorce case, right after he called me for one more favor. I figured if I enlisted your help, I'd have the upper hand on him. And you'd know all about him."

Katz laughed. "What did he think of that?"

"He was furious. After you and I met in Old Town, I met with him out at Gravelly Point. He was apoplectic. Claimed I'd deceived him."

Harding's statement was consistent with what Santana had told Katz. "What did you tell him?"

"I told him it was just a coincidence."

"Did he buy it?"

"What do you think?" Harding got up from his chair and stood behind it. "He didn't say anything. But I knew what he was thinking."

"What was that?"

"That I had double-crossed him, Mr. Katz. That's what he was thinking. That I hadn't been true blue loyal to Il Capo, the great Jack Smith."

There was still one thing bothering Katz. "Why are you sharing this with me now?" he asked Harding. "Why did you lie to me out at Dyke Marsh and again at the restaurant? What's changed?"

Harding nodded his head. "That's a fair question. You have every reason to question my sincerity." He sat back down and rested his elbows on his knees. "I had a visitor today, Mr. Katz. To be honest, he scared the shit out of me."

"A visitor? Here?"

"Here," Harding replied. "He posed as a probation officer. He wanted to know how I was holding up. He told me all the details. He advised me to play along with Jack's ruse for a couple more days. He promised I'd be out on bond by tomorrow or the next day."

This was a lot to digest. Katz started with the visitor. "What's his name?" he asked.

"Fine. I don't know his first name. He's with the agency, works for a woman named June Webster. They both report to Smith."

"What about the meeting left you uneasy?"

"Everything, in a word," Harding replied. "I got the impression they're going to somehow put the rap on me. They only need time to get the net tightened."

Katz wondered how. "This Fine, he promised to have you released in a day or two. You should be elated. Not that I know how he thinks he's going to do that."

"But they're not following the script," Harding explained.

"What script?" Katz asked.

"I was led to believe they were going to crack the case in one or two days. Everything was going to come out in the wash. Now the whole story is changing. They're going to release me under a cloud. I'll walk out of here accused of a crime."

"So?"

"Come on, Mr. Katz. Don't you get it?"

Katz shook his head. He honestly did not.

"They're going to walk me out of here with just enough evidence hanging in the balance for everyone to reasonably believe I killed Libby Lewis," Harding said. "Then I'll suffer some tragedy. Maybe a suicide, or a terrible accident. Something to silence me. The case will be closed. And I'll be the fall guy for a murder that never happened."

Katz would have liked to say Harding had a vivid imagination. "You really think so?" he asked. "I mean, that they'll do that to you?"

"Yes! From the very instant Smith discussed the case with me, I had a sense about it. Something's not right. I know he's trying to catch a terrorist. I believe that. But this mess he's landed me in is too deep. I want out." Harding squinted, as though he were looking into the sun. "You have to believe me," he said earnestly. "Otherwise, I'm fucked."

"Okay," Katz said. "Tell me again about this assassination plot you're supposed to be foiling. From the top."

Harding laid out the facts as best he understood them.

**

"The whole thing is absurd," Katz said when Harding finished.

"It's beginning to look that way, now that reality has caught up with us," Harding agreed.

Katz scratched the back of his neck. He debated coming clean with Harding about the additional things he knew, but decided against it. Instead, he said, "Based on everything you're telling me, I think you're better off staying in jail. Your safety won't be placed at risk here. We can see that you're alone and under the eye of the guards at all times. In the meantime, I can use this fictitious case Smith created to try and figure out what's really going on."

"If you think it best, I'll do it," Harding smiled wryly. "Never thought I'd be asking to stay in a jail cell."

Katz looked at the clock on the wall. It was 6:45. "I'm going to walk over to the Probation Office and see your real PO. I'll let her know we're not going to file a bond motion."

"Will she be suspicious?" Harding asked.

"No reason for her to be." Particularly since Katz intended to tell Abby Snowe the truth about the case.

CHAPTER 24

THE SIDEWALKS WERE GLASSY in the street lights, puddles filling the pavement and reflecting the clearing sky overhead. The rain had stopped completely. Billowing clouds floated in the night, blue and pink, mixed with myriad shades of gray. Favoring his bruises, Katz walked three quarters of a mile to the Probation Office, near the courthouse. It had been a long time since he had been to Abby Snowe's office.

There was a time when he used to drop over all the time, back when they had been a topic of conversation. Things had become strained between them after he went into private practice. She considered his use of legal technicalities objectionable and his opening statement a despicable ploy. Overall, she saw him as conniving and phony.

When Katz knocked on her office door that evening, Snowe welcomed him with a smile. Her office was tiny and dingy and crowded. Folders cluttered the desk, the floor, the window sill and the bookcase shelves. Inside those folders were stories of human successes and failures, onetime screw-ups and permanent derailments, cases that resulted in early dismissals or the imposition of lengthy jail terms. All of it made their disagreements seem irrelevant.

"They let you out quick," she said, rising to greet him. "Feeling better?" Her straight sun-streaked blond hair fell forward and she shoved it behind her ear in a familiar gesture.

"I'm pretty much healed already," he replied.

"You better be careful," she said. "Knowing you, you'll tax yourself and end up in a hospital suffering from dehydration or something within a week." She touched the sling supporting his injured arm.

"Ouch!" he yelped.

She laughed.

"Listen," he said, "is there some place we can talk, privately?"

They walked over to the courthouse, empty now, with only the hall lights lit. Waved in by the night guard, who recognized two familiar faces, they climbed to the top floor, where they sat on a bench in a cavernous half-lit hallway.

"Listen," Katz began. "I'm going to tell you something. It's going to sound unbelievable. Except it's true."

"Try me."

"This Harding case isn't what it appears to be. First, there was no murder. The body they pulled from the water isn't even Libby Lewis. It's some unclaimed, nameless person from the morgue. This is all a fabrication, part of a sting operation on the part of some federal spooks who are trying to catch a terrorist."

The hall suddenly felt chilly. "Why are you telling me?" she asked.

"I have to tell someone," Katz responded. "You're part of this case. Plus, we've known each other a long time. I can trust you."

"Why didn't you tell me at the hospital?"

"I'm learning this stuff in waves," he answered. "Honestly. I came right over from the jail, after visiting Harding, who leveled with me for the first time."

She shook her head, not disagreeing, but rejecting involvement. "You need to go to the police."

"I don't think I can," Katz said. "The story's too damned preposterous. And there's a good chance some of the cops are involved. Besides, I don't have enough facts to back what I know. I have to let this thing play out, Abby."

He told her about his initial meeting with Nate Harding at Dyke Marsh, about Santana's spying on Harding's rendezvous with Smith, and about Harding's confession at the jail.

She expressed dismay when he finished. "Layer upon layer upon layer. Do you actually believe Harding's story? I mean, I know this guy is a power in the bureaucracy, but that doesn't mean he's not a complete psycho, Mo."

Katz did not believe Harding was psychotic. Scared, yes. And he had a right to be; Katz knew Jack Smith better than most people.

Snowe went on, "Do spy agencies even have access to a morgue where they can just check out bodies for their espionage capers? Is that our tax dollars hard at work? Like Rent a Dead Girl?"

"Listen, I know this sounds close to spy fiction," he replied. "But the facts I do know check out. There's been something out of focus about this case from the beginning. I felt it even before Harding came clean. He's leveling with me, at least about what he's been told. No doubt about it."

"So what's your next move?"

"I'm not going to proceed with any bond motion," Katz answered. "It provides a modicum of protection for my client, staying in Kevin's jail. And that will give me more time to fish around and try to figure out what the hell is going on here."

He left out any mention of the flash drive, in part because he was unsure of its significance, but primarily because it raised serious questions about Bullock's motivations and Cook's trustworthiness. If he told her about it, she might force him to cough it up to the police, something he was not ready to do. The same held true for the tiny photo recovered by David Reese.

"Are you going to tell Kathy?" Snowe asked.

"I'm not going to tell her the truth, if that's what you mean." Katz hesitated. "At least not yet. I have to see how it all shapes up."

"No, I mean about the bond motion. You'd better let her know you're withdrawing it right away."

Katz was slightly taken aback. "I'll let her know first thing tomorrow," he said. "There's no rush. Nothing has been filed. It always takes a couple of days to move the bureaucracy, even in a courthouse that prides itself as the state equivalent to the U.S. District Court's rocket docket."

"Except it's already on the docket," Snowe informed him. "For tomorrow afternoon. At one p.m."

"It's what?" Katz felt a jolt of panic. "Are you sure?"

"I'll show you."

Together, they descended through the echoing halls to the second floor, where the next day's docket was printed and posted on a bulletin board behind a plate of glass.

There it was, clear as day. *Commonwealth of Virginia v. Nathaniel Harding.* Courtroom 1. The Honorable Daniel Osborne, District Court Judge.

Katz stared at it like someone who needed to absorb the ink off the paper to believe in the authenticity of the printed words.

"Obviously, you didn't know anything about this," commented Snowe, with a laugh.

"When did this happen?" Katz asked.

"Kathy called late in the afternoon," Snowe explained. "The judge wants her to put on some evidence. Sort of like a preliminary hearing. I thought it was a little strange when she mentioned it to me. Very unorthodox, you know."

This was exactly what Nate Harding had predicted. The creation of a false narrative, with just enough to cast a shadow of guilt. And then the defendant would be released. Katz wondered if someone had gotten to Judge Osborne.

"What is it?" Snowe asked, sounding anxious.

"Nothing," Katz said. "I've got to get back to the office. I've got to get ready for this hearing."

He kissed her on the lips and left.

**

Katz made his way to his office, zigzagging through the streets and alleys, grateful that the rain had stopped. It seemed to him that the sky and the earth had melded into one dark shade of blue, except above him shone the stars and the once full moon, now missing a sliver of its shiny orb. The trees were nearly bare of leaves, exposing gnarly branches that looked like fingers that came to life while the city slept.

As he walked, Katz's mind wandered, sorting and ordering his impressions of Nate Harding, Harry Bullock, Jordin Deale and the drowning at Daingerfield Island. Bullock and Deale were pursuing a case against Harding, who was nothing more than a piece on some elaborate chessboard devised by Jack Smith.

With memories swirling through his mind, Katz looked at the illuminated store fronts along King Street, the main artery on the east-west axis through the city. Clothes, furniture, books, coffee shops, crafts, wigs, more clothes, more food, bars, artwork, and jewelry. He turned the corner, where the shops ended and clusters of residential and professional townhomes began.

The dark blue was fading to black as night crept in, wrapping itself around him like a cloak. The light from the streetlamps illuminated the night as though there was a fog. "What the fuck are you up to, Jack?" he murmured to himself. "What are you really up to?"

CHAPTER 25

"MR. SMITH."

Hearing his name called, Jack Smith turned.

Derek Fine was loping toward him. "Mr. Smith," he repeated. He slid to a stop when he caught up with Smith. "I just finished reading a speech you gave awhile back," Fine said. "I listened to the podcast. It had to do with identifying the threat posed by domestically situated terrorist cells."

Smith smiled contentedly. He could almost hear himself presenting that speech.

It was 1995, six years before 9/11. A National Intelligence Estimate had concluded terrorists were going to strike the U.S. on its own shores. It concluded that the first World Trade Center attack – the one that occurred in '93 – had been intended to kill scores of people. It said that terrorists were bound to try to strike America's symbols of democracy and capitalism, from the White House to Wall Street.

Yet no one had listened. No one got it.

The 1995 NIE called them "transient groupings of individuals," people who operate "outside traditional circles but have access to a worldwide network of safe havens."

Such people were all around us, as the Jack Smiths of the world could testify. They stand next to us, waiting to do harm.

"What you talked about in that speech, sir," Derek Fine continued. "That's what's happening now. It's the work of domestic terrorists." He hunched his shoulders. "You predicted it and now it's happening."

They reached the cafeteria. It was closed this late at night, except for the vending machines. Smith slotted coins in for a cup of coffee. Black. He offered Fine something. The young man declined.

They sat down at a corner table in a small section of the large cafeteria that was still open. A metal grate that stretched from ceiling to floor closed off the remainder. The entire room was filled with empty tables and chairs. Salt and pepper shakers stood on each table, tiny sentries waiting for the onslaught of morning.

Fine perched on the edge of his chair. His legs were long and his knees knocked against the table's edge. He rested one elbow on the laminate surface.

Time to impress the man.

"By the way, I took steps today to make certain that everything remains on an even keel with Mr. Harding."

Smith slid back in the plastic seat.

"What exactly?"

"I visited him in the Alexandria jail," Fine said proudly.

Smith hunched over and looked intently at the dregs of his coffee. He could not afford to display any anger. This room might be empty, but the walls had eyes and ears.

"I'm sorry," Smith said calmly. "What did you just say?" He reached in his pocket for his phone.

Fine elucidated, pleased with his initiative. "I felt it was important to make sure Mr. Harding remains calm and doesn't panic and start sharing information with his attorney. So, posing as a probation officer, I visited him at the jail."

Smith was only half listening now. His mind was reeling. What had this fool done?

Smith spoke into the phone as soon as June Webster picked up. "June, I'm glad you're still here. I'm sitting with one of your protégés, Derek Fine. He's shared some rather intriguing information. We need to talk. In five minutes. My office."

**

AS JUNE WEBSTER put down the phone, she tried to collect her thoughts. Smith's tone had been disconcerting. When he sounded calmest, it usually meant things were starting to fall apart. She felt it. And that presented a danger. Smith would find a way to blame

136

any failure on her. She needed to trek up to the Hill in the morning and see whether she could begin some damage control, maybe take some heat off of herself and salvage her career.

Quickly, she made a call. She did not expect anyone to answer on the other end at this hour.

"It's June," she spoke to the message recorder on the senator's private line. "I'm going into a meeting with Jack Smith. I know he's slated to testify before your committee next Tuesday, senator. Perhaps I can meet with you before then, to discuss a few issues you might want to raise with him in a public forum? Please have your scheduling secretary give me a call." He had her number.

When she clicked off, her heart was pounding as though she had jogged a mile at a forty-five degree angle.

**

SMITH AND FINE were both waiting for her in Smith's office.

While he waited, Smith had contemplated the situation from all angles. In any operation, one misstep and everything begins to teeter. This was a misstep. There was no way on earth he could have anticipated it. If he had, he would have prevented it. Now it was too late.

"Do you know what this young man has done?" Smith asked Webster as she closed the door behind her. "He had the audacity to visit Nate Harding in jail, posing as a probation officer."

He turned to Fine. "A criminal offense, I might add, impersonating a law enforcement officer." Fine flushed deeply but was silent. Then back to Webster. "Did you authorize this?"

"This is the first I've heard of it," she answered.

Smith's eyes burned. "Who told you to do this?" He was scowling at Fine. "Who gave you permission?"

"I took initiative, sir." Fine was shaking, all his earlier confidence drained away. "I wanted him to know he was going to be released soon. That everything was okay."

"Initiative!" Smith screamed. "Initiative! You're not paid to take initiative. You're paid to take orders, to do as you're told. No one, no one is authorized to go outside the lines of authority and pull a stunt like that. What kind of idiot does that?"

Silence. Followed by insubordination.

"You do, sir," Fine replied. It was as audacious a statement as it was unexpected. "I've studied your career," he continued. "I've read everything you've written, listened to every speech you've given. You go outside the lines all the time. It's how you established your reputation. How you became a legend."

Smith was too angry to succumb to a strategy of flattery. "The last thing I need is for an underling to imitate me," he hollered. "You're not to draw comparisons between us, do you understand? The risks I've taken and the path I've blazed are not something you can duplicate. You will only ever mess it up. Do you understand?"

Fine appeared about to cry. He was glancing toward the door as though his dearest wish was to leave that room.

Webster felt embarrassed. She looked like she wanted to slap Fine. Wanted to slap both of them, actually. "Whatever possessed you?" she shouted at Fine. "What's wrong with you?"

Turning to Smith, she added, "This is partially your fault, Jack. If you hadn't conjured up this harebrained operation, faking a drowning and creating a phony crime, none of this would be happening. What did you expect? All Derek is doing is marching down the road you've blazed."

"I was only trying to help," Fine interjected, unable to keep a whining tone at bay.

Webster and Smith both glared at him. "Don't you both realize we had everything under control?" Smith insisted. A bit of hyperbole, wrapped in pique. "Nate is our guy. He isn't just some person picked out of a police lineup. I've groomed him for years. I spoke to him about this operation when it was launched. He knows the score.

Or at least he did before you marched in and probably spooked him."

Smith continued to glare at Fine. At the same time, he balanced his current exasperation with admiration for Fine's ingenuity in switching the photo Reese had attempted to send to Katz. That had turned out to be a lifesaver. He realized he could not afford to alienate Fine or Webster, not right now. "Maybe I am partly responsible," he said wearily. "Maybe this is all my fault. I'm sorry, Derek. I know you were only trying to help. It's just that this is such a delicate operation. You understand that, don't you?"

Fine nodded, sagging with guilt.

"I know you do," Smith continued. "Let's see whether it makes any difference in the morning." Smith prayed it would not, but realistically he was not so sure.

Although Smith admitted to no ulterior motive in arranging for Harding to be released, it was perfectly understandable if Harding saw it otherwise. The likely scenario: put on a court hearing; allow just enough evidence for the public to believe Harding was guilty of something; release Harding; and then have something tragic occur. If Harding envisioned a trap of that sort, then he would run into Katz's arms. He would tell everything to the attorney. And Katz would necessarily become even more of a problem.

CHAPTER 26

Thursday, November 4

DEREK FINE was the last person Smith wanted to see early the next morning. Yet there he was, sitting outside Smith's office, slouched over in the same posture as the previous night, riddled with guilt and self-doubt.

"What is it?" Smith asked without any cordiality as he swiped his badge over the cypher to access his office.

"I neglected to tell you something else," Fine reported, his voice tentative.

Smith dreaded what might come next. "Tell me."

"I think Harding's attorney has the thumb drive," Fine said.

Smith stopped in his tracks. Bullock had reported getting rid of the thumb drive. A narrative had been created attributing Moultrie's murder to its theft. Events planned for next Tuesday were predicated on the lone wolf knowing the contents of the drive.

Smith invited Fine into his office. Fine explained seeing 'Lewis Drive' flash across Katz's computer screen shortly after the head shots had been switched. Smith assessed the implications as Fine was talking, and immediately texted Hughes to drop by his office as soon as he arrived.

**

A CARNIVAL atmosphere filled the courthouse by noon, making the art of acting all the easier.

The television vans were back on the street with their transmission poles extended three stories into the sky. The myriad wires in all imaginable colors – red, yellow, black, green, white, blue – were back. Bright lights. Large transparent umbrellas, and dozens of media people – reporters, producers, camera crews, anchors, and writers – crowded the sidewalk.

Inside, reporters who fed the media juggernaut waited for the curtain to go up.

"All rise," the clerk announced. "The General District Court of the City of Alexandria is now in session, the Honorable Daniel Osborne presiding. Please be seated and come to order."

Judge Osborne took the bench and settled his black robes around him.

"*Commonwealth versus Nathaniel Patrick Harding,*" the judge read from the paper in front of him. "Are both sides ready to proceed?" Kathy White nodded from behind the prosecution table. So did Katz. "Very well," Judge Osborne addressed the prosecutor. "Call your first witness."

"David Reese," Kathy White replied to the judge's instruction.

"I'm sorry, Your Honor," Katz interrupted, standing. "We're not here for an evidentiary proceeding. I move that we dispense with it and consider the issue of bond."

"Motion denied," the judge said firmly. Followed by "Proceed," directed to the prosecutor.

David Reese, tall and gangly, took the stand and was sworn in. He straightened his unfamiliar tie and shifted his shoulders inside his jacket. He glanced out at the spectators, Mai Lin among them. She gave him an encouraging smile.

"Mr. Reese, can you please tell the court where you were on Halloween night, October thirty-first?" White asked her witness.

"I was on the bike trail that parallels the George Washington Parkway," Reese said. His voice cracked. "I'd traveled across the 14th Street Bridge and I was headed south toward Old Town."

"And did you run across anything unusual on your ride home that day?"

"Yes. As I rode across Daingerfield Island, I saw what I thought was a body in the water."

"And what did you do?"

"I stopped and dismounted." He was obviously reliving the moment, both his fear and his bravery. "When I first saw it, I just stared. I hoped it wasn't what I thought it was. But it was. It was a body in the water. I knew I couldn't just ride away. So I called for help."

"You called 911?"

"That's right."

"How long did it take before emergency crews arrived?"

"Only a matter of minutes."

White showed Reese a photograph. He glanced down at it and nodded. She walked across to defense table and showed the photo to Katz. The photo showed a woman bathed in blue light lying still in the grass surrounded by EMTs, her wet dress clinging to her body and a necklace wrapped around her neck.

White asked Reese, "Do you recognize this photo, marked as Commonwealth Exhibit Number One?"

"I do," he answered. "It's a photo I took of the woman who was pulled from the water."

"Later identified as Libby Lewis," the prosecutor added.

**

SITTING AT THE DEFENSE TABLE, Harding was certain of Jack Smith's endgame. Katz had said it was safer for him to stay in jail. He would have to take matters into his own hands to make certain that happened now.

Suddenly he jumped up on top of the defense counsel's table, turned his back to the judge, his arms flailing, and began screaming to the assembled.

"The truth is I'm an innocent man," he hollered. "The truth is I will accept nothing less than full and complete vindication. I have no doubt that I will be exonerated. No jury of my peers would find me guilty of a crime that I didn't commit."

Katz instinctively understood what Harding was doing, and made no effort to restrain him.

"I abhor the use of technicalities in criminal cases," Harding yelled at the speechless audience. "I say let the evidence in. You've all heard the expression 'The truth will set you free.' I believe that. I also believe that failing to tell the truth leaves you in shackles."

Nate Harding's voice thundered. "I am not going to be free until my reputation is restored," he screamed. "And that's not going to happen unless and until I am completely exonerated of any criminal wrongdoing. To hell with holding a preliminary hearing in this case. I want it fast tracked for a jury trial."

"Order!" Judge Osborne bellowed. "Order in the courtroom! There will be order!" He slammed the gavel on the wooden bench. "Order!"

Chaos reigned.

The judge turned to the bailiff, "The defendant will be removed from the courtroom and returned to the lockup. Now!"

Deputies, coming out of their thrall, swarmed Harding. They grabbed him by his legs, tipped him sideways and carried him like a battering ram to the holding cell. His shouting voice receded. Judge Osborne threw down his gavel.

If the Harding case had been a real criminal prosecution, Katz would have immediately asked for a psychological evaluation and considered filing an insanity defense. Instead, after a pause for everyone's blood pressure to settle, he asked for a continuance.

"I need a little time," Katz implored the judge. "I'm as baffled as anyone by my client's conduct. I request a recess until tomorrow. I will meet with him in the interim and, hopefully, we will be able to make sense of things by then."

White, looking a little shell-shocked herself, added, "Make that a joint motion."

The judge found his gavel and continued the case to 10 a.m. the following Tuesday. Then he quickly departed the bench.

The reporters and others packing the courtroom clamored for an explanation. No one stayed around to provide one. Katz was escorted out the back entrance of the courthouse by the deputies, enabling him to avoid reporters stationed around the main entrance.

As Katz left, Reese and Lin were waiting to speak to him.

"Will you take us up on our offer?" Lin asked. "Can we help you?"

Katz leveled with them. "I appreciate it, but there's no way I allow either of you to assist me in this case. David is a witness for the prosecution. I need to maintain an arm's length relationship with him. If I have either or both of you helping me with this case, I'll be accused of influencing a witness and be thrown off the case."

"Of course," Reese said. "I'm embarrassed I didn't think of that myself."

Undeterred, Lin asked, "Once the charges are dismissed against Mr. Harding, can we help you then?"

Katz smiled. "Yeah," he said. "You can help me then."

CHAPTER 27

AS KATZ RETURNED to his office, Tony Fortune was rummaging through the attorney's desk. Fortune was not entirely sure what he was supposed to be looking for. But those papers he had seen the other night looked enticing.

Suddenly, an arm reached out and grabbed him. "What the hell!" he screamed.

Papers flew off the desk. Thunderbolt, who was trailing Fortune in search of treats, scampered under the desk. Wrestled to the ground, Fortune pleaded for mercy.

"Okay. Okay. I give!"

Curtis Santana loosened his grip on Fortune, who promptly tried to break free, which proved to be a mistake. Santana pounded a fist into Fortune's rib cage. Then he picked Fortune up and flung him against the wall.

When Katz arrived a few minutes later, he found Fortune curled up on the sofa in pain and Santana hovering over him. He looked at both Santana and Fortune for an explanation.

"I found this little shit poking around your desk, going through your folders," the investigator said.

"I can explain," Fortune winced. He checked that Santana had backed away before straightening up on the sofa. "The cop, the last time we were in court. Remember?"

Katz remembered their last court case together. "What cop?"

"Guy with a big belly and huge head."

"Phil Landry?" asked Katz.

"Yeah, that's his name," replied Fortune. "He took me aside when we were in the courthouse. When I was running late, remember?" Fortune rubbed his ribcage. "He told me he could fix the case. I wouldn't have to go to jail, he told me. I only had to do one small favor for him. If I did it, everything would be dropped."

"What are you talking about, Tony?" Katz asked, annoyed. "I

got that case dismissed because a police officer didn't show."

"Not true, Mr. Katz," Fortune corrected him, looking virtuous. "Landry did. He said all I had to do was keep tabs on you. He asked me to drop over to your office a couple of times and nose around the place. If I saw anything that looked unusual or out of the ordinary, I was to report to him immediately."

Katz was incredulous. There was no way Landry got Fortune's case dismissed, no matter how many contacts or how much clout he had. Joey Cook had notified Katz of the weak link in the prosecution's case the night before trial. It was impossible for Landry to have arranged things. "And you thought that was a great idea, Tony?" Katz was outraged.

"I never seen you like this before, Mr. Katz." Fortune feigned laughter. "I wasn't going to rat on you. Honest! You don't think I'd do something to hurt you, do you? You done a lot for me, Mr. Katz."

Fortune stood, then bent over slightly for a minute before standing upright.

"I was going to tell you about this before," he continued. "I swear. The only reason I didn't was I knew you'd get mad. Really, Mr. Katz, I would never do nothing to hurt you, not after all the good things you've done for me through the years."

"Shut up," Katz said. The tumblers turned in his mind. Phil Landry left the masquerade party in a hurry on Sunday night. Moultrie's body was recovered a short distance away, so there was a good chance Landry had been summoned to the murder scene. Katz also remembered Wolfe mentioning the next day's scheduled court case. As a result, Landry knew where to go. He must have done some digging right before trial, maybe in the clerk's office.

A perceptive cop would have found the defect in the case. Landry must have used that information to broker a deal with Fortune, setting him up as a stooge. And the stupid kid fell for it! But why was Landry suddenly interested in the contents of Katz's office?

Katz looked at Fortune. "I'm not going to call the police, but I am never going to represent you again, Tony. Ever."

"Come on, Mr. Katz," Fortune whined. "That's harsh."

"Harsh?" Katz could hardly believe the kid's nerve. "You make a deal with a cop about one of my cases, and you don't tell me about it?"

Fortune gave him a lopsided grin, still thinking he could charm his way out of this.

"You think this is funny?" Katz lost his temper for real. "Get out! And stay out. Don't you ever ask me for help, you little fuck! Out!"

Fortune took a few steps backwards, looking devastated. "You can't be serious, Mr. Katz."

Katz was merciless. "I am deadly serious, Mr. Misfortune. You are *persona non grata*. No more legal assistance from this office. If I ever see you here again, I'll have you up for trespassing. Now get out of my sight."

"Don't do this to me," Fortune pleaded. "Don't put me out."

Katz had touched something primal. Instead of relenting, and despite his deep feelings toward Fortune, he accelerated. "You have completely betrayed my trust. You don't deserve my representation. Ever. Now get out! And stay out!"

**

MID AFTERNOON, June Webster was ushered into Abe Lowenstein's office. The senator extended a warm hand. Webster moved past it and hugged him.

Lowenstein's office was located on the fourth floor of the ornate Russell Senate Office Building. Its large windows looked out through bare tree branches at the white marble façade of Union Station. The late afternoon's setting sun reflected through the windows.

"How bad are things?" he asked.

"Slightly out of control," she replied. She sank into a blue leather sofa. "No," she corrected herself. "Seriously out of control. Ever since that drowning out on Daingerfield Island, it's been one thing after another. Jack's acting with impunity. Subverting the criminal justice system with a phony trial. Running around trying to catch the terrorist by setting a new trap along the railroad tracks when Jumma al-Issawi comes to town next Tuesday."

"It's insane," the senator said.

"I agree, Abe. But Smith gets away with all these machinations."

"What can I do to help?"

"Your congressional hearing," she said. She knew the senator had been briefed on the operation. "Make him divulge his operation to arrest the lone wolf. Expose his foolishness."

Lowenstein nodded politely, as though thinking it over. He crossed his legs and studied her carefully.

She crossed her own shapely legs and returned his stare. "You'll come across as a heavyweight," she told him, "as someone who's willing to ask the hard questions about possible malfeasance in our national and international security operations."

Lowenstein smiled. "Possibly," he said. "And what's in it for you?"

She said nothing.

He leaned forward. "You want to take him down, don't you? I mean, it's a blood sport, June."

Yes, Webster told herself, staring at him. It is a blood sport. Pernicious. "You have him in a cage by calling that hearing," she said. "Hold him accountable. Expose him. I can help you do it. I think I know what he's up to."

**

KATZ BORROWED Santana's car and drove back to the Alexandria City jail to visit Nate Harding, who had been returned to the jail. His own car was in the repair shop after being towed from the LBJ Memorial Grove.

Katz had to wait a few minutes in the attorney-client conference room before Harding joined him.

"There are CCTV cameras overhead, but no sound," Katz said as Harding entered. They could be seen, but not heard.

"Got it," Harding said, avoiding any gesture of friendship.

"That performance of yours in the courtroom was a thing of beauty," Katz said, smothering a grin. "It was awesome."

"Thanks," Harding replied.

Katz needed answers to what was going on, and he was reaching for straws trying to do so. "Do you know Phil Landry?" he asked. "It turns out Landry pressured one of my former clients to snitch on me."

"I know him, and it sounds just like him," Harding replied. "Landry is one of Abe Lowenstein's henchmen. No official connection, of course. But he does the senator's bidding."

Katz remembered seeing the senator on television. "I heard an interview with Lowenstein." He tried to recall where and when. "When I was being released from the hospital after my accident."

"Lowenstein is wired into everything to do with the intelligence community," Harding said. "He was Libby Lewis's boss. According to Fine, he's scheduled a hearing next Tuesday about the terrorist threat."

Katz wondered if the timing was coincidental.

"I suggest you confront the senator, Mr. Katz," said Harding. "Find out what's going on while we're both still breathing."

"I'll go over there now," Katz replied.

CHAPTER 28

KATZ LOCATED a parking space on First Street, along the east side of the Russell Senate Office Building. He tucked Santana's Fiat against the curb and walked toward the building's front entrance. Across the street, on the other side of Constitution Avenue, the dome of the U.S. Capitol shone through the claws of bare trees against the background of a clear late afternoon sky, the sun beginning to dim.

Katz bounded up the stairs to the main entrance. He tried to be patient as he went through security, a constant source of delay in the city. Then, in lieu of taking the elevator to the fourth floor, he decided to take the stairs. Years of use had polished the stairwell's granite steps; an ornate banister wrapped its way around, like a ribbon. The staircase door on the fourth floor opened onto a long hall of the rectangular building.

As Katz turned the corner to Lowenstein's office, he bumped into a woman. He apologized and slowed down. The woman slipped around the corner heading to the elevators. Katz took three steps down the hall. He stopped. That face, the thin, stern lips and dark eyes. He could not remember where, but he had seen her before.

He turned and followed her. Trim and well-tailored, she stood waiting for the elevator. He walked over and extended his hand. "Excuse me," he said, putting all his warmth into his voice. "I'm Elmo Katz. Do we know each other?"

"No, I don't think so," she replied, automatically shaking his hand. The elevator bell rang. The door opened. With a polite smile, she stepped onto the elevator and was gone.

It was true. They did not know one another. But he remembered where he had seen her face before.

Katz stood motionless by the elevator. He tried to process the information, sifting through the facts as he knew them to be. She was the same woman whose photo Reese had found by the bulkhead on Daingerfield Island. The one he later emailed to Katz. Who was she? And what was her connection to Libby Lewis?

Slowly, Katz retreated from the elevator and walked down the hall to the senator's office.

"Can I help you?" the receptionist asked when he stepped into the room.

"Say," he started, pretending to look at someone over his shoulder. "Didn't I just see," he muttered. "Wasn't that what's her name? I just saw her in the hall leaving this office?"

"Oh, June Webster," answered the receptionist with an attractive smile. "She's on the talk shows a lot, discussing national security. She's a bigwig at the CIA. Highest ranking woman, I think."

"That's right, I knew I'd seen her before," Katz said, adding, "The senator, is he in?"

"No," she answered. "He left a few minutes ago."

"But I just saw Ms. Webster leaving."

"I'm sorry," she said, sounding less friendly. "Can someone else help you?"

The moment was about to become awkward, but suddenly a man stepped into the reception area, seemingly from out of nowhere.

"I'm Mike McCarthy," he said. "Folks call me Mac. I'm the senator's chief of staff. He's already gone. He left as soon as his meeting was over."

"Hasn't he gone back to the Pale Horse?" asked the receptionist, trying to be helpful.

"I'm sorry," McCarthy said, as though he had not heard her. Then, to Katz, he said, "I'm just headed out for a cigarette. Nasty habit. Care to join me?"

Katz and McCarthy walked down to the C Street exit, facing toward Union Station. McCarthy lit up.

"We appreciate your stopping by," he said.

"So you know who I am."

McCarthy laughed, a smoker's laugh, low and guttural. "You're a minor celebrity. Everyone's been talking about your case over in Alexandria with that crazy client of yours."

"You heard about it already?" Katz sounded as though he were flattered.

"Along with half the other folks who work here on the Hill."

"I'm surprised," Katz smiled. "No one stopped me for an autograph on my way up here." He gazed at the smoke from the cigarette. "Nate Harding was pretty amazing, I have to say."

McCarthy laughed again. "You want one?" he asked. Katz took a cigarette. McCarthy lit it for him.

The senator's aide took a deep drag. "Nate Harding. That man's certifiable." He coughed. "A lot of the legislative aides up here are attorneys, you know. We know him through his job, and we all think the guy is off his rocker. I feel sorry for you, representing a nut case like that."

But McCarthy had not invited Katz outside to talk about Nate Harding.

"You know June Webster?" McCarthy asked casually.

"Vaguely," Katz replied. "I once represented a divorce client who worked with her."

McCarthy expressed interest, taking another deep drag on his cigarette.

"I'd like to share the details, but I really can't," Katz said. "Privileged information, you know."

"I understand," McCarthy said, but his tone clearly indicated 'not really.'

Despite the calendar, the early evening had grown warm. Katz unbuttoned his wool suit jacket and slipped out of it. His painful left wrist made him wince as he hung the jacket over that arm.

The conversation shifted back to Harding.

"He's a little eccentric," Katz admitted, adding, "but innocent, of course."

McCarthy squinted as smoke got in his eyes. "I suspect that's what every good defense attorney says about his or her client," he said, taking another drag on the cigarette.

"They do," Katz laughed. "All the time. The difference here is the client is telling the truth."

"How do you know?" asked McCarthy, a slight edge in his voice.

"It's easy," Katz replied. He decided to gamble. "You see, Mac, there was no murder in this case. A body was dumped in the river. It was part of a ruse, a clandestine operation to lure a bad guy to that location, supposedly a terrorist."

McCarthy feigned surprise. "That's a shocking statement to make. Do you have any proof of it?"

"You don't have to pretend," Katz replied. "I'm sure you and your boss know all about it."

McCarthy took another drag on his cigarette, his eyes watchful.

"I find it surprising that there has not been any news about a memorial service for Libby Lewis," Katz continued. "Don't you find that odd?"

"Her family is planning something in a few weeks," McCarthy said. "A festival of life, that sort of thing, I think."

"I think the mourning has been put on hold because she's going to rise Lazarus-like from the dead shortly," Katz said.

"What else do you think you know?" McCarthy inquired.

"Someone is planning to carry out a terrorist act," Katz told him. "It's going to happen in the next few days."

Katz watched McCarthy's expression.

"You don't seem particularly concerned," Katz said. "So can I talk to your boss? Is he around? That's what I came here to talk about with him."

"He really isn't around," McCarthy said.

"The receptionist said something about Pale Horse?" Katz asked, continuing to watch the other man's expression.

"That's right," McCarthy admitted. "He's over at the Pale Horse Warehouse in Georgetown, at one of the SCIFs scattered around town. He's there for a briefing."

Katz knew that SCIF stood for Sensitive Compartmented Information Facility. He was vaguely familiar with them. He knew there were several SCIFs located on Capitol Hill and all around the city. Why go to Georgetown?

McCarthy could probably guess what Katz was thinking. He said, "The senator has a fundraiser tonight in Georgetown. Close proximity for scheduling purposes. That's all."

Katz smiled.

McCarthy snuffed out his cigarette. Katz did the same. They dropped the butts in a trashcan.

"I'll set up a meeting for you and the boss soon," McCarthy said. "He'll be interested in your assessment of the case."

They shook hands and Katz plodded back to his borrowed car.

**

KATZ HAD TOSSED his jacket on the back seat and was strapping himself into Santana's car when a Capitol Hill policeman tapped on the driver's side window. "This your car?"

Katz lowered the window. "Yes officer," he replied, hoping Santana was not sitting on a stack of unpaid parking tickets. "Is there a problem?"

The officer pointed to a taxi sign on a rubber stand. "This is reserved parking," he said. "I was about to write you up for a ticket. You arrived in the nick of time. They're a hundred bucks a pop."

It should have occurred to Katz there might be a reason he had been able to park in a choice space so close to the Senate. He looked dumbly at the cop and shook his head. "I never would have parked here if I'd known it was reserved," he said. "I don't know how I missed it."

"Just go," the policeman ordered, unsure of whether or not Katz was personally connected to a member of Congress.

"Thanks, officer." Katz complied by starting the car.

Without delaying to close the window, Katz pulled out into traffic. He stopped at Constitution Avenue, waiting for the light to change. Ahead were the U.S. Supreme Court and the Library of Congress. Opposite them lay the Capitol grounds. He heard a motorcycle roar up behind him, its engine revving.

The light finally changed, and Katz made a right turn down the broad swath of Constitution. The motorcycle stayed close behind him. Katz glanced in his rearview mirror. The biker's face was unidentifiable behind a black helmet and impenetrable visor.

The lawn of the Capitol was on Katz's left, with the glittering marble tower of the Taft Carillon and its park to his right. Katz heard the motorcycle coming up on his left.

A buzz like a dive-bombing bee suddenly tore through the open window beside him. Something exploded against the plastic display on the dashboard. Katz flinched, causing the car to swerve violently to one side. He gripped the wheel and tried to straighten it. Bullets. His mind was screaming.

The next shot zoomed within inches of his nose and hit the passenger side window, shattering it. Shards of glass flew everywhere.

Katz glanced down at his arm in disbelief. Above his wrapped wrist, the white cotton of his shirt had bloomed red with blood. Instinctively, he dragged the wheel sharply to the right and gunned the car onto an avenue bordering the park.

His quick reaction had taken his pursuer by surprise. The bike's roar faded slightly. Katz knew he was only a couple of blocks from Union Station. Its traffic circle would be clogged with taxis and buses, making him a sitting duck.

Another avenue was ahead, transecting at a more than ninety-degree angle. Over the pounding of his heart, he could still hear that nightmare roar as the motorcyclist drew close again, hunting. Halfway across the intersection, Katz yanked the wheel right and stood on the accelerator, fishtailing onto his new route.

Somewhere nearby was a park with crisscrossed walkways. He

found it. A park full of trees, but with a wide sidewalk cutting across it diagonally.

Katz slowed slightly, allowing the motorcycle to draw even with the rear of his car. He feared permitting that gun to creep so close again, but he needed to put this guy out of commission. The bike was in perfect position as the vehicles zoomed in tandem, ignoring shouts and the shriek of brakes from all directions.

The bike rider's arm was upraised with a bulging silencer aimed his way when Katz deliberately fishtailed the little car in another right turn. Its back end swung violently to the left. For a second, Katz thought he had gone too far and the car might roll, but it worked perfectly. The motorcycle was thrown sideways, shoved off the road like a beaten pawn on a chessboard. And the car was still on its wheels.

Katz aimed the Fiat straight for the corner of the park, where the handicapped curb cut should be. He hit the accelerator, felt a slight bump as the car ran up onto the sidewalk, and never let up speed as he headed for the far corner of the park. With hardly any leeway between the width of the car and that of the sidewalk, Katz gripped the wheel hard, desperate to keep straight and true. The scattered trees flew by like fence posts. Before he knew it, he had reached the other end of the diagonal and shot back onto the street.

Katz let his foot relax on the pedal for the first time, tapped the brakes to slow to a sedate pace, and glided gently to the intersection. The light was red. Still jumpy, he looked to the side, half expecting to hear the growling sound of the motorcycle beside him. Instead, only silence.

Sweat dripped into his eyes. He reached with his bandaged wrist to wipe it. As he did so, he noticed the soft cast of his left arm was now saturated with blood.

Katz rolled up his sleeve and tried to slide his fingers under the cast to probe the wound without success. Removing his tie, he wrapped it around his arm, just below the elbow, directly over the laceration. He tightened the noose as firmly as he could with his right hand, then wrapped the tie around the left arm again.

Despite most of the car windows being shattered, the bullets had not penetrated the tires or the engine. No hoses were hissing or electric cords sparking. The passenger window was a jagged hole, with shattered glass showing all around. Nothing he could do about the gouge in the windshield from yet another shot he hadn't heard.

Under cloak of darkness, Katz headed to the 3rd Street Tunnel which provided egress onto the Southeast Freeway. That would carry him safely over the 14th Street Bridge to Virginia.

CHAPTER 29

DAVID REESE heard the sound of a key being inserted into the door lock. He put down his Kindle and turned with a smile. That had to be Mai Lin.

She had gone out to buy dinner and promised to be back by seven. The local news was ending. No new developments in the Lewis case. David could picture her fiddling with her keychain and its assortment of keys, ornaments, baubles, plastic slinky things, and other junk. He smiled wider, thinking of it always falling to the ground.

He rose and walked over to open the door. He was still three feet away when the door opened.

His first reaction was puzzlement, which turned into startled paralysis. It took him a second to recognize that it was not Lin who had opened the door. It took another second for him to make sense of the gun pointed at him. Behind it stood a man in dark clothing with no face.

The man grabbed Reese and violently turned him around, twisting his arm and pushing the hard, cold muzzle of the firearm against his neck.

"You say one word and I'm going to kill you," the man whispered.

Reese gulped for air.

"Where is it?"

"Where is what?" Reese replied. He tried to sound earnest, while knowing there was only one thing the man could want from him.

At that instant, a wild shriek pierced the stillness in the hallway. The man with the gun twirled around, spinning Reese in front of him like a shield. A woman's form flashed across the doorway. Seconds later, the building's fire alarm erupted in a cacophony of disturbing noise.

**

FIFTEEN MINUTES LATER, SAFE ON Virginia's shore, Katz headed toward his office. He would call Joey Cook from there. The incident must have been reported on the regional police radio. Cook would know the lay of the land.

Katz pulled up to the curb under a street light in front of his office. Before he could turn off the ignition, the passenger door flew open. Reese and Lin peered in at him. Reese appeared disheveled and they were both shaking uncontrollably.

"Someone attacked us!" Lin cried. "Threatened us!" She stared down at the glass on the seats, console and dashboard, at the starred front window, and finally at Katz's bloodied shirt. "What's happening?" she cried hysterically. "Why is there blood? What's going on?"

"I'll explain later," Katz said. Using a manila folder lying on the floorboard, he scraped shards of glass littering the interior and told Reese and Lin to get in the car. Reese slid into the back seat while Lin, clutching her purse, collapsed in the front seat. As Lin pulled the door shut, Katz put the car in gear and sped away.

"I went back to the apartment," Lin told him. "There was a man there, threatening David. He was holding a gun to David's head. I pulled the fire alarm," the girl sobbed. "He ran away."

"We trusted you," Reese said. "So we came to you."

Katz wasn't sure how he could help them. "You're going to have to go to the police," he told them.

"I don't want to go alone to a police station or anywhere else," Lin wailed. "I'm afraid."

Katz suddenly made a U-turn. A plan was materializing in his head. "I have a friend who might help," he told them.

Lin huddled in her seat, tears quietly slipping down her cheeks. "I don't understand why they did this," she said. "What do they want from us?"

Katz did not have an answer. "You're safe now," he said in a falsely calm voice. "It's going to be all right." He knew he had to end the Harding case tomorrow, before more people were injured or killed.

CHAPTER 30

KATZ PULLED INTO THE CARPORT behind Abby Snowe's townhouse. He took the key from under the back door mat, opened the door and ushered Lin and Reese inside.

"Where are we?" Lin asked.

"In a safe place," he answered. "This is my friend's house. She's a probation officer. She works long hours, but she'll be here soon. You're going to have to go to the police. She'll help you through it."

They walked through the kitchen to the front of the house. Lin flopped on a couch. Reese went upstairs, collapsed on a bed in one of the smaller bedrooms, and, tucking his head between his hands, began crying.

Katz's cell phone rang. It was Joey Cook.

"Thank God you're all right," Cook said. "I've been worried."

"You heard about the shooting?" Katz kept his voice low as he strolled to the kitchen.

"I heard about a Fiat and a motorcycle involved in a high-speed chase up on Capitol Hill," Cook replied. "I figured it was Santana's car as soon as I heard the make and model. And I assumed you were the driver. Man, what is it with you and cars?"

Katz looked at Lin. She had fallen asleep on the sofa, her hands on her lap. Something was lying in her open hands. It looked like a thumbnail-sized photo.

"What are they reporting?" Katz asked. He lowered his voice while asking the question and moved closer to the sofa.

Cook said, "Just an altercation of some sort between a motorcyclist and a motorist. The preliminary report said that gunshots might have been exchanged. It sounded like some type of drug buy gone awry."

Katz squinted at the photo in Lin's hands.

"The follow-up reports didn't mention anything about gunfire," Cook continued. "They said some crazy kids were drag racing around the Hill on a lark. A fraternity prank. No one seems particularly alarmed about it."

"Nothing about what became of the motorcyclist?" Katz asked idly.

"He must not have been hurt too bad," Cook answered. "No mention of him being dragged off to a hospital, anyway. By the time the local police got there, he'd disappeared."

No response.

"By the way," Cook continued. "I've got some interesting news for you."

More silence on Katz's end.

"Are you still there?" Cook asked.

Katz was staring at the tiny photograph, his mind ticking slowly. It was the size of a picture that would fit in a locket, like the one worn by the woman whose body was retrieved from Daingerfield Island.

The photo was definitely not of June Webster. Katz suddenly realized someone had been monitoring his computer in real time, and had intercepted and substituted Webster's photo for the one Reese had sent him. Someone was manipulating evidence, first the thumb drive, now the photo.

Lin opened her eyes. She looked up at Katz.

"I said I've got some interesting news for you," Cook was insisting.

"What news?" Katz asked, his mind elsewhere.

"No charges were ever filed in that case," Cook informed him, satisfaction in his voice. "There's not even an incident report. Nothing. It's like it never happened."

"What case are you talking about, Joey?"

"The case with Harry Bullock," said Cook. "The wreck on I-395."

Katz felt woozy. "That's not possible, Joey," he said. "I'm guessing you don't have anything because the initial buy took place on federal property."

Thoughts sped through his mind. It could also have something to do with jurisdiction. The line between Arlington and Alexandria cut across Interstate 395. Katz added, "They may have been outside of Arlington County, in the City of Alexandria. Plus, the drug buy was along the parkway, so that should be in the U.S. District Court."

"Nope," Joey replied emphatically. "Zilch. Nada."

"What do you mean?"

"I checked the neighboring jurisdictions," explained Cook. "The crash happened right around Arlington Ridge. It's close to the line, but clearly within Arlington's jurisdiction. And nothing has been filed in federal court either."

The front door opened. Abby Snowe walked into her living room, stopped and stared.

Across the room, Lin stood up, the photo cradled in her hands. Katz looked from one woman to the other. Snowe glanced at Lin, then viewed Katz's bloody shirt.

"What's going on, Mo?" she asked.

"Listen, I have to go," Katz said to Cook.

"Okay," replied the cop. "But before you go, just remember. This sort of shit doesn't happen around here. Someone is messing with the process, controlling outcomes. It all started on Halloween, and it's not letting up. You be careful, understand?"

"Yeah," Katz replied. He steadied himself. Snowe was by his side, inspecting his arm before going to the medicine cabinet.

**

ABBY SNOWE returned from the bathroom, having put away the gauze and hydrogen peroxide. Katz's arm was pretty much patched-up. He sat up, cradling his arm.

It was time for the whole truth.

He told her about the thumb drive delivered by Joey Cook, the trip to Senator Lowenstein's office, and the motorcycle chase, which

162

explained the shot-up car in her carport. He also explained about arriving at his own office to find Reese and Lin in a total panic, and the break-in at their apartment.

Snowe stared into space. She had no idea where to begin. "Why would anyone go after the witness to a drowning? Does David have some connection to this flash drive, which appears to be what someone's interested in?"

"It wasn't about the flash drive," Katz replied. "At least not for David."

He shared his suspicion with her. "The dead woman wore a locket pendant. It must have opened during the rescue effort. A photograph fell out onto the grass and David recovered it."

"He told me about it. He sent a copy of the photo in a PDF file to me. Only thing is, the photo I opened on my computer isn't the same photo Mai's got now."

"How can that be?" asked Snowe.

"Someone intercepted the communication and substituted another photo."

"Who?" Reese was now standing at the foot of the staircase, having been awakened by their conversation.

"Someone who didn't want you, or me, or anyone else to see the photo that fell out of the pendant," Katz answered.

"This picture?" asked Lin, joining the conversation, clutching the photo. "It's important enough to kill for?" She handed it to Katz, who carefully studied the eyes in the photo staring back at him.

Katz looked up. He could see the utter senselessness of it on Lin's face. "I know," he said. "It doesn't seem right, does it? I wish I had a better explanation. Except I don't."

Snowe looked over at Lin and Reese. "You've got to make a statement," she told them. "I need to take you to the police tonight. Even if you don't have much to tell, there's been an assault and threats to kill."

Although Reese protested, Snowe was insistent. As they departed, Katz called Curtis Santana, who was still at Katz's office. He agreed to get a ride to Snowe's place.

**

"SHEE-IT!" Santana screamed.

Hearing the private investigator's voice, Katz walked out to the carport, lit by a couple of halogen lamps attached to the house.

Santana stared at his car. One front window was shattered. The windscreen had a starred hole in the center. The glaring light magnified the scrapes and dents in the body.

Santana looked at Katz. Then they both started laughing. Good, Katz thought to himself. They were not going to be intimidated. They were going to stand together and fight their way through this.

They walked over to Snowe's tiny patio and sat down.

"I got an ID for the woman whose photo you received in the PDF," Santana told the lawyer. "She's June Webster, a senior career officer at the CIA who works for Smith. The photo is the same as the one issued a couple of days ago by the Virginia DMV."

"I know," Katz said. "I ran into her coming out of Senator Lowenstein's office."

"I'm sorry?"

"She was there late this afternoon," Katz explained. "No doubt they'd been talking about the hearing."

"What hearing?" Santana asked.

"When I was in the hospital," Katz explained, "I saw a news clip. Lowenstein is holding a hearing on the terrorist threat. His witness is going to be Jack Smith."

"Senator Lowenstein is turning out to be an interesting guy," Santana observed.

Katz agreed. "There's some sort of cat and mouse game going on between him and Smith. Webster is probably taking Lowenstein's side, feeding him information detrimental to Smith's interests."

"What makes you say that?" asked Santana.

"It's how Washington works, Curtis. The ambitious crawl over other people's bodies."

Katz then explained the discovery of the photo in Lin's possession. "Someone didn't want the picture in the locket to be transmitted," Katz said. "When Reese sent it, some spook out there was already watching my computer, or maybe his. Webster's photo must have been readily available, maybe in a photo directory or something."

"It's a little crazy," Santana observed.

"And they probably know I have the contents of the thumb drive," Katz added. "I plugged it into the computer when Joey brought it over, then removed it when he told me it was encrypted."

"Did the contents show up on the screen?"

"I can't remember for sure," Katz said, "but I assume so."

"Then it's more than a little crazy."

Katz nodded. "I met one of Senator Lowenstein's staffers, a guy named Mac," he continued. "While I was with him, mention was made of a place in Georgetown called the Pale Horse Warehouse. It's a SCIF."

"What was the context?" asked Santana.

"It was a remark dropped by a receptionist. Mac had no choice but to repeat it to me later, probably to remove any suggestion that it was significant."

"And you think it might be."

"I do," Katz replied. "I need you to check the place out."

"Okay."

Suddenly a creaking sound made Katz and Santana stop speaking. They waited for the sound of footsteps. There were none. Perhaps it was the wind.

Santana put a hand on his sidearm. Katz got up and looked over the five-foot-high patio fence. Darkness stared back.

By mutual consent, they went inside and locked the back door. It was getting too cold anyway. Two bar stools stood near the kitchen island, and they settled there.

"Another thing," Katz added. "Joey says the accident on I-395 was never papered."

Santana considered the implication. "What about the drug buy at the LBJ Memorial Grove?" he asked.

"Not that either," Katz replied.

Santana whistled. "Sounds like the car chase was intended to take you out of commission," he said. "Just like the chase around the Capitol. And whoever's behind this has Bullock on his side."

Katz did not want to admit Bullock's involvement, not even to himself. "Not necessarily," he said.

"You got to quit kidding yourself, Mo. Bullock almost got you killed."

"The guys we chased could have been set up by someone other than Bullock," Katz retorted. "It might even have been coincidental."

Santana refused to buy it. The conversation went silent. In the awkward moment, Santana and Katz grasped for something else to say to one another.

"I almost forgot," Santana said. "Suzie asked me to give these to you." He reached into an inner pocket of his bomber jacket, produced a three-page motion in the Smith case and handed it to Katz. "Eve Smith's pleadings."

Katz shook his head. "When is she going to let it go? The court has already rejected her arguments more than once. No attorney would put a motion back on the docket without new evidence, and there isn't any here."

"Harassment," Santana said with a shrug.

Katz opened the folded document and scanned its contents. Then he walked over to Snowe's computer, which sat on a kitchen desk, and accessed his office files through a cloud program. Katz searched around a moment and opened an electronic folder.

"What are you doing? Santana asked.

"I'm looking for an old motion in the Smith case," Katz said.

He found the document and sent a copy of it to Abby's laser printer.

Before he had a chance to retrieve the document, Santana said, "By the way, I've got a friend who'll be able to open that flash drive of yours, no matter how much protection they've wrapped it in."

"Who's that?" Katz asked, putting down the papers.

"Roscoe Page."

While Katz did not know Page, the name was legendary in IT circles. Page ran a major cybersecurity operation at Tyson's Corner, one that had made him a millionaire several times over. If anyone could break into the flash drive and open its contents, he was the one.

Santana gave Katz a number to reach Page, and Katz dialed it.

"Curtis says you can help me," Katz said cryptically after Page answered.

"It shouldn't be a problem," Page replied. "We can meet tonight, if you like. Say in an hour, at ten o'clock." Page then asked: "Are you still at your girlfriend's house?"

Katz started. "How the hell do you know that?" he asked.

Page laughed. "Santana told me that's where he was going to meet you."

"No, I mean how did you know she's my girlfriend?"

Page laughed again. Instant allies. "If you want," he said, "we can meet at Haines Point. Santana tells me he's got a favorite spot out there."

"That will do fine." Katz glanced at the clock. 9:10 p.m. "I'll see you there," he said. As he hung up, Katz heard the sound of Snowe's car, returning from the police station. Just in time, he thought to himself.

CHAPTER 31

THE LBJ MEMORIAL GROVE was quiet when Katz arrived. He steered Snowe's car into the same place he had parked his own car earlier, then walked through the dark to where the *Won Way* was floating. Although yellow tape surrounded the yacht, no guards stood sentry. Katz slipped under the tape and climbed aboard.

Twenty minutes later, he was driving down the K Street corridor in the heart of the District's financial and lobbying hub. A few blocks up Connecticut Avenue, Katz turned right onto M Street, and then into an alley adjacent to St. Matthew's Cathedral. He parked Snowe's car and walked up the alley to Massachusetts Avenue, hailing a cab to take him to Arena Stage in Southwest. Katz then flagged another taxi to get to the Tidal Basin.

He walked to the bench beneath the 14th Street Bridge facing the Potomac. The underbelly of the bridge echoed like a steel drum as cars glided over it in the dead of night.

"Took you a while," Page's voice said as Katz approached the shadow on the bench.

"I wasn't taking any chances," Katz answered.

"Except with me," Page replied with sarcasm.

Katz sat down next to Page. "I'm pretty much operating on blind faith with you."

They were both facing the water. Neither looked at the other. Katz felt a blast of chill air sweep over him. A Metro train rushed out of the tunnel from L'Enfant Plaza and up onto the trestle overhead. The six-car train ran parallel to the 14th Street Bridge and the Amtrak Bridge across the Potomac, where it would snake back underground.

"Did you bring the thumb drive?" Page asked.

Katz pulled it from his inside pocket and handed it to Page, who plugged it into a laptop he had with him. The screen lit up; Page's fingers danced across the keyboard.

"You know how to open this thing?" Katz asked, amazed at Page's casual manner.

"It isn't protected very cleverly," Page replied. "Just enough to prevent a smart amateur from breaking the code." He glanced at Katz for the first time. "Then again, I don't think anyone expected it to be taken from Lou Moultrie's house by some interfering amateur."

Katz's thoughts scrambled. "What did you say?"

"My contacts tell me that Lou Moultrie retrieved the thumb drive from Libby Lewis's purse on Sunday night and took it home with him. Next thing you know Moultrie's dead and the thumb drive is missing."

Page looked inquisitively at Katz, who realized that Page did not know the thumb drive had remained in the purse and been delivered to the property room of the Alexandria Police Department. *Who created the false narrative*, Katz asked himself. *And why?*

"Mind telling me how you ended up with this thing?" Page asked.

"I can't do that," Katz said.

Page continued stroking the keyboard at lightning speed, pausing from time to time, like a finger on the trigger of a machine gun.

After about fifteen minutes, Page told Katz, "Looks like this file provides the date, time and route of a train carrying some precious cargo to Union Station, namely a controversial figure by the name of Jumma al-Issawi." Page continued to study the information on the screen. "There's a key vulnerability marked on the route. The book depository, if you will. In the hands of the wrong person, this information could result in a political assassination."

Katz's muscles contracted like rubber bands.

Page continued to study the information on the screen.

"I think we need to turn it over to someone," Katz said. He was not sure who. Jack Smith? Phil Landry? Jordin Deale? U.S. Attorney Helen O. Douglas?

"Not my responsibility," Page retorted. "I didn't filch it from anyone. I bear no responsibility." He shifted the laptop screen. "I'm going to leave it with you."

Katz repeated his concern. "In the wrong hands, as you say, it could result in disastrous consequences. We have to do something."

Page shrugged. "I'm an observer of life, not an action hero," he said. "Al-Issawi's fate is no concern of mine. What's his safety to me, or you?"

Katz looked across the Potomac River. Another Metro train burst out of the tunnel. It clanged across the bridge toward Virginia. A freight train filled with coal began lumbering across the river toward the coal-fired utility on the House side of the Capitol.

A breeze rushed down the river's bank, picking up leaves, like sheet music, and tossing them in all directions.

"You don't want me to give up the drive and the information in it," Katz said, confusion filling his mind. "Why?"

The screen ignited the darkness, lighting both their faces. At this angle, Katz could read it. The date was Tuesday morning, the time 10:30 a.m. There was a map with a circle showing the railroad track where it ran through a tunnel near the base of the Masonic Temple in Old Town.

"Here's a question for you," Page said. "If this information exposes a vulnerability, and if people know the information is missing, why don't they just change the route?"

Katz felt a twitch of pain in his bad arm and rubbed it.

Page closed the laptop. He unplugged the thumb drive and handed it to Katz. "I've removed all the passwords so you can access everything," he said. "Good luck."

The two men went in separate directions. Katz walked to the intersection of Independence Avenue and Raoul Wallenberg Place, where he was able to hail a cab. He had the driver take him up 14th Street to Thomas Circle and then to M Street. He got out along Connecticut Avenue, looked around as he paid his fare, and then walked the remaining distance to the alley next to St. Matthew's, where Snowe's car was parked.

He drove back to the LBJ Grove.

If there were guards around, they were at the far end of the marina. He climbed onboard the *Won Way* and stashed the drive in its previous hiding place behind the clock. Then he quietly exited the boat, still the invisible man.

"Not a scratch, on me or your car," he said as he handed Snowe the car keys an hour later when he returned to her place. He looked around for Santana.

"He's gone," Snowe said. "And David and the girl are sleeping upstairs in my guest room."

She put her arms around him. "You're welcome to spend the night, if you'd like. Unless, of course, you foresee a potential conflict of interest when Harding's case resumes tomorrow."

Katz laughed. "I think we're good on that," he said. There would no longer be a case after tomorrow. They headed upstairs, their hands entwined.

CHAPTER 32

THE PALE HORSE Warehouse sat at the end of a row of nondescript three-story buildings nestled along the far end of the Georgetown waterfront, in the shadow of Key Bridge and the elevated Whitehurst Freeway, where the lively streets in the area had all run out of pavement and faded into dead ends.

Shortly before midnight, Tony Fortune surveyed the area around the warehouse. Natural barriers – parked cars, bins piled high, shrubs and trees – camouflaged the place at street level. Shadowy figures with long guns walked the perimeter.

That was interesting.

The roof appeared to provide the only way inside.

He had waited outside Snowe's townhouse just long enough to catch a snippet of the patio conversation between Katz and Santana. Reference to this warehouse had sounded significant. If he could turn up some valuable information there, maybe Mr. Katz would return him to his good graces.

Redemption was worth the risk, even though he knew he really belonged at the hospital with his girlfriend, Maggie, who was about to give birth to their child.

Fortune tramped back up the alley to M Street and followed it to the edge of the Key Bridge. From there, he had access to the Whitehurst Freeway. Suspended on high pylons above the old waterfront, it bypassed Georgetown's narrow streets and carried traffic from the bridge to the K Street corridor and points east.

He pulled out his phone and tapped a text into it:

Checking out the Pale Horse for you.

He sent it to Katz.

A car's horn blared in the night as Fortune began maneuvering along the wisp of sidewalk at the edge of the Whitehurst Freeway. No one walked on this sidewalk, which was nothing more than a concrete tightrope.

"Get the hell off the road, you fool," a driver yelled, half-drunk. Fortune tottered but avoided falling onto the road by an inch. He slid along the edge of the freeway until he guessed he was directly above the old buildings. The lights along the freeway only hinted at them, squatting in the darkness below. He jumped up on the cement barricade, balanced and steadied his lanky frame. Then he leapt off the highway onto the adjoining roof.

Anyone watching would have thought he had just plunged to his death.

Fortune landed on a rooftop and fell to his knees on a pebbly surface. No bones were broken. He struggled up and dusted off his clothes. He walked to the street front and squinted down. Yes, he had judged it just right. This was the building.

A skylight, pried open a moment later, offered entry.

Fortune let himself down and pulled out his pencil flashlight. Casting its tiny light around, he stumbled through a dusty attic. The building still had electricity, since neon EXIT signs glowed at the various stairways, enabling him to navigate without tripping over cardboard boxes and wooden crates.

He chose a metal staircase at the back of the attic. It led down to a large open room with a wooden floor. A long bank of two-story high windows stretched from one end of the building to the other, their frames peacefully rusting. Ghosts of textile workers haunted the floor, working on long, narrow tables forming cotton into finished products.

Fortune descended another staircase to the next level. This had a wide central hall with rooms on either side, each of them behind a firmly closed wooden door. Light shone from beneath one of the doors, filtering across the floor.

Fortune was drawn to the room like a moth to a flame.

The light from under the door illuminated the tips of his shoes. He placed his ear on the dusty wooden door. Voices murmured, but the thickness of the old oak muffled them.

Suddenly the door flung open. Electric light flooded into the hall. Fortune, almost blinded, had a quick glimpse of a man and two women seated at a table. They turned startled faces to stare.

Fortune had no idea who the distinguished looking man and the two women were, or whether they were important. But the muscular man who opened the door was a type he knew only too well. He fell backward, heart pounding.

Fortune turned and sprinted down the hall to a lobby. He raced across the checkerboard floor, through the front door and into the night. He ran the length of the warehouse yard, jumped over a waist-high fence and found himself on a side street. He turned up the sidewalk, then angled across the two lanes of road into an alley. He knew this led to the trail along the C&O Canal that ran through Georgetown, below M Street. Fortune scurried along the alley until he came to the canal towpath. He jogged unseen along the towpath through shadows of blackened buildings and leafless trees.

A few blocks away, the canal intersected with Rock Creek. If he could get there, and across the water, he could disappear in the shadows under the concrete bridges of Interstate 66. From there, he could easily vanish into the city.

He heard footsteps behind him on the hard clay. He was being chased. He could not turn around. His pursuer was only a short distance behind him. He raced by one of the locks and dams along the C&O Canal.

A small sign beside the canal read LOCK 3.

He kept running at top speed.

Without street lights, it was reasonable to assume his pursuer could not see him. Shadows hung heavily along the canal. He hoped the shadows would render him invisible. He had run another quarter of a mile, past another lock.

LOCK 2 read the sign.

Then a light caught on the back of Fortune's head. It lit his entire figure, casting a long shadow down the bed of the canal. It shone like a prison light.

Tony Fortune was running faster than he had in a lifetime of fleeing. Only a short distance to go. Ahead, he could hear the waters of the canal and of Rock Creek swirling into one another.

LOCK 1.

The first shot rang out, ricocheting off the canal's stone wall.

Fortune was at the water's edge, the bottom of his shoes stumbling against stones, loosening pebbles and rocks from the wet mud, his feet losing traction on the wet surface.

Fortune twisted his head, his eyes wide with fright. He lost his footing and fell into the water. He lifted himself up. A second bullet rang out, cutting into him. He saw his blood mixing with the blackish water. Tony Fortune started to cry. He prayed he would not die.

**

TEN MINUTES LATER, Maggie Moriarty gave birth to a baby girl.

CHAPTER 33

Friday, November 5

WHEN KATZ ARRIVED at the courthouse for the resumption of the bond hearing at 10 a.m., the army of reporters was back, and so too were the news towers, satellite dishes, white vans and webs of colored cords taped to the brick sidewalks.

Before going to the courtroom, Katz stopped at the circuit court clerk's office and obtained a notice to appear form. After filling out the form, he phoned the sheriff. "Kevin, I need a favor."

"Anything you want, Mo."

"I need a deputy in your office to serve notice in a divorce action set down for next Friday. It's got to be served today."

"No problem," said the sheriff. "Happy to oblige."

Katz noticed a text from Tony Fortune on his phone.

Checking out the Pale Horse for you.

Katz stared at the message, confused over how Fortune was directed to the Georgetown warehouse. Then he remembered the noise outside Snowe's townhouse the previous evening.

"By the way, you any closer to bringing this insanity to a conclusion?" the sheriff asked.

Katz looked up. "Yeah," he said. "A lot closer."

**

HIS EYES WERE clear and calculating, his voice strong and commanding. "I move to dismiss the case based on a lack of jurisdiction," Katz said.

A few minutes before, Katz had finished meeting with Harding in the cellblock. He had explained the lay of the land. The time had come to end this case and get the flash drive back to the authorities.

The motion caught Kathy White off guard. She protested, explaining she was not prepared. The court should not entertain Katz's entreaty and a process existed for motions of this nature, she argued.

"The prosecution is correct," Judge Osborne acknowledged. "We're not scheduled to argue a motion to dismiss in this matter."

Katz was undeterred.

"Under normal circumstances, I wouldn't argue, your honor," he responded. "But a court cannot continue a proceeding outside its jurisdiction." He had the prosecutor's full attention now, as well as that of the judge. "My argument is simple and straightforward. The charges were brought under Title Eighteen of the Code of Virginia, but the body was not recovered within the confines of the commonwealth."

White was searching for the charging documents.

"The body in this case was recovered in the Potomac River," Katz explained. "The jurisdictional border between the District of Columbia and Virginia is the western shoreline of the Potomac River."

He let it register, and then continued. "The evidence is irrefutable. The body was recovered in the water off the bulkhead at Daingerfield Island. That's outside the Commonwealth of Virginia."

The judge ran his hand through his hair. "Do you have evidence supporting your motion?"

Katz's phone vibrated. He glanced at it lying on the counsel table. Joey Cook was calling. Whatever information the town crier had could wait. Katz looked up at the judge.

"Judge, do you really want me to go out and get a map of the District of Columbia's boundaries? We all know, or should know, where the line is drawn between Virginia and the District. It's the Virginia shoreline."

Judge Osborne looked at Kathy White.

"I believe defense counsel is obfuscating the issue," she said. "Even if the body was recovered outside the confines of Virginia, the prosecution will show the murder occurred in Virginia."

"I don't know how that's possible," Katz said. "The Commonwealth's theory is that Mr. Harding struck and killed Ms. Lewis onboard the *Won Way*. Whether the act occurred at Dyke Marsh, off Daingerfield Island, or someplace in between, it was outside the jurisdiction of the Commonwealth."

As the judge contemplated how best to proceed, the courtroom door opened and Commonwealth Attorney Deale, accompanied by U.S. Attorney Helen O. Douglas, rushed in. They stepped inside the railing and leaned over Kathy White, whispering in her ear.

A moment later, White addressed the court. "The prosecution asks for a five-minute recess, your honor."

The four lawyers huddled out in the hallway, speaking in hushed tones. "Mo, we'll move for dismissal of all charges, with prejudice," Deale said. "That will be followed by a formal letter of apology to Harding. Additionally, my office will provide a complete explanation, after we've run the traps with DOJ and others, that this case was about an attempt to expose a terrorist cell and stop an act of terrorism."

"Why the sudden change in approach?" Katz demanded.

"We were lied to and kept in the dark about a counterterrorism case," Douglas explained.

"Plus we want something," Deale explained. "And it can't wait."

"What do you need?"

"The thumb drive," replied Douglas.

"Thumb drive?" Katz asked innocently.

"No need for that," Douglas admonished him. "Joey Cook told us what happened in the property room with Bullock."

"Why is that of interest to you?"

"The thumb drive contains critical information about a terrorist plot, and we can't risk it getting into the wrong hands," Douglas explained. "This trial was supposed to buy time to identify and capture the terrorist. But there's a diminished sense that the strategy will work, and I'm not going to subvert the criminal justice system to advance a dubious strategy."

Katz reasoned the JTTF had shared some information with Douglas, while withholding salient details. As a result, she had decided to uncover the truth by other means. It had little, if anything, to do with preserving the integrity of the system.

"I should have fought bringing these charges against Harding from the beginning," Deale added. "It never felt right. Frankly, a lot was kept from me. It was a mistake. It's time to stop playing games."

"Okay," Katz said. "I'll get Jimmy Wolfe and ask him to stand in for me."

"So we have an agreement?" Douglas extended her hand.

"I'll get you the thumb drive," Katz replied as he accepted the hand. "But I need you to make a call out to the Columbia Island Marina. And I need a set of wheels."

"The marina?" Deale asked, puzzled.

"Yeah," Katz replied. "The flash drive is on the *Won Way*."

Everyone looked at Kathy White, who displayed a confused look as she asked, "Why didn't anybody tell me about this?" Grudgingly, she handed Katz the keys to her brand-new Mercedes sedan. She made him promise to return the vehicle unscratched.

Katz put the keys in his pocket. "I don't want Nate Harding released," he said. "Promise that he will be stashed in a safe place once he's free. There's a killer out there, and Harding needs to be under protection for the next few days."

"Okay," Deale agreed. "We'll find a cooler to store him in."

They all returned to the courtroom. Katz whispered to Harding the case would be dismissed, but had no time to give him any details. When Katz turned to leave, White was informing the judge that new counsel was on his way. Judge Osborne seemed bewildered, but game.

Katz, with the help of one of the deputies, found his way to the back of the courthouse and to White's Mercedes.

CHAPTER 34

KATZ PARKED at the LBJ Grove. A few other cars sat unattended, but on a weekday afternoon no one seemed to be around. He walked over to the marina. One lonely police officer was standing sentry.

"Ahoy," Katz called. No need for secrecy now.

The officer waved back and strolled toward him. Katz walked along the row of boats toward the *Won Way*.

"I'm Elmo Katz."

"I got a call you were coming," the officer said as Katz reached him. "Also, it's all over social media and the news."

Katz nodded. He had heard the official spin on the car radio while driving over.

Following a dismissal of all charges, Jordin Deale had held a brief press conference. She claimed that new, undisclosed evidence had exonerated Harding. Deale promised a full explanation would be forthcoming, and then abruptly ended the press conference without answering any further questions.

"I mean, it's really amazing," the officer said. "One day they're accusing the guy of murder, and the next day they're releasing him, saying it was a mistake."

"Truth is sometimes stranger than fiction," Katz replied as he climbed on board the *Won Way*.

A wave rocked the boat. They both stopped for a second. Katz found his footing.

"Mind if I go down below and retrieve something?"

"Be my guest," said the officer. "I was told to give you free rein."

Katz went below. The officer followed. Katz went into the bathroom. The policeman waited outside. Katz reached behind the clock on the wall and removed the flash drive from its nook.

The officer nudged the door and watched from the doorway.

"You were protecting the most important evidence connected

to the case," Katz said. He held up the flash drive. "This is the heart of the matter."

Katz and the guard climbed back up onto the deck.

"By the way," the policeman said, "Let me introduce myself. I'm Cecil Dixon. You got a case dismissed on Monday when I didn't show in court. I got an earful from my supervisor and had to cut short my vacation to stand sentry over this boat as punishment."

Katz was about to say it served Dixon right, when suddenly a gunshot crackled across the parking lot.

Dixon caught the bullet in his neck. Blood spurting, he leaned to the side, then collapsed as his legs crumpled beneath him. Katz automatically ducked and found himself kneeling beside the fallen policeman. He heard engines roaring to life and cautiously raised his head.

Near the entrance to the parking lot a dark green car was swerving away with a squeal of tires.

Katz saw the handle of a pistol protruding from the policeman's holster. He hesitated, uncertain whether to stay with Dixon or give chase. A pool of blood formed around Dixon's lifeless body. Katz grabbed the gun and jumped off the deck.

He raced to the Mercedes. Jumping in, he slammed the car into reverse and flew out of the parking space. Shifting into drive, he pushed the accelerator to the floor.

The green car drove across the southbound lanes of the parkway and crashed through a wooden guard rail. Then the car careened onto the right lane of the two northbound lanes and headed north toward the Memorial and Key Bridges.

Katz swerved out of the lot in pursuit.

He heard the roar of an engine behind him. A white van was visible in his rear-view mirror, rocking as it shot out of the lot in his wake. "Christ," Katz muttered.

Not far from the marina the parkway divided in a V. Two lanes to the right swooped under the Memorial Bridge while a single lane to the left headed toward the traffic circle carrying traffic onto the bridge. The green car swerved right while Katz opted for the left column of the V, positioning himself like a wingman off the left side of the escaping vehicle.

With Katz in his blind spot, the driver of the escaping green car took his foot off the gas pedal for an instant. Gaining ground, Katz executed a sharp right turn onto a lane of traffic under the bridge parallel to the other lanes.

Out of nowhere, the Mercedes came flying toward the green car, angled to lunge right at the driver's side of the vehicle, a page right out of Bullock's driver's manual.

"Brace yourself, Mo baby," Katz yelled to himself. Foot still pinning the pedal, he curled himself low behind the wheel, hoping the airbag would deploy.

The Mercedes knifed into the green car. Oil, steel, glass, rubber and plastic erupted into an inferno of smoke and fire. The Mercedes' hood ground into the body of its quarry, propelling the other car across the traffic lanes and toward the river's bank. With a scream of settling metal, the two vehicles slid to a stop inches from the water.

Katz opened his eyes and surveyed the wreckage. The cars were melded together, smoldering. He wiped his forehead to remove the sweat and blood that blurred his vision, clearing his eyesight enough to see Lieutenant Landry exit the green car. Katz had lost track of the van that had been behind him.

Katz struggled with the twisted driver's side door but managed to shove it open. The pistol he had retrieved from the policeman's body was in his hand. Dizzily, Katz clutched the door with his free hand as he braced himself.

"I should have known it was you," Katz shouted. "You persuaded Tony to turn on me. You're going down now, Landry. It's over."

"You have it all wrong," Landry yelled back.

Katz saw a gun in Landry's hand.

"Drop it," Katz ordered. "Drop your gun!" he shouted, pointing the pistol he was holding. Katz felt a punch as he fired.

The lieutenant staggered, his arms flailing, as he twirled and fell face down on the ground.

Katz suddenly became aware of someone about ten feet behind him in a direct line, gun raised, and running toward him. The physical beating he had taken the past week was conspiring against him. Katz was having difficulty breathing. He closed his eyes and crumpled to the ground.

His pursuer reached into Katz's pocket.

CHAPTER 35

"MR. KATZ." Katz opened his eyes. Tony Fortune was bending over him.

"What happened to you?" Katz managed to whisper.

"They came after me," Fortune said. He pulled up his shirt, showing a dark spot where a bullet had entered his side. "I didn't just sustain a flesh wound in the shoulder, like you. I was seriously hit."

This was no time to compare wounds.

"What happened?" Katz asked again, struggling to sit upright.

"It's not important," Fortune replied dismissively. "The thing is that we both came through it." He clutched Katz's hand. "They're going to have to fire a lot more lead if they expect to take us down. Isn't that right, Mr. Katz?"

Katz laughed weakly.

Fortune looked at him beseechingly.

Katz suddenly felt no animosity. Truth be told, he loved Fortune like a baby brother.

"I understand your being angry, Mr. Katz," Fortune said. "You'd have every reason to be angry if I really intended to, like, spy on you, and then report back to that Landry dude. Except I wasn't intending to do that at all. And I got shot trying to help you."

Katz accepted Fortune's statement at face value. "Yeah, yeah," he said.

"Say, listen, Mr. Katz." Fortune drew close. "Can I ask you something?"

"Go ahead."

"All those cases you do," Fortune began. "You know how you're always saying that line about there always being a way around everything?"

"*Fatta la legge, trovato l'inganno,*" Katz smiled.

"Yeah, that's it," Fortune said. "You use that line all the time. You tell those juries you don't subscribe to that sort of lawyering."

"That's right, Tony. That's what I tell them."

"But it's not true, is it?" Fortune continued. "The truth is you use exactly that kind of technique. And you swear that you don't. I mean, not only do you always look for a way around things, but you do it while saying that you don't."

"Where is this going, Tony?" Katz asked, irritably.

"Don't get me wrong, Mr. Katz. I'm grateful. Plenty grateful. But I can't say I'm impressed. In fact, it's always bothered me. The way you play with people, I mean. Telling them one thing while you're doing the opposite. Deceiving them."

Katz was visibly annoyed. "I'm a lawyer, Tony. I'm licensed to do anything that helps my client, within the rules. I don't consider it deception."

"Then what is it?" asked Fortune.

"It's a tactic," Katz explained. "A ploy. A means to an end."

Fortune nodded. "That's pretty good, Mr. Katz. I guess you can call it all those things. To me, it's a lie."

Tony Fortune never spoke that way to Katz. Never. He was always deferential. Respectful. To call this uncharacteristic was an understatement.

"I think I've had enough," Katz said. "Let's change the subject."

"Before we do, let me just put an exclamation point on it," Fortune continued. "I'm not trying to disrespect you. You just need to hear the truth. It's time to change your tactic, Mr. Katz. Time to take a different route to where you're trying to go. To where you drive other people."

Suddenly Fortune reached out and grabbed Katz. He had both hands on the lawyer's shoulders. He was shaking Katz and yelling.

"Can you hear me, Mr. Katz? Can you hear me? Wake up, Mr. Katz! Wake up!"

**

KATZ FELT a jarring sensation and a sharp pain in his shoulder. He was stirring, coming out of a dream. He opened his eyes.

"He's awake," called Suzie Marston.

A nurse rushed into the room. Katz was in a hospital bed. Behind the nurse, Katz saw Joey Cook standing next to Marston. They were both leaning toward the bed, concerned looks on their faces.

"Where am I?" Katz asked.

Then everything went blank again.

CHAPTER 36

Tuesday, November 9

KATZ OPENED his eyes again. He felt the needle in his arm and an ache in one shoulder. His surroundings were shadows melded with darkness.

"Hey." Abby Snowe was beside him. She took his hand. Hers was warm and soft. "How are you feeling?"

"Okay," he answered automatically.

He felt restless, wanted to get up and move around. He knew it was not advisable, attached to an intravenous bag, so he just turned his head and studied her outline.

"How long have you been here?"

Snowe stood and reached over to click on a bedside lamp, then sank back into the visitor's chair. In its yellowish glow her face looked tired and strained.

"Since midnight," she said. "We've been taking shifts."

"It must be the middle of the night. Who's we?"

"Joey Cook, Curtis, Suzie, and that young couple, David and Mai," replied Snowe. "The usual suspects."

"How long have I been out of it?"

"Since Friday," she told him. "Today is . . ." She hesitated. "Tuesday, I think." She quickly calculated the time. "Yes. It's Tuesday morning. About 4 a.m."

"Tuesday, November ninth," Katz announced.

"You can rest comfortably," said Snowe. "They've caught the would-be assassin."

"Fill me in on what's happened these past few days," Katz implored.

The abrupt ending of the trial, the murder of Officer Dixon guarding the *Won Way*, and the shooting of Phil Landry had hit Washington like a tsunami, she told him. Landry had survived being shot through one lung. The doctors were keeping him in an induced coma to give him a chance to recover from blood loss.

"People are still trying to piece it all together," Snowe said. "The whole thing is surreal."

"What about the other man at the Memorial Bridge?" Katz asked. "Who was he?"

"The authorities are still trying to figure out what happened after you and Landry collided," said Snowe.

Katz tried to move. The sides of the bed were raised, like an infant's crib. He was caged in. Plus he was bandaged. And there was that intravenous tube dripping antibiotics and who knew what else into his veins.

"Where's the thumb drive?" Katz asked, panicked.

"Take it easy," Snowe warned.

They stared into one another's eyes. Katz sensed something was wrong, worse than the missing thumb drive. "What is it?" he asked.

Snowe hesitated. "Tony," she answered softly. "Tony Fortune's dead."

Katz tried to sit up, but found himself too weak to do so.

"When did it happen? He was just here the other night."

"His body was found in the C&O Canal in Georgetown," she explained. "He was gunned down last Thursday night or Friday morning. You've been calling out his name a couple of times while I've been here."

"What do we know about it?" Katz asked.

"Not much. A service is being held at St. Jude's in Georgetown."

"When?"

"This morning at eight."

Katz looked at her. "You've got to get me out of here," he insisted. "I don't know what Landry's involvement was, but it's not over."

**

THREE AND A HALF HOURS LATER, Katz had freed himself from the doctors' clutches, dodged a squad of policemen avid to question him, and landed in Joey Cook's car on his way to the funeral service.

"I tried to tell you when I first heard about it," Cook said. "Sorry I wasn't able to get in touch with you."

"Don't worry about it," Katz said. "It was my fault. I saw your message while I was in the judge's courtroom, arguing about jurisdiction in the Harding case. I should have thought to call you back."

Katz wondered if it would have made any difference if he had found out sooner about Fortune's death.

Traffic crossing the Key Bridge was heavy. The church was located a short distance from the Pale Horse Warehouse and the place where Tony Fortune's body had been recovered. Cook dropped Katz off in front of the church and remained in the car.

The large wooden doors to the church were tall and thick, better suited for a medieval castle in England than a neighborhood church. Opening them required all of Katz's strength. Even with two good arms, he would have had trouble moving them.

He eventually squeezed through and slipped inside, expecting the church to be empty, since no cars were parked in front. Instead, it was packed with people.

As he surveyed the crowd, Katz realized this was an army of homeless people, disenfranchised and alienated, the world's petit misdemeanants, all come to pay their respects. These people did not have cars. They were an army of walkers.

A large African American priest, caressing a beard of gray and white, was speaking. Katz tried to blend in with the hushed assemblage.

"He would begin by saying, *Fatta la legge, trovato l'inganno,*" the priest said. "Then he'd pause and ask the jury, 'Do you know what that means?' The jurors were rapt and attentive. Tony used to tell me that, at that moment, he'd know the case was won."

Katz moved further inside. Warm smells of the overflow crowd surrounded and enveloped him. Unwashed bodies, whiskey, soiled pants and stained shirts, greasy and matted hair, clothes slept-in and gone too long without a washing.

As he maneuvered toward the left side aisle, Katz reached out and picked up a funeral card from a small table.

The priest continued, "The attorney would say, 'Actually, I don't know where that expression originated, but that's beside the point. I'm only concerned with its meaning, which loosely translated is that every law has its loophole'."

The priest stroked his beard. "Anthony had heard those words repeated so many times – at his own trials, having had about a half dozen over the past three years – that he knew the attorney's opening statement verbatim. And he'd recite the part about there always being a loophole, a way out."

The throng murmured acknowledgement. Some of them also knew the lines by heart, from personal experience with Katz serving as their counsel.

"I tell you that because those words are so apropos to Anthony Fortune. He was all about running himself head on into problems and finding ways out. About facing walls, and climbing over them. Falling into ditches and getting out of them. Caught by storms and getting through them.

"Maybe he didn't have a lot of sense about staying out of trouble, but he was all about one critical ingredient in all of us. Survival."

Katz edged down the side aisle, recognizing faces in the crowd. They were the clients referred to him by Fortune. Most were *pro bono* clients.

"Survival is more than a code," the priest said. "It is a creed. It is like faith, but without the need to suspend disbelief. It is like love, without the attachment. And it is like hope, without the whimsical desire to see something desirous come to fruition."

Katz's eyes drifted to the front of the church. It was lit by white and gold candles. The coffin was placed in the aisle, an American flag draped over it. Katz tried to recall Tony ever speaking about his military service.

He saw Maggie Moriarty seated stoically in the front pew. She was dressed in black, a lace kerchief on her head. A sleeping newborn nestled in her arms.

"The truth is that Anthony loved each of you," the priest continued. "In his own way, he cared for you. He didn't have enough money to pay his own bills – including his legal bills, which were always piling up – but he always had an extra ten or twenty in his pocket to give you. Didn't he?"

An "Amen" rose from the lips of some. Nods from others. Smiles broke out on many faces. Memories were rekindled.

"And for a man who always looked thin and hungry, he always had a basket of food in his car to hand over to you when you were in need, or a blanket when the night swept in and you were cold lying on a grate."

"Amen," more voices called out.

Katz was surprised to find himself engulfed in grief. He lost his bearings and found himself standing in the front of the congregation. The casket was a heartbeat away.

"Elmo Katz?" asked the priest.

Katz nodded.

"I thought so. I saw you when you entered the church. Anthony drew you here to be near him. Would you like to say a few words?"

Katz cleared his throat and moved next to the casket. He looked out at the crowd. They were blurry from the water puddling in his eyes.

"I don't know a lot about the Catholic religion, but I do know St. Jude is the patron saint of hopeless causes," he began. "Tony constantly reminded me of it. He kept a prayer card of St. Jude in his wallet. He'd pull it out from time to time when we'd go to court. He'd tell me how the case was hopeless or how life itself seemed hopeless, but things always worked out if you had a little faith."

Katz read from the card he had picked up a few minutes earlier.

"*San Judas Tadeo, intercessor en todo problema difícil, consiquemeun trabjao en que me realize como humano, y que a mi familia no faltalo suficiente en ningun aspect de la vida.*"

The crowd applauded proudly.

Katz did not know the English translation of the words he had just recited, although he had a pretty good idea. He glanced over to the priest, and then at Moriarty and the baby.

He wondered if they knew there had never been any such conversation between him and Fortune. Yet, here he was, at a funeral, performing his old tricks. He questioned whether Fortune would approve.

Outside, Joey Cook waited patiently in his car. A DC Central Kitchen delivery van was dropping off hot meals across the street. The phone rang. Cook glanced at the number. It was a pal from the police lab. He answered the call.

Inside the church, Katz continued to address the crowd.

"In the middle gray of life, where every hue and gradation imaginable exists, Tony and I were able to persuade juries that the law is not some immutable thing, but that it's permeable. People can be forgiven for their mistakes and excused for certain behaviors that are nonconforming in nature.

"In doing that, Tony actually taught those jurors a thing or two about life. He reminded them a little bit about themselves. He showed them that a man could be good without being perfect, and that an imperfect man has a lot of good inside."

After the service ended, Katz waited for an opportunity to talk with Moriarty. She held her newborn baby close as they spoke. The tiny girl glowed. She was the most beautiful child Katz had ever seen. Her skin was soft as silk. Her eyes shone.

The baby waved her hands toward Katz.

"Her name is Katzerine," Moriarty. "I call her Katzie."

Katz welled up again. Not just his eyes this time, but his whole face. His entire being.

"How are you doing?" he asked, his voice rough with emotion. He knew she would say she was getting by. So he added, "Seriously."

"Not well," Moriarty confided.

"I'll see what I can do about it," Katz said.

"You don't have to do anything, Mr. Katz. We'll manage. I'm going to start working again in a couple of months, just as soon as Katzie can get into a co-op."

"I'll see what I can do," Katz repeated. He pressed her hand, and the baby's.

Five minutes later, he was back in Cook's car.

**

"SORRY I TOOK so much time." Katz was sniffling when he got into the car. "You should have come inside with me."

Cook stared at him. Katz was teary. He wiped his eyes with the palm of his hand and then ran his palm across his lap as he sat in the passenger's seat. "Oh, man," he sighed.

Cook started the car. He traveled through Georgetown toward the bridge and Virginia. Neither of them said a word.

Then Katz started reciting a litany of apologies. "I'm sorry I berated Tony for being conned by Landry," he said. "Sorry I made him feel obligated to repay me for a breach of trust. Sorry I opened my big mouth talking with Curtis, so the kid could overhear me mention the Pale Horse Warehouse. That had to be why he went there."

Katz had started shaking. "And I feel terrible about Landry. I can't believe I shot him, Joey. It's just he had a gun pointed at me. What was I supposed to do?"

Cook glanced over with concern, then pulled the car into a service lane and over to the curb. Locking it in park and keeping his foot on the brake, he turned to look at Katz. The man should have stayed in the hospital.

"Look, you shouldn't feel responsible, Mo. You didn't shoot Landry."

"What the hell are you talking about?" Katz replied angrily. "Of course I shot Landry. I pulled the trigger. Landry fell to the ground."

"I got a call from ballistics just now, while you were in the church," Cook explained. "The handgun you took from the officer on the *Won Way* was an M9 service pistol."

"So?"

"So the bullet that struck Landry was a .45 millimeter, which was the same caliber used to shoot the officer."

Katz processed the information, his forehead furrowed.

"You missed the target, Mo."

Katz tried to connect the dots. "Then what did happen?" Katz still could make no sense of it, so Cook explained it to him, based upon the preliminary findings of last Friday's events.

"Landry followed you to the marina, along with someone else, who shot at you and hit the policeman. Then he probably turned his gun on Landry, who hightailed it. You pursued Landry, believing he had shot the officer."

Katz closed his eyes as he listened.

"After the collision," Cook continued, "the other man stopped behind you. When Landry drew his firearm, it was the other guy who fired past you and wounded Landry. Landry's shot went wild. The two guns discharged at the same time, disguising the fact that both had been fired."

Katz sat stunned.

"You're lucky the guy was a bad shot," Cook said. "He tried twice to kill you."

Katz was about to ask whether anyone had identified that other person when Cook's cell phone rang. It was Santana. Cook handed the phone to Katz.

"Pay dirt," the private investigator said.

"What have you got?" asked Katz.

194

"When I give you these details, you'll freak."

"I'm putting you on speaker," Katz said, switching the receiver. "I'm in the car with Joey. We're on our way back from Tony's funeral."

Santana began, "A positive identification has been made on the driver of the white van. His name's Charles Hughes. His vehicle exited the parking lot on Halloween night about the same time David Reese found the body."

"Okay," Katz said, waiting for more.

"It's the same van that was parked by Little Hunting Creek the night Moultrie was murdered, and that pulled up at your house last week. And an eyewitness identified it as the van that stopped at the Memorial Bridge right after the collision last Friday."

There was more. "Hughes worked for the agency, reporting directly to June Webster, the woman in the PDF that Reese emailed to you. And, as we both know, Webster works for Jack Smith."

Katz suppressed growing excitement. "That's helpful information," he said. "Now I've got something for you."

Katz shared the ballistics information Cook had just given him.

"The local police and a lot of other people are going to want to talk to you," Santana said.

"I can't right now," Katz replied. He looked at the clock on the dashboard. 9:25 a.m. "Do me a favor and swing by my office," Katz continued. "Suzie will have some papers for you. Bring them to U.S. Attorney Douglas's office as fast as you can. And call the commonwealth attorney and tell her to meet us there."

Cook pulled out into traffic as Katz ended the call. He then rang Marston.

"Snooze," he said, "you okay? Yeah, yeah, I'm dancing around like Fred Astaire. Now, drop whatever you're doing and retrieve the Ashford settlement. I'll hold."

Once she had opened the file on her computer, he continued. "Scroll down through the document for the paragraph that begins

Settlement Amount. Have you got it? Put in two million dollars. No, two million. I'm going to need a few other changes."

Marston's hands were typing a mile a minute.

CHAPTER 37

"THE COMMITTEE is now in session," Senate Intelligence Committee Chairman Abe Lowenstein announced as he gaveled the hearing to order at 10 a.m.

Committee members filled the dais. Members of his party flanked Lowenstein to the right, the minority to his left. If the shooting of two law enforcement officers and the circumstances surrounding the dismissal of the Harding murder trial had the city on edge, it had the Hill frantic.

Jack Smith was the sole witness in the well.

He had been here before, having made a generation's worth of appearances. As a result, Smith understood the system better than most of the men and women he faced.

Smith had known some of them during their service in the House. He had watched them cross over to the Senate. He had also seen movements and priorities come and go.

He knew no one in this town wanted to cede power and everyone possessed an ulterior motive. It was why he felt so at home here, why he had thrived in the Washington environment for so long.

As he sat calmly in his seat, Smith rehearsed his statement. He would build them up, appeal to their patriotism and restore their confidence. He poured himself a glass of water as photographers snapped his picture.

"The committee will come to order," Lowenstein began.

"We are here this morning to inquire into a series of events, commencing with the reported drowning of Libby Lewis and culminating in the shooting of two law enforcement officers, one resulting in a fatality.

"To assist us in our inquiry today, we welcome Jack Smith, whose accomplishments at the Central Intelligence Agency need no introduction. It is my sincere hope that, by the time we have concluded this hearing, we will be in a better position to understand why our national security personnel undertook their recent actions, and whether those actions have eliminated the threat of a terrorist act."

Smith turned on his microphone and took the oath to tell the truth.

"Thank you, Mr. Chairman," he began. "Your prescience is of note. I suspect it was not simply fortuitous when the committee set today as the hearing date. I believe you had a premonition. And it was that feeling of danger, of foreboding, that compelled you to seek information as a way to protect the American people and their elected officials from forces that would do us harm."

He cleared his throat. It was a strong opening. Now, it was time for him to set the stage.

"A generation ago, Orlando Letelier, a former Chilean cabinet minister, and Ronni Moffitt, his American assistant, were assassinated on Massachusetts Avenue, a short distance from here. The sound of the bomb that blew up his car on September 21, 1976, reverberates in this town to this day.

"I remember the explosion. I was a young man and had just arrived in Washington. I remember thinking that day that these sorts of things don't happen in Washington, not in this town, not in the capital of the western world."

He surveyed the senators facing him. He had them. The same was undoubtedly true of the crowd seated behind him.

"Today we are faced with another murderous threat, even more apparently ominous than that one," he continued. "The threat of the lone wolf."

He glanced at his watch.

10:05 a.m.

**

AN AMTRAK TRAIN running from Richmond to Washington ripped along the rails, passing through Fredericksburg without stopping. This was a special, with four cars overflowing with security people and no stops until it reached the safety of Union Station.

Katz had just arrived at the U.S. Attorney's office. Santana was waiting for him in front of the building, holding the papers Marston had prepared. Katz accepted the documents. Together they entered the building. To the far left, a circle of U.S. marshals stood idly beside a metal screening machine. Stacked on a table beside the machine were a pile of containers for the keys, smart phones, cash clips and metal wallets, security badges, watches, spare change, jewelry, and other metal objects removed by defense attorneys, witnesses, law enforcement personnel, jurors, clerks and others who entered the office.

"I'm Elmo Katz," he announced to the receptionist.

The U.S. marshals standing against the wall suddenly woke up, as though a gun had fallen to the floor and fired.

"We've been expecting you," one of them said. "Come on through. Ms. Douglas is upstairs. She's got the commonwealth attorney with her."

Bypassing their own security, two marshals escorted Katz and Curtis down the hall, around a corner, down another hall, and to an elevator, which they rode to the fourth floor.

When the doors opened, four more U.S. marshals were waiting. They closed ranks. The phalanx marched swiftly down a long narrow hall and into the large, ornate office of the U.S. attorney.

Helen O. Douglas entered, accompanied by White and Deale. The U.S. attorney signaled the marshals to leave. She waited for the door to close, then let loose.

"We had a deal, Mo," she said, her face flushed with anger. "I kept my side of the bargain. You, on the other hand, never delivered the thumb drive. I'm sorry about all that's happened. But you've left me in a hell of a difficult position."

Katz took a deep breath. Had Douglas forgotten that people had been shot last Friday when he was trying to deliver the flash drive?

"I retrieved the drive, just as promised," Katz said, trying to sound calm. "I had no idea what was going to unfold aboard the *Won Way*. I could have gotten killed, you know." Katz looked at the clock on the wall. "Do you realize what's about to happen in a few minutes?" he asked.

The government attorneys appeared confused.

"I take that as a no," Katz said.

"A lot has gone haywire in the past week," the U.S. attorney admitted. "That's a story for another day. Where is the thumb drive?"

"I don't have it any longer." Katz watched as their expressions turned from confusion to anger. "Don't worry, Helen," Katz said, tapping his index finger on his temple. "It's all right up here. Date and time and place of a planned terrorist assassination."

"And?"

"And I'll provide it as soon as we take care of a little unfinished business."

**

KATZ PLACED an agreement on Douglas's desk. This was the business of the bargain. He removed a pen from his coat pocket and placed it on top of the papers.

"This is for the widow and baby of the man killed in Georgetown trying to help me out by spying on the Pale Horse Warehouse," Katz said.

"What are you talking about, Mo?" Douglas laughed.

"An annuity," Katz explained. "An agreement between the parties and the U.S. Government for Maggie Moriarty. Two equal installments, one million each. One million now and the other million when her child reaches the age of majority. Consider it cheap, for a life lost."

Douglas swatted the papers off the desk. They fell to the floor. "No!" she thundered. "We're not going to be blackmailed into paying you for information. Either you're a patriot or you're a fraud who will permit an innocent man to die. Which is it going to be?"

Katz retrieved the papers from the floor, favoring his still wrapped wrist, and placed them back on the desk. He took up a pen and struck a few lines. Then inked some substitute language.

"Now, it's four million for Maggie and the baby, in equal payments of two million each."

"This is blackmail, Mo," Deale said.

"I know what it is," Katz answered. "I also know there is likely to be an assassination in. . ." He glanced at the clock, which read 10:18. ". . .in twelve minutes. At least there will be if you don't act quickly." He turned to the window and wagged his thumb. "It's going to happen right around the corner, in the shadow of your office. Is that the story you want in this evening's news?"

"You can't extract this kind of revenge," Douglas said.

"This isn't revenge, Helen," Katz explained. "This is justice. It's about an innocent party gunned down because of the hubris and insanity of our government." He glanced at the papers. "Go ahead and sign or I'm going to increase the price tag by another million."

**

TWO MINUTES LATER, they exited the elevator on the ground floor, Katz tucking the signed papers inside his jacket pocket as they ran. On the way down, Katz had informed Deale, White and Douglas that the assassination attempt was planned to occur in the train tunnel beneath Callahan Drive. In turn, they summoned a battalion of U.S. marshals, who met them a moment later in the lobby, led by Sergeant Chester Olshanski, a crewcut and sinewy ex-Fairfax cop and Marine.

"Hurry up," Katz called to the new arrivals. "We don't have a minute to spare."

The entourage raced out the door and into three black Suburbans that carried them down the street toward Amtrak's rail tracks and the train tunnel under Callahan Drive.

"We've got a terrorist in the tunnel," Olshanski shouted to the officers in the lead Suburban. "Either he's planted an IED on the tracks for a train traveling up from Richmond, or he's got a shoulder-fired missile and is going to hit the train as it passes by."

It took six minutes for them to get to the railroad tracks leading to the tunnel. As they emerged from the vehicles, the whistle of the special Amtrak train sounded. 10:26. Right on schedule.

The train was racing through the Eisenhower Valley. Its blaring horn was signaling its pending passage through the tunnel. In four minutes it would fly by them.

Suddenly, more law enforcement officers were appearing from the left and right. They funneled into the group racing toward the tunnel. Katz spotted Roscoe Page, the IT guru who had unlocked the thumb drive for him. Page turned his head and acknowledged Katz with a nod. Then he sprinted forward to the head of the pack.

The group had picked up the pace once the whistle blew.

They reached the tunnel entrance.

Olshanski stopped. The others slowed as they came abreast of him. The group included uniformed and plainclothes cops, special agents, U.S. marshals, detectives assigned to the U.S. attorney's office, FBI agents from the Joint Terrorism Task Force, and a couple of assistant prosecutors packing heat. Most had their weapons drawn, held cocked upward in two hands.

Each had a mental clock ticking in his or her head. About two minutes left.

Someone handed Olshanski a white bullhorn. Raising it to his lips, he aimed the bullhorn into the train tunnel.

"The person you're expecting is not on the train," he shouted. "He got off in Lorton and is traveling the remainder of the route by car. It's time to give it up!"

He lowered the bullhorn.

Silence answered his entreaty.

"Is that true?" someone whispered.

Olshanski turned, dismissing such naiveté with an insulting stare.

Surveying the rest of his posse, the U.S. marshal said, "The terrorist may have set up an IED in the tunnel to slow down or stop the train. It may be too late."

"Not necessarily," replied one of the policemen. "If he's got a sidewinder, which is the other possibility, he's somewhere up in the rafters of the tunnel, armed and waiting. We could go in and take him down."

It made sense, particularly with thirty seconds to go.

Suddenly someone called out from the tunnel.

Olshanski stepped forward and fired several rounds in the caller's direction.

A deafening barrage of firepower followed, all of it directed into the tunnel. Bullets struck the cement and steel underpinnings of the entrance, ricocheting and setting off sparks. A rain of ammunition filled every dark corner of the tunnel.

The thud that came from inside the cavernous hole was the unmistakable sound of a human body hitting the ground.

Suddenly the train appeared, hurtling toward them. The group scattered. The train raced through the tunnel and past the small train station at the foot of the Masonic Temple, then snaked off in the direction of Braddock Road, Crystal City and the bridge that would carry it across the Potomac River to Union Station. The clattering and clanging receded and then died in the distance.

As the train disappeared, Katz turned to find Douglas staggering. She had been struck by a bullet, unnoticed in the whirling activity of the moment. She crumpled, falling to her knees, then collapsing on the ground.

Olshanski crouched beside the U.S. attorney. Deale did the same, trying to administer first aid. The others divided into two camps. Half crowded around the U.S. attorney. The other half sprinted into the tunnel.

Katz hesitated before joining the group heading down the tunnel.

Harry Bullock lay on the side of the tracks, his body riddled with bullets. Flashlights flicked across the darkness. A cautious search found that Bullock had no weaponry strapped to his body. A gun lay near him. LEOs searched for explosive devices.

Nothing was there, except the residue of urban litter. A grocery cart, a couple of old, bald tires, fast food wrappers and empty plastic water bottles and beer cans.

Katz squatted beside the fallen cop, careful to touch nothing. "What the hell, Harry," he muttered. Around Bullock's body were scattered a large number of cigarette butts. He had waited for hours.

Katz rose, feeling sore all over. He turned around and walked back slowly, thinking hard. Stepping out of the tunnel into the sunlight was like coming out of a dark movie theater into the street. He squinted.

"You see something?" asked an agent suddenly at his side.

"Just the sunlight," he replied. "It's blinding."

A second later Page appeared beside him. "What was it?" he asked. "What did that guy want to know?"

"Whether I saw anything," Katz replied.

"Did you?" Page asked.

Katz lowered his voice. "Only a guy waiting to stop a train with a handgun."

Page headed into the tunnel. Katz watched him stop beside Bullock's sprawled body and turn around. He walked back along the railroad track, turning to look at the officer who had approached Katz.

Page rejoined Katz. "You're right," he said. "He wasn't here waiting to stop the train. Maybe he was here intending to stop someone else from stopping the train."

**

MEANWHILE SERGEANT Olshanski was holding his hand like a spoon under Douglas's head to cushion it from the rough ground. The bullet had entered the prosecutor's stomach and exited her back. Blood had already soaked through her clothes and was welling from her mouth.

Medics arrived and quickly circled her body, hoisting it onto a stretcher. It was a race against time. The prognosis did not look promising.

As the ambulance pulled off, Katz patted its back door, hoping Douglas would pull through. Then he walked over to Roscoe Page and said, "I thought you said it was all in my hands."

Page smiled. "I couldn't leave you all alone. Once I knew the time and place, I had an obligation to help."

"I appreciate your coming," Katz said.

"Not a problem," Page replied, adding, "It turns out we weren't alone. Apparently a lot of others were prepared to greet a terrorist before the train arrived."

Katz said nothing.

"By the way," Page continued, "I'm going up to the Hill in a few minutes. Join me. Abe Lowenstein's holding a congressional hearing now."

Katz remembered hearing Lowenstein announce the time of the hearing, when he was recuperating in the hospital from the crash with Bullock. That was before Katz ever met Page, before Page ever saw what was on that damned thumb drive, and before a lot of people died.

"I wouldn't miss that for the world," Katz said. They walked toward one of the Suburbans. Katz looked around. "Quite a crew," he said, his eyes directed at the LEOs swarming around the area.

"Not all of the members of that posse are mine," Page explained. "It turns out Jack Smith had a bunch of operatives in place as well. We found one another about an hour ago, as we were taking position. An army was assembled to stop this one."

In the far distance, they could just hear the train's horn signaling.

**

THE TRAIN HOOTED its horn as it rattled across the trestle that ran adjacent to the Metro tracks over the Potomac River.

Jumma al-Issawi looked out the window at the shimmering water. He had wondered who all the people were standing by the tracks as the train raced through Alexandria. What was that about?

CHAPTER 38

THE NEWS HAD FLASHED across every television and computer screen, iPad, smartphone and pager in the Capitol. A terrorist plot had been foiled, a would-be assassin had been killed, and the U.S. attorney for the Eastern District of Virginia had just died from a wound sustained in the daring operation to stop the terrorist.

Mac McCarthy approached Lowenstein and whispered in his ear. People in the audience and staffers sitting against the wall read the headlines on the screens of their electronic devices. The news was seeping into the room like an invisible gas.

Jack Smith observed the distractions. Yet he continued speaking. "The situation in Washington has been understandably tense, and with good reason," he said, appearing oblivious to what was swirling around him. "Rumors have been rampant about the existence of a terrorist cell. I think people have a right to be apprehensive.

"I'll be honest. I'm worried. I've got a battalion of dedicated public servants working 24/7 trying to determine whether there is any legitimacy to this thing. I've got a premonition there's something else out there."

Lowenstein cocked his head, indicating Smith should sum up.

"I actually believe that a heightened state of concern is a good thing," Smith concluded. "It keeps people focused. If we're attentive, the odds are in our favor."

"Thank you, Mr. Smith," Lowenstein said. Then he added, "Your words could not be more prescient. I have just received word that the United States Attorney for the Eastern District of Virginia has been killed attempting to prevent a terrorist attack."

The room erupted in chaos.

Smith looked up at the clock behind the dais. It was 10:45.

"So let me ask you, Mr. Smith," Lowenstein said, leaning his leonine head forward. "Did you have more than a premonition about a terrorist attack that was planned to occur earlier this morning?"

"Mr. Chairman," Smith said. "My preference is for the committee to go into executive session. I will acknowledge that a terrorist act was planned for this morning, one which has apparently been foiled by federal authorities. However, since I do not know the outcome of that situation, I am reluctant to testify about it in this open hearing."

Lowenstein agreed. "The committee stands in recess," he said. He would have liked to have caught Smith in a lie, but the man was too clever to say anything on the record.

The news was now everywhere. A U.S. attorney had been gunned down three blocks from the courthouse. A local Alexandria homicide detective was the shooter, and a renegade intelligence official was being sought for the two shootings that occurred the previous Friday at the LBJ Grove and the Memorial Bridge.

Lowenstein invited Smith to a small anteroom adjacent the hearing room.

"I'm in disbelief," Smith said. "Douglas was an exceptional attorney. She was a good woman."

The senator stared intently at him. "You knew this was coming," Lowenstein said accusingly. "Why didn't you secure the vulnerable area under the bridge earlier? Why did you let it unfold like this?"

"Let me put the same question to you, senator," Smith retorted. "We all knew it was coming. I could tell from the way you questioned me a moment ago. You planned this hearing to coincide with the timing of the plot."

Lowenstein had underestimated the situation. Smith would not accept any responsibility. He would simply obfuscate and spread the blame.

"I let this happen, senator, because it enabled me to catch a terrorist," Smith continued. "But you let it happen because you thought it would embarrass me, or maybe expose me and my agency. I'm not sure which. But it was you, not I, who has been disingenuous. So please do not lecture me about failing to take appropriate steps to avoid the situation in the first place."

Smith studied Lowenstein's face. Intimidation was not working. So the chameleon changed colors.

"On reflection," Smith continued more softly, "I suppose I could have done more." He now sounded contrite. "With the benefit of hindsight, yes, I should have. At that time, however, I believed keeping the plans intact presented the best opportunity to uncover and apprehend the terrorist. And I always felt we would catch him before he was able to carry out the plot."

Not sure whether he had neutralized the senator, Smith kept talking, providing details of the operation.

McCarthy appeared at the senator's side. "Do you want to call the hearing back to order and offer an explanation as to what happened?" he asked. Then he whispered something else into the senator's ear, something about Charlie Hughes.

Smith had not anticipated the hearing being called back into session. On one level, he was concerned; on another level, intrigued. Always an opportunist, Smith saw a possibility to craft the narrative.

"You have an opportunity here," Smith said before the senator could reply to Mac. "You can provide an explanation of what happened. Explain that we were working in concert to foil the plot. I would have no problem with that."

"I should say something," Lowenstein acknowledged. "I certainly want to offer an explanation, but do you really think it's appropriate to say we were working together all along?"

"It's not whether the statement's accurate, senator," Smith replied. "It's whether it's believable. People need assurance now. They don't need truth. A week from now, no one is going to hold you to an explanation you made on the spur of the moment."

"I see," Lowenstein said, turning to reenter the hearing room.

To use Smith's explanation would be to seal their fates to one another. Once he started on that road, the senator would never be able to separate himself from it. It certainly served Smith's interests, but not Lowenstein's, and it did nothing to explain the whole truth of what had occurred over the past couple of weeks.

**

LOWENSTEIN returned to the rostrum and gaveled the hearing back to order.

"A short while ago, we learned that the U.S. attorney for the Eastern District of Virginia has been killed," he began. "Most, if not all, of you have received the same information on your electronic devices. The news has already been broadcast on the major networks.

"This comes on the heels of the shootings of two law enforcement officers last Friday. And only days before that, a body was found floating in the Potomac River. Many of you may be asking what in the world is going on in our nation's capital.

"From a distance, these may appear to be unconnected acts of violence. I want to take a moment to share with you some of the facts we know about these events, however, and to explain why we believe they are related.

"At the outset, I want to tell you and the American people that all the information has not yet been collected. As in the fog of war, some of the facts as we know them may be incomplete or even inaccurate. Nonetheless, I believe we have an obligation to the American people to be transparent in our actions."

Lowenstein looked for Smith, who had returned to his seat in the well. Then he looked up at the entrance doors. Roscoe Page was in the room, accompanied by Elmo Katz.

Seeing the chairman distracted, Smith turned. He and Katz made eye contact with one another.

"Two people died today," the senator explained. "As much as we mourn the death of the U.S. attorney, it may be that the death of the other individual is the one that will make the biggest headlines. His name was Detective Harry Bullock, and we have reason to believe he was a conspirator bent upon unleashing a terrorist act, blowing up a train traveling to Washington that carried the target of an assassination plot."

The room exploded in gasps. The senator had confirmed the rumor circulating the past half hour.

"We have further reason to believe that an intelligence officer named Charles Hughes was responsible for both shootings that occurred last Friday, injuring Philip Landry, a Homeland Security executive, and killing a policeman at one of the local marinas," the senator added.

He summed up with a stunning conclusion.

"As to the reported death of Libby Lewis, well, the truth is that Ms. Lewis never drowned at all. She's very much alive. A cadaver was placed in the water to draw the then unknown terrorist to Daingerfield Island a week ago in a failed attempt to end the plot before it could be hatched. While that undertaking failed, our security personnel and local law enforcement can be applauded for working together to stop Bullock's terrorist act in the eleventh hour."

He didn't elaborate about how much he had known, including his meeting with Lewis the previous week in Georgetown. Jack Smith barely glanced at the senator as he rose to leave the chamber.

**

THE MUCH MOURNED Libby Lewis held a brief press conference just before heading over to Senator Lowenstein's office. Her presumptive drowning provided a Lazaruslike air to her appearance in front of the cameras.

Following the press conference, Lewis found her way to Lowenstein's office, where she was waiting when the senator arrived, bringing Katz and others with him. She was a trim woman of about forty, with a mass of dark hair gathered into a low ponytail. For a corpse, she looked remarkably healthy.

"It's amazing how quickly the whole thing has taken on a life of its own," said Lowenstein after he introduced Katz and Lewis to one another.

Then he addressed Katz, "You're going to have a busy couple of days yourself fighting off the media. Then it's back to work, young man. I hope you're ready for it. Because it's only going to get more interesting from this point on."

"What's on your mind?" Katz asked.

"I'm going to ask you to consider serving as the next U.S. attorney for the Eastern District of Virginia," the senator replied. "We need to fill the vacancy quickly. I will confer with the chair of the Judiciary Committee, of course, but I do not foresee any problem. You're the logical choice. It shouldn't be a problem."

Katz hesitated, then said, "I need to think that over. It's quite an offer."

"Think it over carefully," the senator agreed. "Then get back to me. I'll talk to the White House. We'll get the nomination going before the end of the year."

Lewis shook the lawyer's hand. "You've been through so much," she said. "I'm sorry about that young man, Fortune. I feel partially responsible for his death."

The senator bowed his head. "I regret that as well," he whispered. "Libby and I were meeting at the Pale Horse with June Webster when he burst into the room. My security team assumed it was someone who wanted to harm us." He paused and then added: "He was a casualty for a cause greater than any one of us."

Whatever that means, Katz said to himself.

The meeting finished, Katz ran into McCarthy and Page talking in the senator's reception room.

"Is the case finished from your point of view?" McCarthy asked.

"I still have some loose ends to tie together," Katz replied, his tone flinty.

"Like what?" Page asked.

"This and that." Katz ran a finger across his jaw. "In fact, there's one thing you can help me with."

"Name it," Page said.

"I'd like to do a quick forensic study of whatever electronics we've got," Katz said. "Bullock's phone, for starters, along with his computer, and Moultrie's, if we can find them."

"What are you after?" asked McCarthy.

Katz felt he could trust them, or at least he hoped he could. "I don't think Harry Bullock had any intention of harming anyone on that train. In fact, I doubt he was a terrorist at all."

"How can you say that?" McCarthy asked. "He was a bad cop. He was responsible for the shooting of a U.S. attorney in the tunnel under Callahan Drive."

"I know that's the way it looks," Katz admitted. "But here's the thing. And it's been bothering me all along about this case. The dispatch that was issued to retrieve the body found on Daingerfield Island." Katz looked at McCarthy and Page. "Do you two know what I'm talking about? The kid who called the police, David Reese."

They looked at him stone-faced.

"David Reese called the police," Katz explained. "Except by the time that call was made, the dispatch had already been placed. I've got a private investigator who discovered the emergency vehicles were on their way before Reese picked up the phone and called 911."

"So what does that prove?" asked McCarthy.

"That someone always intended to disrupt the planned apprehension of the would-be terrorist," Katz explained. "Someone created an expectation that a terrorist was going to be nabbed. Except there was never going to be any capture."

"You've got it wrong," McCarthy objected. "This whole thing was put together to arrest a terrorist. That was the whole point of the exercise."

Katz did not really expect to win McCarthy over, or Page, for that matter, at least not here.

"I understand that's how you're looking at it, Mac," Katz said. "But suppose I told you that no one intended to kill al-Issawi. Suppose I told you this is all a play within a play. And that the evil genius – the one who perpetrated a real murder – is about to slip away undetected."

Page was beginning to understand. "I'll help you any way I can," he said. "How much time do we have?"

"It's Tuesday afternoon," Katz answered. "We've got two and a half days."

"Why is that?" asked McCarthy.

"Because Jack Smith has a court hearing Friday on a divorce case," Katz said.

"No he doesn't," McCarthy objected. "That's not what he told me, anyway. When we were prepping for today's hearing, he said he had a flight to catch out of Dulles on Friday morning."

"You sure?"

"Totally sure," Mac answered. "Smith has a flight back to the West Coast on Friday morning at 8 a.m."

"All right then," Katz said. "I'd better get to work."

CHAPTER 39

KATZ SPENT the next two days trying to make a coherent case out of the pieces of a scrambled jigsaw puzzle. Santana, Reese and Lin joined him, working Wednesday and through the November 11 Veterans Day holiday on Thursday. Katz was lucky to have their help.

In the meantime, Nate Harding's sham prosecution became the talk of the town. No one was repulsed by it. Actually, quite the opposite. People found the make-believe case imaginative and entertaining.

Harding and Libby Lewis both attained immediate celebrity status. In particular, Harding's collaboration with his counsel made a compelling story for the crime cable channels. And Lewis's willingness to be 'used' as the victim of a drowning created an absolute sensation.

Judge Osborne was applauded for his handling of the case. Privately, Katz wondered whether Jack Smith had pressured the judge to get Harding released. Because of Harding's courtroom theatrics, no one would ever know for sure.

Government officials had balked when Katz produced the agreement signed by Douglas. Given the publicity surrounding the case, however, the politicians decided to support the agreements by doubling down on the benefits for Moriarty and baby Katzie. It showed compassion and sealed Douglas's legacy. Additional monies were also promised to the Public Safety Office Benefits paid to Officer Dixon's widow and four children.

For the most part, Katz and the others remained holed up in his office, piecing together the fragments of a madman's puzzle. Or trying. They started where all good preparation for trial work commences, at the beginning.

Jack Smith had devised a trap to catch a terrorist on Daingerfield Island. He was an expert on the subject of the threat posed by lone wolves. He seemed to be using that knowledge to advance his own sinister advantage. Libby Lewis was used to offer the bait, detailed data concerning upcoming travel by Jumma al-Issawi. Through texts and emails, she lured the supposed terrorist to the island, offering him a flash drive containing the required information.

According to Lewis – whom Katz interviewed in his office on Wednesday and again on the phone on Thursday – Smith micro-managed all the arrangements. This included the chat rooms, flash drive and travel route. It was as if he understood what the terrorist wanted, Lewis explained. Lewis used words like "uncanny" and "surreal" to describe Smith's orchestration, which extended so far as to organize a demonstration against al-Issawi to create the illusion of widespread hatred toward the activist in advance of his trip to Washington.

Lewis's description was corroborated by both June Webster and Derek Fine, both of whom had been ordered to cooperate with Katz or face removal from the agency and, for Fine, possible criminal prosecution for impersonating a federal officer.

Webster acknowledged she thought it ludicrous to utilize a dead body in the shallow waters off the island when the trap was set Halloween night. She saw no need for it, and Fine agreed. The bloom on Fine's hero worship had been wilted by recent events. He admitted that it was an innate desire to protect Smith that led him to impulsively switch the photograph Reese emailed Katz following Harding's arraignment, and to visit Harding in jail afterward.

Hughes, the agency's 'fixer,' could have offered invaluable information as well, but he had disappeared, probably fleeing the country.

There were many odd circumstances about the goings-on at Daingerfield Island. If staging a phony drowning had never made any sense, as Webster believed, placing the body in the Potomac had to have been done for some other purpose. To do it simply as a reason to sound an alarm and abort the caper made no sense at all. And one thing Jack Smith definitely was not was crazy.

216

Harry Bullock had been on Daingerfield Island that night. He had interviewed David Reese. It was easy to attribute Bullock's presence to the fact that he was the terrorist, the orchestrator of the plot. But what if Bullock was innocent, at least of that? Katz wondered. What if there was another explanation for Bullock's appearance at that location, at that time? Or, for that matter, what if there was another reason for Bullock's presence in the tunnel under Callahan Drive at the moment the train flew along the tracks on the way to Union Station? Or his concealment of the thumb drive, which was located at his apartment?

In reviewing the contents of Bullock's computer, Page uncovered a series of emails between Bullock and Jack Smith in the weeks before Halloween. In their communications, Smith referred to past years when the detective had been on his personal payroll and aided him in schemes that never came to light. This time he was enlisting Bullock as a rogue agent to assist in the apprehension of a terrorist planning an attack on Washington. And Bullock had apparently swallowed the story whole.

While Katz toyed with the idea that Bullock had been duped by Smith, a call came in from Joey Cook.

"Those two lowlifes Bullock rammed on the interstate, turns out they did end up being charged with drug distribution," he informed Katz. "There was some kind of snag in the paperwork, that's all."

That fact added to Katz's theory of Bullock's innocence. Or at least it seemed less likely that he had deliberately tried to get Katz killed in the car smash. Which was some comfort.

There were so many twists and turns, Katz had a hard time keeping it straight in his head. With assistance from Reese, Lin, Santana, and Page, some startling facts began to emerge.

Some of those facts were discovered in Lou Moultrie's computer, which was located at Hughes's home. A comprehensive diagnosis of computer's emails confirmed a series of communications from Smith's ex-wife. In those emails, inexplicably diverted to the spam folder and never retrieved by Moultrie, Eve had threatened to disclose secrets about Smith's operations shared with her during their marriage.

As Katz knew, a clause in the Smiths' divorce decree prohibited either from disclosing personal details about the other. But Eve was past caring about consequences. If Smith was unwilling to voluntarily reopen the case and provide her a more equitable distribution of their marital assets, she swore she would disregard the clause and cast fate to the winds. Let her husband and the CIA try to come after her.

In those emails, Eve also revealed her long-time extramarital affair with Harry Bullock.

"I can't fucking believe it," Santana said. "Harry Bullock? I mean, really?"

It was as much a shock to Katz, maybe more. The affair had apparently been going on for years, including the time Katz and Bullock worked cases together in the prosecutor's office, as well as during the divorce proceedings.

"You never uncovered any evidence of Eve Smith having an extramarital affair during the divorce, did you?" Katz asked Santana, who had been his private investigator at the time.

"We never looked," Santana reminded him. "Jack Smith didn't want us investigating it, remember?"

"What if Mr. Smith knew about his wife's infidelity all along?" Lin postulated. "What if the whole terrorist sting was a big phony operation created to discredit Harry Bullock?"

"And kill him," added Reese.

They decided it was more than a theory. Jack Smith had conned Harry Bullock into hunting down an imaginary terrorist. All the while, Smith wanted to punish Bullock for having an affair with Eve and for destroying his marriage. Smith succeeded in turning Bullock into the would-be terrorist, resulting in Bullock's death and the tarnishing of his reputation.

"Geez," Lin said. "Mr. Smith is one of the most diabolical creatures on the face of the earth."

**

At one point, Katz slipped out of the office and walked down to Contrabands and Freedmen Cemetery on Washington Street to attend Officer Cecil Dixon's burial. Police officers from every jurisdiction in the commonwealth and the metropolitan D.C. area, along with hundreds of police departments across the country, filled the old cemetery, hallowed ground containing the remains of African Americans who escaped slavery during the Civil War and settled in Alexandria during the Union occupation. Katz avoided friends and colleagues. No one had accused him of responsibility for the officer's death, yet he felt personally complicit. The bullet that struck Dixon in the neck was intended for Katz.

Following the playing of "Taps," Katz walked back to the office. He passed by stores he looked at nearly every day. The ones filled with clothes, food, furniture, books, coffee, crafts, wigs, art and jewelry.

Jewelry.

He rushed back to the office, alarming Santana, Lin and Reese as he raced to the computer on his desk.

"Do you recall the three-page motion you handed me the night we were over at Abby's place?" he asked Santana. "The one Suzie gave you."

Santana did not remember.

"Just before you mentioned Roscoe Page," Katz said, trying to jog the investigator's memory.

"Yeah, I remember now," Santana said.

"We have to find that filing," Katz said.

Katz's hands ran over the keyboard. Within minutes, he found an electronic version of the filings Marston had obtained for the upcoming hearing in the Smith divorce case, and compared it to an old document in *Smith v. Smith*.

"Look at this," he said excitedly.

Everyone huddled around the computer screen. "They're identical," Reese pointed out.

"What's the significance of that?" asked Lin.

"These court papers were never intended to be used in an actual court proceeding," Katz explained. "The motion was part of a masquerade, nothing more."

Katz began digging through his hard copies of court records in the bookcase against the far wall, searching for an old file, *Smith v. Smith*. He found it, and poured several photographs onto the desk. Pictures of Jack and Eve Smith, standing together, smiling happily; of Jack alone in his office; and of Eve with her mother.

Katz took one of the photos and showed it to the group. It was a full-length picture of Eve's mother, wearing a white gown with lace and a necklace. He placed the photo on top of the desk.

"Do we have the locket photo?" Katz asked Reese and Lin.

Lin reached into her purse and retrieved the tiny image of Eve's mother, placing it beside the photo on the desk.

Everyone fell silent.

Katz remembered the photo that Reese and Lin said they had dropped off at his office the afternoon of the I-395 crash. He asked them to look for the photo. Reese found the manila envelope among the clutter on Marston's desk and gave it to Katz.

Opening it, Katz removed the photo that Kathy White had introduced at Nate Harding's bond hearing, the photo bathed in blue light that Reese had taken on Daingerfield Island showing a woman's face shrouded in wet hair, a necklace around her neck, the black dress clinging to her.

He placed the photo on the desk next to the other two photographs.

They looked at the matching necklaces worn by Eve Smith and by her mother, and of Eve's mother's face in the full-length picture and in the locket photo.

"Oh, my God," Lin exclaimed. "Oh, my God."

CHAPTER 40

Friday, November 12

DULLES INTERNATIONAL AIRPORT was already a beehive of activity. Cars, buses and shuttles were streaming by the ribbed cage of the colossal structure designed by Eero Saarinen. Inside, passengers queued for departure while others disembarked from arriving flights, everyone moving in all directions at the same instant.

In the midst of this ordered chaos, a taxi carrying Jack Smith pulled up to the curb. He was carrying only one bag, traveling light. He paid the fare in cash and threw the bag over his shoulder as the taxi pulled away.

Smith stopped at a trash receptacle outside the airport and removed the notice to appear form from his jacket pocket.

He had prepared the motion as part of his own subterfuge, copying it verbatim from one of the original filings in the divorce case.

When a deputy sheriff had served him the notice to appear, it was as though the hand of death was reaching out to touch him. Of course, it was nothing more than a computer-generated notice, automatically issued. But it was eerie, nonetheless.

Smith crumpled the court paper into a ball. He tossed it in the trash barrel. As he walked into the terminal, he saw someone out of the corner of his eye. He paused. Then he turned, pivoting awkwardly. "Elmo," Smith said. "What in the world are you doing here?"

Katz glanced toward the sliding doors through which Smith had entered the terminal. And the trash can on the side of those doors. "What did you just throw in the trash?" Katz asked.

"Just some papers," Smith said.

"That wasn't the court summons, was it? You're really not supposed to toss a court summons away so cavalierly."

Smith, caught off guard, embraced Katz like a fighter trying to keep down the arms of his opponent.

Here they stood, client and counsel, erstwhile collaborators in an ugly divorce case. Smith had never seen anyone quite like this lawyer, save for when he looked in the mirror.

"How long has it been?" Smith asked. He broke the embrace and stepped back. He needed a way out.

Katz pressed him. "Seriously, was that the notice to appear? Why did you throw it away?"

"I don't have to be in court," Smith replied, without answering the question. "The judge isn't going to do anything, anyway. A date will be set for a hearing. That's all. It's not a hearing on the merits. Plus, it will infuriate the hell out of her. My not being there."

"That's pretty good, Jack."

"It's the truth," Smith said.

They moved to one side, away from the steady stream of airport passengers and personnel rushing in all directions. Smith noticed that Katz held a folder. He was suddenly aware of the presence of others, who formed a perimeter around the two men.

"I knew the moment Nate Harding brought you into this case that there was going to be a problem," Smith said, recalling his conversation with Harding at Gravelly Point.

"Harding brought me in as insurance," Katz replied. "He figured you'd jettison him as soon as he was no longer useful. Thing is, he didn't realize just how much he'd complicated things for you."

"Complicate things, Elmo?" Smith queried, his eyes sharp. "You mean by bringing in such a talented attorney?"

Smith glanced at the men and women standing closest to them, and figured they were probably FBI.

"It's not my talent that bothered you," Katz said. "It's the fact I had the photos. If the right set of circumstances occurred, I could figure it out."

"There is nothing to figure out," Smith said, defiantly. Menacingly. He glanced around, checking if anyone had recording devices. No, just mechanical men and women in gray suits.

Katz opened the folder he was holding. Smith looked down and saw emails from his ex-wife addressed to Lou Moultrie.

"Where did you get those?" Smith asked, for the first time exhibiting a look of concern.

"Moultrie's computer. It's why you really sent an assassin to his house that night. You probably deleted the emails yourself when your guy Hughes brought the computer back from Moultrie's, before you told him to destroy the computer. Except the dumb shit kept it, brought it to his own house. Too bad for you."

Smith tried to brush it off. He looked at the agents with Katz. "Listen, I really do have a plane to catch. Good try, but I have to run."

The agents blocked his way.

Smith raised his voice. "Really, Elmo, I must insist. You're a very competent attorney. I was fortunate to have you in my corner. But espionage is not your strong suit. I don't have the faintest idea what you're trying to do now. I have to go. I have a flight waiting."

Holding the file in one hand, Katz reached into his pocket with the other and removed his phone. He tossed it to Smith, who caught it automatically.

"Before you go, call Eve, will you? Call and ask if she's heading out to Circuit Court for her motion to be called."

Smith stared down at the phone. "I'm not going to give you or her that satisfaction."

"This has nothing to do with satisfying me, Jack, and you know it," Katz said. "That motion wasn't filed by Eve. It's a rewrite of one I prepared for *you*. You filed the motion yourself to create the impression she's still alive."

"What the hell are you talking about?" Smith demanded.

"It's all part of your charade, the charade you created to extract vengeance for Eve's betrayal, for her affair with Harry Bullock. You

224

wanted to punish her, and you wanted to punish him. So you killed her, and then you had him killed in a bizarre case of mistaken identity. It doesn't get any more ruthless than that, Jack."

"This is crazy, Elmo. You may know your way around a courtroom, but not out here. You don't have the faintest idea what you're talking about."

"Then enlighten me."

At first it appeared Smith was going to speak. Then he reconsidered and shook his head. "I'm not going to speak candidly if the rumors are correct about you becoming U.S. attorney for the Eastern District. It would be suicide on my part."

"Not if you're innocent," said Katz.

"You've already said that I'm guilty of killing my wife," Smith replied.

"I can be persuaded otherwise. Just call her."

"I'm not going to compromise whatever small amount of doubt exists in your mind," Smith said. "You're crazy if you think you can link a murder to me. I'm not involved in anything that sinister. Not as a coconspirator, not as an accomplice, not as a principal."

Smith sounded persuasive, but Katz was undeterred. "You're not walking away this time," he said.

Smith chuckled.

"This isn't funny, Jack," Katz said. "You killed your wife. You had her body placed in the Potomac and claimed it was a cadaver used as a prop to unmask a terrorist plot. I can prove it."

"It'll never hold up," Smith said with contempt.

"And why is that?" asked Katz.

"Because I wasn't present, that's why. I was in an airplane landing at Reagan National when the body was discovered off Daingerfield Island. I was at headquarters when Lou was murdered. And I was testifying before Congress at the time Bullock was shot, if you recall. Charlie Hughes is the guy you need, but he's on the run. As for Bullock? He was a terrorist, gunned down by the police after he shot and killed Helen O. Douglas.

"I mean, Helen was your friend, wasn't she?" Smith pressed on. "Or was she just a competitor? Maybe you're happy she's dead, so you can replace her. You always did covet becoming U.S. attorney, didn't you?"

Smith prepared to toss the phone back to Katz. As he did so, he saw something in the palm of Katz's hand. It was a pendant on a fine silver chain.

Katz tucked the file under his arm and opened the pendant. Inside was a miniature photograph, replaced where it had always belonged. A photo of Eve's mother.

Smith reacted as though a cell door had just slammed shut. "What is that?" he asked.

"A conviction," Katz replied.

**

KATZ LAID OUT the case for Smith.

"You had Hughes call the EMTs to Daingerfield Island before David Reese got off his bike. The call was made from the satellite parking lot at Reagan National. You needed to have a foil because, after all, there was never any terrorist to be apprehended at Daingerfield Island.

"You concocted the whole thing, beginning with the intelligence analysis that reported the existence of a lone wolf plotting an attack on Washington. You planted that story and then you devised the plan to arrest the terrorist, knowing all along there was no terrorist, only a figment of your own imagination. You even masterminded a protest against the target to add credibility to your plan.

"You were devising a plan, alright, but it was to murder your wife, not to catch a terrorist. The entire operation was nothing more than an elaborate disguise to hide your wife's murder, to hide it in plain view, and then to kill her paramour. You must have been laughing every step of the way.

"Your people unwittingly tricked the chief medical examiner when her body arrived at the morgue, explaining that the body was a cadaver used as part of a sting operation to catch a terrorist. Then Eve's body was transported to a crematorium, where it was burned. You destroyed the evidence, or at least the corpus, before anyone could properly identify her."

As Katz spoke, fear coursed through Smith's body.

"Harry Bullock was enlisted to assist you in catching the terrorist," Katz continued. "You selected Bullock because he's over-rambunctious and stupid, and because he was fucking your ex-wife. It's why you didn't let Santana investigate adultery as a ground for divorce. You didn't want anyone to spoil the fun for you. You must have been plotting Harry's demise for a long time.

"Poor, dumb Harry. It never occurred to him that you were setting him up in the role of the terrorist. You placed him on Daingerfield Island on Halloween night. He thought he was looking for a terrorist, and he might have even suspected Reese. Then he destroyed a thumb drive for you without realizing you'd attributed Moultrie's murder to its theft.

"Finally you positioned him in the tunnel under Callahan Drive to wait for the arrival of the terrorist. Imagine his chagrin when a posse of armed LEOs charged over the hill and mistook him for the terrorist. You knew the trigger-happy crowd would begin firing before Harry could shout out an explanation from up in the rafters. I'm not sure he figured out what you'd done before his body fell onto the tracks riddled with bullets."

The agents moved inward, like plastic melting on the edges.

Katz wasn't finished. "When they pulled Eve's body out of the Potomac," he continued, "she was wearing this pendant. When you had her body cremated, the pendant was removed from her neck and placed in an envelope to be retrieved by the next of kin. You forgot, or didn't care, or didn't dare send anyone to pick her things up. Curtis Santana was able to get it from the crematorium late yesterday afternoon.

"David Reese took a photo the night Eve's body was dragged out of the river. She was wearing the pendant around her neck."

"I'm not sure what that proves," Smith said, conceding nothing.

"I found some old photos from your divorce file," Katz said. "There's a photo of Eve with her mother. The old woman wore the pendant during her lifetime. When she died, Eve must have inherited it. She began wearing the pendant and placed a photo of her mother inside of it.

"The photos taken at Daingerfield Island obscure the victim's face. But the pendant is clearly visible."

Next Katz removed the tiny photo from the pendant. "David Reese found this in the grass where the EMTs performed CPR. One of your people, Derek Fine, will testify he intercepted this photo when Reese tried to email it to me. A photo of June Webster was substituted.

"Reese gave the original to his girlfriend Lin, who kept it for safekeeping. Too bad for you, she had it the night you sent Hughes to shakedown Reese."

Smith's face was expressionless, signifying nothing.

"I was the one person who could string it together, provided it fell in my lap, which it did," Katz said. "That was the reason you wanted to kill me as well."

"You know, Elmo, if God likes you," Smith said, "He gives you something that you ask for. But if He loves you, He denies you something that you want."

Katz responded with a blank stare. *A sermon. Now? Really?*

"I wanted to survive at the agency," Smith continued. "And I did. At the time, I thought it was a prayer answered. But it actually wasn't. Because that survival convinced me I could get away with anything. And, for the longest time, I did. Do you understand what I'm saying?"

"Not really," Katz said. "All I know is you murdered Eve and got others to kill Bullock, believing he was the lone wolf.

"The murders were pretty ingenious. I have to give you credit for that. Devising a phony terrorist plot as a subterfuge to carry out two murders, and doing it in plain view."

Katz placed the tiny photo in the pendant and snapped it shut.

The agents surrounding the two men closed in finally and placed cuffs on Smith.

Katz watched as they led Smith out of the terminal and into an unmarked vehicle. Next stop would be the courthouse, where he would be arraigned for his wife's murder and conspiracy to murder Detective Harry Bullock.

EPILOGUE

HELEN O. DOUGLAS'S FUNERAL was held the next Monday at her family's church outside Boston in Watertown, Massachusetts.

Katz and Snowe flew up together. Both the vice president and the attorney general attended. Snowe remained in Massachusetts a few additional days at her sister's place in Ipswich, along Boston's north shore, while Katz rented a car and drove home.

He took I-90 across the Bay State and into New York, then turned south on the Taconic State Parkway. He intended to visit his folks, who had retired along the Hudson River, but veered away from the exit ramp at the last second and just kept driving south to Virginia.

About an hour after he avoided the exit ramp, somewhere around Perth Amboy, New Jersey, Katz called Lowenstein's office. He got McCarthy on the line. "I decided to accept the offer to serve as Douglas's successor," he said.

"What made the decision for you?" asked McCarthy.

Katz didn't feel a need to tell him the truth. *Fatta la legge, trovato l'inganno.* It had been a game to outsmart the prosecution and win acquittals. Suddenly the expression wasn't so amusing to him. In fact, Katz vowed to lay down new tracks, a commitment he made during a visit to the makeshift memorial established along the tow path for Tony Fortune, filled with flowers, bottles of wine and votive candles.

"It's just time for a change," Katz answered McCarthy. "Time to get back to best practices."

**

JACK SMITH retained Jimmy Wolfe as his attorney.

Nothing happened in the case until Katz was sworn in as U.S. attorney. The next day, Wolfe filed a motion to have the Alexandria commonwealth attorney, the U.S. attorney and their entire offices recused, arguing conflict of interest. The court agreed. Privately, so did Katz.

A special prosecutor was appointed. Within a month, the case was in shambles. Granted, it was complicated. And the public never could quite embrace it, content to believe Washington had been rescued from an actual terrorist plot.

Eventually Wolfe worked out an Alford plea, maintaining his client's innocence but acknowledging the evidence was strong enough to convict him. Courthouse commentators expressed surprise, at least until the agreement became public. The plea was to a single conspiracy count. Smith's pre-sentence investigation called for the maximum twenty years of incarceration, which he received, with fourteen suspended and six to serve.

Six short years before Smith was back on the street. It was a sham and a shame. The case involving Eve Smith was circumstantial, but it tied together well enough. The inability to locate Hughes weighed heavily on the prosecution, but that was no reason to dump the case. Properly handled, Katz believed a conviction could have been sustained for murder in the first degree.

Worse still was that fact that no charges were brought against Jack Smith for any of the other murders. Smith had been right when he told Katz that all of the loose ends and dead ends would make it impossible to prove guilt beyond a reasonable doubt. He had done too good a job of muddying his own trail. And while Smith feigned acceptance of responsibility for the mayhem he had created, Katz knew he secretly vowed revenge against Katz for his imprisonment, a score he might try to settle six years from now.

Landry came out of his coma, and returned to work at the Joint Terrorism Task Force. He blamed Katz for Hughes's shooting him. Katz didn't even bother trying to straighten out that one.

Katz had achieved what he wanted, namely exposing Smith. The man who was a cancer on the agency had been removed. His pension and government benefits were taken away. And even though he only got six years behind bars, he would pretty much be a pariah once he was released.

Elmo Katz settled in as U.S. attorney without much difficulty. He brought along his entourage. Santana was hired as a special assistant. McCarthy came over from Lowenstein's office as deputy U.S. attorney for the criminal division. Suzie Marston became Katz's administrative assistant, Lin became a research aide, and Reese was hired as a clerk.

Since Thunderbolt was ineligible for the government payroll, he was adopted by Jimmy Wolfe's legal staff and continued to patrol the alleys around the courthouse for them. Santana dropped by from time to time with treats.

Abby Snowe moved in with Katz. It was serious, though neither was yet willing to commit for keeps. The only vow Snowe was willing to make, along with White and Santana, was never, ever to lend Elmo Katz an automobile of any kind.

AUTHOR'S NOTE

Thank you for reading Daingerfield Island.

To write and publish this book, or to accomplish anything meaningful in life, the most important thing is persistence. It's not creative genius or superior talent, neither of which I possess to any large degree. It's believing in the story and not losing faith. Eventually a winning combination comes along – a reader, an editor, a publisher – and it happens. So my advice to any aspiring writer or dreamer is simple: Never stop trying. Never stop turning to others for assistance. And, never cease helping others fulfill their dreams. In the end, that may be the way your own vision finds expression.

I welcome hearing from you. Email me at AlendronLLC@aol.com. Let me know what you think about the book, and how future Elmo Katz stories can be improved.

ACKNOWLEDGEMENTS

I am indebted to several wonderful people whose individual and collective contributions were key to the completion of Daingerfield Island. Peggy McLaughlin and Ken Atchity, the 'story merchant,' provided editorial guidance on early drafts. Andrew Egerton rejected an early version submitted to BrickHouse Books, but then encouraged me to submit a revised version that was favorably received. Adele Nichols, Howard Louis McMillan, Michael Cora and Miriam Kotzin, author of 'The Real Deal,' offered critical comments. Special thanks to Zoe Russo, Laurel Abell, and Daniel Flannery, whose editing was masterful; Doritt Carroll, Esq., for legal advice; Ace Kieffer, graphic designer and associate editor; prose editor Charles Rammelkamp, a constant source of inspiration and support; and Clarinda Harriss, editor and publisher of the Baltimore-based indie print house, who never stopped saying "Onward!" A special shout out to the folks at New Columbia Distillers—including Michael Lowe, John Uselton, and Travers Lingle—who hosted our 'release' party at the Green Hat gin distillery in Northeast DC. Finally, gratitude to my wife, Robin, my best friend and love of my life, who knows me better than I know myself, and our sons Alex, Andrew, and Aron, whose unique individuality and extraordinary genius are an endless source of inspiration to Robin and me.

Elmo Katz will return in
Jones Point.

234